CAUGHT
A MAI

Like blood-drenched gravestones were those Subterrane signposts to Satan's underground empire, and Weston Craig would transcend the brain-spanning scope of a mad scientist's deadly disrupter disk to salvage a beautiful girl's stark loveliness from the fiend's lusting devices, and secure for the world of tomorrow modern science's greatest invention!

"Mistress of Machine-Age Madness" appeared in Robert Erisman's Marvel Tales *magazine way back in 1940. It's a wonderful, nearly forgotten pulp science fiction-weird menace tale featuring a sadistic mad scientist and a plethora of monstrous beasts, all victimizing a hero and his often naked heroine companion. It is a story much in the same vein as Henry Kuttner's marvelous (pun intended) "The Time Trap," which had appeared in an earlier Marvel publication in 1938.*

FOR A COMPLETE SECOND NOVEL, TURN TO PAGE 75

AUTHOR PROFILE

JACK WILLIAMSON

Jack Williamson, 1908-2006

MISTRESS OF MACHINE-AGE MADNESS

By JACK WILLIAMSON

ARMCHAIR FICTION
PO Box 4369, Medford, Oregon 97504

*For more information about Armchair Books and products, visit our
website at…*

www.armchairfiction.com

Or email us at…

armchairfiction@yahoo.com

CHAPTER ONE
The Woman and the Whip

SHRIEKING with terror, and quite aware of her complete nudity, Ann Tancred appeared in a second-story window. The weird greenish glare of the laboratory conflagation spotlighted the full roundness of her young breasts.

In the laundry truck that he drove to pay for his engineering course, Weston Craig rounded the street corner and came upon the scene. Amazement drove his foot against the brakes.

Yawning in the side of the old brick house was a round, four-foot hole—as perfectly circular as if it had been cut out with a monster punch. Uncanny greenish flame was gushing out of it, and from the explosion-shattered doors and windows on the ground floor.

The fire department, as usual in the sleepy little university town, was late. Singed and smoking from the accident, Professor Tancred was running back and forth in the street. A lean little wisp of a man, he reminded Craig of an excited ant. He was babbling frantically:

"The disk—it's out of control! My precious disk!" Keen enough to win the Nobel Prize in physics, his mind seemed to have deserted him. "My notes! My daughter! My disk! Somebody—do something!"

Craig guessed what had happened. He was student assistant in Tancred's physics laboratory classes. He had helped wire the weird-looking atomic disruptor disk, and he had listened to hours of Tancred's ravings about the possibilities of the invention.

The disk would liberate atomic power, to run all the world's industry. It would manufacture neutronium out of the disrupted atoms—a wonder-substance, a million times stronger than steel. It would bore mines to incredible depths, cut tunnels under the oceans.

So the excited little scientist had promised.

Just now, however, something seemed to have gone very much wrong with the wonderful new invention. It was time indeed, Craig saw, for somebody to do something.

For an instant his eyes clung to the screaming nude girl in the window. Ann Tancred was just sixteen. He had regarded her only as a dark-eyed, dark-haired little mouse of a freshman. But the slim softness of her young body kindled something in him.

His foot went from brake to accelerator. The laundry truck veered across the lawn, beneath the deadly thrust of the disintegrating ray. Narrowly missing the frantic scientist, Craig backed it against the burning building.

He scrambled to the top of it, beneath the window where Ann was leaning out. The choking green chemical smoke was now pouring out above her head. Pain added terror to her screams. Still unconscious of her nakedness, she threw herself down into Craig's arms.

Her slender body was still cool and dripping from the shower she'd been taking when the explosion had surprised her. They both fell off the truck, and sprawled together on the lawn.

"Oh—" she gasped at him, "Thank you—for saving my life!"

They got up. The girl turned away from Craig, trying to cover her breasts with small hands, Craig draped her with a bath towel that he grabbed from the truck. Slim and long-limbed in the green glare of the ray, she ran away from him, toward a neighbor's house.

That was Commencement week, four years ago now. The disruption ray had sliced through trees and a neighbor's roof. There were damage suits, and Professor Tancred left the university, to carry on his experiments in a more secluded place.

CRAIG graduated, and became a fellow in the engineering department. He received several letters from Tancred, postmarked somewhere in Arizona, requesting him to look up data or buy pieces of equipment.

Craig wrote a few times to Ann. He received no answer. The girl, he guessed, had not recovered from her embarrassment. But he could not forget her.

Then came the last, strange appeal from her father. The frantic phrases of the scientist's letter haunted Craig:

My dear Weston:

Come to us—for God's sake!

You will be interested to know that the disrupter disk, after all these years and disappointments, is at last perfected, I am installing the completed model on a new boring machine. I know that the Subterrane *will accomplish all that I have dreamed of.*

The new "mole," as we call it, can carry us down through Earth's crust, to the mother lode of all treasure. The years of poverty and effort can soon be ended. We can all be millionaires—billionaires—there is no limit!

But we need you, Weston. All my years of work may lead only to tragic disaster, unless you come to aid us. For I have reason to mistrust my present associate—Dr. Hugh Maddrey.

Ann is afraid of Maddrey. She believes the promise of unimaginable wealth is transforming him into a madman. He is certainly becoming more and more violent.

I must have the Mexican cook take this letter out, without his knowledge.

For Ann's sake, Weston—come at once!

> *Desperately.*
> *Tancred*

Craig wondered about the *Subterrane*. He had always been a little skeptical of Tancred's invention. And the letter sounded half-crazy to him. Craig had no desire for millions. But he did need money for a new cyclotron.

And, across four years, memory of Ann Tancred's long, full-breasted nude body, still tantalized him. He locked up his laboratory and caught the next plane west.

The bus that he had to take from Phoenix stopped at a dusty, sun-faded ghost town at the desert's edge. Craig told the wrinkled, sun-blackened man at the gas pump:

"I'm looking for old Professor Tancred. Know him?"

The man stared, letting gasoline run on the ground. Craig saw the shadow of fear darken the deep-sunken eyes. Suspicious mistrust brought the thin, sun-parched lips together like the jaws of a trap.

"What's the matter?" Craig demanded. "Don't you know Tancred?"

The wrinkled desert rat stopped the wasting gas. He stepped back from Craig, his eyes narrowed watchfully.

"Know him well enough," he muttered. "Him and that devil, Maddrey!" The words jerked out, violently. "That Maddrey—he's a coyote! A hydrophobia-skunk!"

"I don't know Maddrey," Craig said, "Where does Tancred live?"

"In that devil's den!" The man spat the words. "If you got to go there—get off the bus at the mail box, twenty miles up. You'll see the road. And you'll meet Maddrey!"

The sun was low when the bus left Craig at the mailbox. There was no one waiting—he had decided not to send a telegram, lest it fall into the dreaded hands of Maddrey.

The box stood on its post alone in the middle of a vast sweep of barren mesa. There was no tree or house in view. Craig could see no living thing—until he saw an ominous black bird wheeling, far away south.

He looked at the box again. Black-lettered on the side of it was the name, *Dr. Hugh Maddrey.* Above was a thin smear of wet red paint. Dimly, through it, Craig could read Tancred's name.

He shuddered, and his fingers groped unconsciously for the heavy little automatic that he had bought in Phoenix. Suddenly Craig wished that he had a more formidable weapon—and knew more about its use.

He found two narrow wheel tracks that led straight south across the sere brown vegetation of the mesa. They ran between the monument-like sandstone buttes that towered here and there, and on toward the black wheeling bird.

Only now there were three of the birds.

Uneasily, Craig started walking south, along the dusty tracks. He couldn't help wanting to turn back toward the safety of his laboratory, where problems could be solved with a slide rule, and uncertainties checked in a test tube.

Always, Weston Craig had led a sheltered life. Always he had been afraid, even of fear itself. Sometimes he had spurred himself to reckless feats. But he had never conquered fear, and he thought he never would.

Now his whole body was tensed and goose-fleshed with an intuition of monstrous peril waiting for him. His throat was dry. A cool wind of evening sprang up across the desert, and suddenly he was shivering to the chill sweat of fear.

But he plodded ahead, gripping the little gun with sticky fingers. He had trained himself to go ahead, in spite of fear.

Once, he remembered, he had saved Ann Tancred's life—with no thought of fear.

He knew that he would risk a great deal for her again.

He counted the black specks again that wheeled in the sunset sky ahead. Now there were seven. He remembered reading how the desert's carrion birds will gather above anything dead. Was their object just a rabbit or a coyote, he wondered. Or—something larger?

THE face of the desert changed, as the sun dropped lower. The naked buttes became pillars of ominous red—they were like blood-drenched gravestones, Craig thought, in a giants' cemetery. Purple light flowed up, and drowned the red. And a dust-red moon rose beyond them.

Craig's feet were getting sore. Still he could see no sign of any habitation. He began to wonder how much farther it could be to whatever dwelling or laboratory Tancred and his alarming assistant had established here—and abruptly he stopped.

Listening…

It came from far ahead, an unfamiliar sound. It had the drumming quality of a powerful aero engine. But Craig could find no light in the moon-flooded sky. And he had a curiously disturbing impression that the roaring came from *beneath*.

The ground seemed to quiver under his aching feet. He dropped his ear to a boulder, and the sound was louder. A quivering tension drew upon his nerves. His heart began to skip.

But it couldn't be—not Tancred's *Subterrane!*

Then he stared at the base of a purple butte, half a mile ahead. There was a flare of greenish flame—that carried him instantly back four years, to that laboratory accident and the memory of Ann Tancred's naked childish loveliness.

The flame died, and something burst out of the rock. A bulky, clumsy-looking metal thing, shining dully in the moonlight. It rocked ponderously on massive caterpillar tracks and came sliding down a talus slope.

It was cylindrical, except for the tracks. It looked a little bit like a submarine, with conning tower and other obstructions removed. Except the nose of it, which was a palely glowing greenish disk.

That was a disruptor disk, a huge copy of the one he had helped Tancred wire. This strange machine was Tancred's "metal mole!" The *Subterrane!*

A small dark opening appeared in the side of it. Craig glimpsed two small figures moving swiftly. The machine, he realized, must be far larger than he had at first thought.

That mighty drumming had ceased. Now another sound ripped through the moonlight—a scream, torn by the fangs of agony from a woman's throat!

Crack!

For an instant Craig was puzzled by that sharp, rifle-like report. But it came again. And he knew, from the shriek that followed, that it was the sound of a whip.

Chill apprehension prickled along Craig's spine. He wished that he had taken time to practice with the little automatic. But he went forward, at a weary, stumbling run, and met the screaming girl.

Long-legged and slender, she came fleetly across the mesa. Cruel mesquite and poisoned Spanish Bayonet ripped at her clothing. The full moon caught the flash of a smooth white thigh, and gleamed on the full roundness of a naked breast— and it was black on the whip's bleeding tracks.

Crack!

Gigantic in the moonlight, the man came close behind her. A bull-huge brute, black-haired, black-bearded. His breath

Gigantic in the moonlight, the brute came close behind her, his

was a hoarse bestial gasping. The whip ran through his hands and leapt out in the moonlight, a thin black serpent striking.

The girl shrieked again, and Craig knew the intonation of her voice. Four years had filled out her straight body with the lush curves of womanhood. But she was Ann Tancred.

Craig lifted the inadequate little automatic, shouted hoarsely:

"Hold on—you, there!"

THAT sounded silly. He knew that he should have shot first. But then, unused to using weapons, he might have endangered the girl as much as the man.

serpent-like whip snatching at her clothing, flaying her flesh

The girl checked herself. Her dark eyes grew wide in the moonlight. Her hands lifted instinctively to cover her nudity. Craig knew, from the odd little toss of her disheveled head, that she remembered their last meeting.

"Craig!" She gasped the warning. "It's Maddrey—watch him!"

The dark-featured, gigantic man came panting up beside her, trailing the whip. And Craig flinched before the eyes of Maddrey. They were blue against the moon, blazing—mad! "Well—Mr. Engineer!"

The voice of Maddrey was a deep hollow bellow, again bull-like. Craig shuddered from it. And the old fear flowed like an icy liquid in his veins.

"I read Tancred's foolish letter, for the Mexican was my slave." It was an appalling, effortless roar. "And we've been waiting for you, Mr. Engineer. We may need you to repair the disruptor-disk, somewhere along the way... *Because you are going with us, down to the center of the Earth!*"

The girl came stumbling forward.

"No—no!"

Hoarse with fear, she flung quivering arms around Craig. Her firm breast brought him the rapid thud of her heart. He caught the perfume of her body.

"Oh, Weston—he'll kill you!"

Maddrey moved to follow the girl. The thin gleaming whip leapt forward like a live thing. Craig tried to ignore the fear shrieking in him. He thrust himself forward, lifted the little wobbling gun.

"Stand back," he whispered.

He hardly saw the swift movement of Maddrey's big hand, in the moonlight. He had time to squeeze the trigger of the little gun, just once. But he knew the bullet was going wild.

And the tiny report was drowned in a thundrous crash. He saw the spurt of yellow fire from Maddrey's hip. Then crimson lightning splintered against his head. He felt the girl's frantic hands clinging to him, as he slipped down. He heard, far-off, her anguished scream:

"Don't! Don't! Not the whip!"

CHAPTER TWO
Passage to Madness

CRAIG came back to consciousness, lying in the dark. A dull wedge of agony was splitting his head. He fingered it, gingerly. Maddrey's bullet must have plowed a long furrow through his scalp. The wound had been roughly dressed, but the hair on his neck and the collar of his shirt were still stiff with dried blood.

He sat up stiffly, fumbled about. He was in a cramped little cell. There was no article of furniture. The walls were riveted metal. A flimsy metal ladder ran up one of them.

He would climb it, when he felt stronger.

The metal walls quivered to a deep, drumming roar. Craig felt an uneasy sense of swaying motion. It made him feel a little sick. The noise was like a hammer, pounding the wedge of agony in his brain.

He knew that he was a prisoner aboard the *Subterrane*.

Bound—

Where?

A sudden blade of blue light fell from above, painful to his eyes. It widened to a shining pillar. A trap door was opening in the ceiling of riveted steel, above the ladder. Craig saw a woman's foot, a trim bare ankle.

Her skirt caught on the ladder. Smooth thighs flashed. Then the light was obscured, as she lowered the door back into place. Craig waited, again in utter darkness.

She touched the floor beside him. His nostrils caught the fragrance of her hair.

"Ann?" he whispered.

"*Shhhhh…*" she warned. "Maddrey thinks I'm asleep. He told me not to come near you. If he finds me here, he'll whip me again." She shuddered. "Oh, Weston…"

"We must get away," Craig whispered.

She was trembling.

"But how can we?" Her voice was hoarse with dread. "We're on the *Subterrane*. Maddrey has been boring straight down with us, for hours." She clung to him. "We must be dozens of miles down!"

"*Dozens* of miles?" Craig shook his head in the dark. "That would be impossible. Volcanic heat would roast us. The pressure would crush the machine."

"But you helped poor Dad build the first disruptor disk," she protested. "You know the disrupted atoms form a neutronic film that lines the tunnel. It is less than a thousandth of an inch thick. But it doesn't conduct heat. And it's so dense that the weight of ordinary matter is nothing at all against it. It can stand thousands of tons, and thousands of degrees of heat!"

Craig was interested. The agony of his wound was forgotten for the moment, and their desperate plight. He was the engineer again.

"What about the power?" he asked.

"That comes from the disintegrated atoms," the girl told him. "Escaping electrons are picked up by accumulators at the edges of the disk, to charge the batteries. There is power to spare, for the refrigerator and ventilator systems."

A sob of fear came back into her voice.

"Oh, Weston—what can we do?"

"Your father?" asked Craig. "Can't he help us?"

She shuddered in his arms.

"I'm afraid—about Dad," she whispered. "One day he was gone. Maddrey told me that he had been called suddenly to Washington, about the patents. But he would have surely waited to speak to me. I'm so afraid—"

She sobbed again. Craig remembered the buzzards wheeling above the desert. He was certain that Dr. Tancred had not gone to Washington.

"Twice I tried to run away," whispered the girl. "But Maddrey caught me, with the whip—" Her quivering hands felt cold. "He's mad—a monster!"

"We must try to overpower him," said Craig. "If we can get out of here, and find something to use for a weapon—"

SUDDENLY his voice seemed very loud, and he choked it off. The drumming of the machinery had stopped. Heavy steps rang on a metal deck above, approaching. The girl trembled against Craig, voiceless.

"Oh, Weston!" she sobbed. "He's coming—"

The door was flung open above. Blue light flooded them. Leaning weakly against the metal wall, with his arm about the shuddering girl, Craig looked up. He saw Maddrey's bull-like, black-bearded mass. One gigantic hairy hand gripped a big automatic. From the other trailed the whip.

"Well?" Maddrey's voice was a careless, triumphant bellow. "Mr. Engineer, I see that I must warn you, too. You are not to associate with my ward, Miss Tancred. You two must keep apart."

Craig stared up into Maddrey's black face. He tried to meet those cold, blazing blue eyes. They seemed to shake his very soul, with an insane and ruthless violence.

"Nonsense, Maddrey!" Craig's voice trembled, in spite of his effort to keep it steady. "You've got to turn back."

"Turn back, Mr. Engineer?" Maddrey's voice was as ruthless as the booming of an angry sea. "Turn back—when we are bound for the center of the Earth! Do you know what the core of the Earth is?"

Craig himself shuddered, from the mad violence of that voice.

"Well, Mr. Engineer, I'll tell you. The heart of the Earth is a ball of precious metals, separated by flotation. Gold, platinum, radium!

"Your temporary prison, Mr. Engineer, is also the treasure room of the *Subterrane*. We have auxiliary disks, to cut sections of the Earth's heart to fill it. And your share can be your weight in gold—if you will promise to make any necessary repairs to the disruptors."

"I don't want any share—not from you," Craig told him.

But Maddrey's insanely blazing eyes had left Craig; they moved to the girl's slim, whip-marked loveliness. And Craig saw the terrible glare of an insane lust kindle in them. Maddrey chuckled, thickly.

"My darling, I told you not to come here." His voice had sunk to a thick gloating rasp. "You have disobeyed me. I must punish you for that." He chuckled again. "Or perhaps you enjoy the taste of the whip?"

Deliberately, the giant thrust the gun back into his belt. The sleek black serpent of the whip rippled through his enormous thick fingers. It came hissing down through the narrow opening, and coiled around the girl's white throat.

It left a red welt, and she screamed.

"Don't you think that I am expert, Mr. Engineer?" boomed the great voice of Maddrey. "I used to skin a twelve mule team, from the silver mines. I have cut off a Mexican wench's ear, at thirty feet."

A crimson rage tensed Craig. Reason told him he could do nothing. But fury drowned reason. Unarmed, swaying from that wedge of pain in his head, he swarmed up the flimsy ladder.

Maddrey was waiting for him, chuckling thickly. A great hobnailed boot crushed against his temple. It drove that wedge of agony deeper. The pain was intolerable, paralyzing.

Sick and dazed, Craig fell off the ladder. He dropped back to the metal floor. His head struck the wall. New agony half-blinded him. He lay breathless, half-unconscious.

But still he could hear Maddrey's voice, like the roar of far-off surf:

"Darling, I see that your engineer is going to be no use to me. I think I'll shoot him." Craig heard no sound from the girl. But the bellow came again: "So you don't want him to die? Then strip yourself, and stand up to take your medicine."

Desperately, Craig fought to rise. He slipped back into a red sea of pain. His mind floated groggily on crimson waves, and he felt very ill. But he could see Ann, as if she were far-off.

HE saw her slipping the garments from the rich-curved slimness of her red-welted body. Once she hesitated, with a little sobbing protest. And the whip flicked down. With a pistol-sharp report, it cut a tiny silken strap, and left a tiny fleck of red upon her satin skin.

Then, naked, she stood up to wait for the whip. Craig heard the cruel hissing of it, and the vicious cracks. He saw red marks spring across the firm upturned breasts of the girl, her smooth white back, and the gleaming columns of her thighs.

She held her breath, and uttered no cry. Lifted up to Maddrey, her bloodless face was queerly composed. She was held in an ecstasy of pain.

Wincing from every report, Craig counted the strokes of the whip. It fell nine times, and stopped. The girl made a soft, sobbing moan, and dropped down upon the floor beside him.

Maddrey chuckled, and coiled the red whip in his hands. Craig heard the far booming of his voice:

"Remember, the both of you—*I* am the master. The *Subterrane* is a little world, outside of the law. And I am its king. Don't forget that. If you forget, the whip will remind you—"

Sick, helpless horror drove that agonizing wedge deeper into Craig's brain, and once more extinguished his awareness.

CHAPTER THREE
The Kingdom of Hell

CRAIG was once more dimly conscious when the *Subterrane* fell. Ann Tancred was gone from the little steel-walled room. His throbbing head lay on a pillow, and a blanket covered his stiff body. The girl, he knew, must have brought him those.

The machinery was drumming again. That meant, he realized vaguely, that the metal mole was boring on down toward the Earth's core. And Ann was still at the mercy of Maddrey—insane with his ungoverned impulses, and his lust for unimaginable treasure.

The drumming abruptly stopped—and the *Subterrane* fell.

Craig had a sick feeling in his stomach. He clutched wildly at the metal ladder. It seemed to him that the fall lasted an endless, terrible time. Somewhere above he heard Maddrey's bull-like voice, bellowing with fear and rage.

Then the mole struck, with a savage, crushing force. Craig's splitting head was driven against the metal floor again. But this time he clung doggedly to consciousness.

He heard the crash and shriek of tortured metal. He thought that the machine must have fallen to the floor of some cave, crushed itself with the impact. But it didn't lie still.

For a little time Craig suspected that the toss and pitch that sickened him was all in his own battered head. But the measured creak of metal plates and the roll of his body convinced him at last that the *Subterrane* was adrift upon underground waters.

Nerved with a desperate hope that Maddrey might have been injured by the fall, he dragged himself up the flimsy ladder. But the door above had been locked upon him. His empty hands battered upon it in vain.

He shouted, and listened. But there was no sound save the creak of the plates and the slap of waves. At last, exhausted, Craig dropped back to the steel floor of the little treasure-room.

A TERRIBLE cold fear was growing in him. Was he the only one left alive? Was he doomed to slow death in a metal coffin, floating upon black buried waters that no eye had ever seen?

But at least Ann was freed from the whip.

So Craig told himself. But presently the iron deck above him rang once more to heavy footfalls. Again he heard the bellowing tones of Maddrey. He heard a vicious crack—and then the scream of Ann.

The old, numbing despair settled back into him.

Again he climbed the ladder, battered against the door. But the only response was the distant bellow of Maddrey's laughter, and another scream from Ann.

At last Craig heard the clang and grate of rocks beneath the machine's steel shell. He knew that they must have drifted to the edge of this unknown water. The *Subterrane* lay still.

Another time of intolerable suspense went by. Then Craig heard the click of a key in the lock above, and blue light blinded him. Maddrey's whip hissed and burned across his shoulders.

"Wake up, Mr. Engineer!" bellowed the giant. "I've got a job for you. You had better get about it—unless you want your hide peeled off!"

Craig blinked against the light and stared up into Maddrey's mad blue eyes.

"What's the job?" he demanded.

"The main transformer slipped off its mount, when we fell into this damned sea," Maddrey told him. "And the big disruptor disk burned out. It has got to be re-wired—or we'll all die in this damned hell."

Hope kindled in Craig again. Maddrey had never learned much about the invention he had stolen. Here was a chance to bargain for life. He caught his breath, and his shoulders drew straight.

"If I repair the disk," he said, "we're going to turn back to the surface. And you'll have to surrender your gun—and the whip."

Maddrey's blue eyes glittered cunningly.

"Perhaps I will," he said. "But first we'll inspect the damage. You must convince me that you know how to make the repairs. Come on out."

Craig climbed up the metal ladder. Reeling with exhaustion, suddenly aware of torturing hunger, he walked ahead of Maddrey along a narrow metal deck. They peered down into the engine room, in the nose of the machine.

A chaos of broken machinery and tangled cables lay tumbled about the huge rectangular case of the fallen transformer. Craig surveyed the damage, and slowly shook his head.

Maddrey's voice was lowered, hoarse:

"Can you fix it?"

"Maybe," Craig told him. "But it will take weeks. Possibly months. If you want me to try it, hand over the whip and the gun."

Maddrey stepped back from him, and the mad eyes grew cunning again. He made an animal chuckle.

"I think you'll fix it, anyhow, Mr. Engineer," he said thickly. "I think you'd rather do that than see my whip skin the girl alive—one square inch at a time."

Cold blue eyes drilled into Craig.

"Wouldn't you, Mr. Engineer?"

Weston Craig tried to meet that savage glare of ice and madness. Fear sent a prickling numbness over him. He tried desperately to remember things he had heard about how to deal with madmen. Nothing very hopeful came to mind.

"Speak up!" roared Maddrey.

Craig started, swallowed. He must pretend to yield. That was the only way. Perhaps he would have some opportunity to overpower Maddrey. He licked his lips, and nodded slowly.

"I'll try to make the repairs," he said.

"You *will* make them!" Maddrey boomed. "If you care about the girl—"

A sudden apprenhension stiffened Craig. He peered into Maddrey's dark-bearded face, gasping:

"Where is she? If you've—"

Maddrey's answer was a bellowing call:

"Darling—we are ready to dine."

ANN TANCRED came out of a narrow door, and across the metal deck. She looked pale with fear, and her dark eyes were cast down. She carried a tray, and the dishes on it rattled to the trembling of her hands.

"Lively, now!" boomed Maddrey. "And don't spill it!"

The whip cracked, rifle-like. The pale girl cried out, and started. A glass of water danced out of the tray, splashed and splintered on the deck. Maddrey chuckled thickly.

"Darling—I warned you!"

His terrible eyes stared thirstily at the front of her tight silken blouse, swollen to the full contours of her breasts. The whip flicked out, slashed the fabric like a knife. Firm white flesh pushed through the slit, marked with a line of red.

The girl choked back her sob of pain. Tears fell into the dishes on the tray. And fury rose against Craig's fear. Fists knotted, he swung upon Maddrey.

The giant reached for his automatic.

"Strike me, and you die!" he boomed thickly. "But she shall be the one to pay—"

His roar was abruptly stopped.

Clan-n-n-n-ng!

The iron hull above them rang to a crashing impact. It throbbed again, to a series of battering blows. Gripping whip and gun, Maddrey moved uneasily aft, toward the valve.

"It's something alive!" he croaked hoarsely. "We'll see—"

His great hairy hands spun a wheel. The small, massive oval door swung inward. There was an inrush of air. It was hot, heavy, musty—the fetid, over-powering breath of a rank and teeming jungle.

Peering over Maddrey's great shoulder, Craig looked out into the cave—and shuddered from a sense of evil nightmare.

The *Subterrane* lay upon a flat dark beach. Beyond it was the jungle. A towering wall of livid, luminous, hostile forest. The shapes of the monstrous plants, and their pale glowing colors, were eerily strange.

Above the jungle rose the cave's rugged wall. It was pitted with the dark openings of cliff dwellings. The glowing wings of huge, bat-like things flitted unpleasantly before them.

The dark and cragged roof was low above the *Subterrane*. But, in the distance, beyond a jutting salient of the cliffs, it lifted to an illimitable arch. Beneath it lay the vastness of the underground sea. The uneasy waters shone darkly, like blood made luminous.

"The mother of caves!" Maddrey's whisper seemed apprehensive. "This is the sea into which the underground waters drain. It seems that the things of the Earth's abyss, like those of the deep sea, make their own light—"

Horror choked off his voice.

The automatic crashed four times, deafening in the heavy air. Maddrey stepped fearfully back, and Craig saw the thing that he had shot.

A great, bat-like creature, like those soaring before the caves. As it tossed on the beach, in the agony of death, Craig could see that it was reptilian. Its body was scaled. The broad, leathery wings glowed as if lined with green flame. The teeth were hideous fangs, the lower limbs armed with fearful talons.

THE thing still gripped a heavy copper sledge, with which it must have been hammering on the hull of the *Subterrane*.

Craig swung protestingly on Maddrey.

"Why kill it?" he demanded. "Probably it meant no harm. May have been trying to signal, with the hammer. But now— God knows what will happen!"

Maddrey snapped a full clip into the automatic. He gulped—a little fearfully, Craig thought. But then all the roaring violence of his voice came back:

"I'm the master, here! You say we may be here for months. Well, I'll show these winged devils who is their ruler."

"Looks as if you'll have your chance..." Craig commented. "...right now."

With a trembling arm, he pointed. A horde of the bright-winged troglodytes were gliding down from the cliffs beyond the jungle. Snarling, hissing, grunting, cackling, they swarmed about the machine.

Maddrey fired half a dozen shots into the fantastic bedlam that they made. A copper spear came clattering through the opening. Hastily he spun the wheel, to close the valve again.

Dry-voiced, Craig demanded:

"What now, Mr. Conqueror?"

"Frightened?" Maddrey boomed scornfully. "The beasts have nothing better than copper. The *Subterrane* is an oyster they can't open—not in a thousand years."

Craig tried to wet his throat.

"I am afraid," he whispered. "Maybe they can't open the oyster—but they're going to cook us in the shell! Didn't you see them—carrying torches, and broken branches?

"We've no power to move the *Subterrane*. And fire, in the oxygen of this super-dense atmosphere, will be about ten times more effective than any blaze you've ever known.

"Listen..."

Faintly, through the thick steel hull, they heard the eager crackling roar of flames.

CHAPTER FOUR
The Poisoned Whip

THE plates of the *Subterrane* grew hot. Paint began to bubble and crack and smoke. The air became searing, stifling. The fire outside made a steadily mounting roar.

Maddrey paced up and down the hot metal deck, cursing in a hoarse and frightened voice. Ann Tancred had quietly fainted, from terror and exhaustion and heat. Her white body lay sprawled on the floor, beside the tray she had dropped. Maddrey, passing, cut at her viciously with the whip. She made a sleepy little moan, but did not move.

"Stop it!" choked Craig. "You devil!"

The mad blue eyes of Maddrey swung to him.

"Well, Mr. Engineer," his thick voice mocked, "what else do you suggest? I may die uncomfortably. But at least I intend to have the pleasure of witnessing agony greater than my own."

The whip flicked out again, to make a thin red mark on the exposed curve of Ann's white thigh. Her leg drew up a little, and she moaned again. Maddrey looked back at Craig.

"Unless, Mr. Engineer," his great voice said, "you can repair the disruptor disk and form a new neutronic film to protect us from the heat."

Craig's fists were knotted with impotent wrath. His lean body quivered. That old wedge of pain was driving into his head again, and he swayed from a weakness that he could not overcome.

"I can't fix the main disk." His voice came faint and husky. "But I think I can do something else—if you'll leave Ann alone."

The mad eyes of Maddrey gleamed cunningly.

"What can you do?"

"The auxiliary disks—the ones intended to cut samples from the rocks—don't seem to be injured," Craig told him. "And a rather simple change in the wiring will project the disruption field as a tubular vortex."

He was remembering the laboratory accident, four years ago, and the green ray that had cut through the wall. Perhaps, he thought wearily, it would have been better if he hadn't come along to save Ann.

"Then get at it!" Maddrey's ruthless hand seized his shoulder. "Before we're all cooked alive!"

For an instant Craig resisted. He would only be saving Ann to face further tortures. Then a spark of hope came to his pain-dulled brain. Perhaps he could turn the new weapon upon Maddrey, first.

But the cold eyes of Maddrey watched him, with a cunning alertness, as he dismounted the instrument from its armored port, and labored to alter the wiring behind the shining, foot-wide terminal disk.

The roar of flames without grew louder as he worked. The heat inside the hull passed the limit of endurance. Craig's clothing was drenched with sweat, then dried again. Hot metal blistered his fingers, and the air burned his lungs. A sick weakness dragged him toward oblivion.

Ann moaned again, on the hot deck. Once she struggled, as if suffocating. Unconscious fingers ripped away her blouse. Her whip-scarred breasts stood out naked, jeweled with tiny drops of sweat, quivering to her gasping breath.

Craig swayed over his task. Covertly he watched Maddrey. He hoped that the giant would collapse, give him one second's opportunity. But Maddrey seemed unaware of the heat. His blue cunning eyes never wavered.

That crimson wedge was driving deeper, dulling Craig's brain. His blistered fingers grew lifeless and numb. Maddrey's great hairy hands helped him make the last connection.

And Maddrey seized the disk, gasping:

"Thank you, Mr. Engineer!"

Craig pitched limply down to the blistering deck, and Maddrey went out to fight the troglodytes. Dimly, Craig saw him open the valve. Darkly, as in a glass, he saw the blinding green finger that probed from the disk—and cut a flapping beast-creature in twain.

Then Craig's awareness mercifully faded.

It was a long time before Craig was fully conscious again. Mere snatches of sanity broke his delirium. He knew that fever parched him, spreading from the throbbing agony of his wound.

ANN was allowed to tend him for a time. Memories of her cool tender hands, and the terror-haunted eyes in her pale sweet face, mingled with his mad dreams. But nothing in all his delirium was more terrible than the sound of Maddrey's whip, and the sobbing of the girl.

Presently her place was taken by another, a monstrous nurse.

A troglodyte!

Craig knew, at last, that he had been carried out the *Subterrane*, to a flimsy little frond-thatched hut above the beach. The hideous, leather-winged reptile-thing waited on him there, bringing water and copper bowls of unfamiliar, ill-cooked food.

The very odor of the thing was almost deadly. It was peculiarly acrid, revolting. A concentrated essence, Craig thought, from the snake-house in the zoo. The hut was saturated with it, and the hissing monster haunted his delirium.

In spite of the odor, however, Craig felt at last that the wound was healing. The wedge of pain was gone. Sanity returned, and be began to realize what had happened.

Maddrey had conquered the troglodytes. Their copper weapons had failed against the terrible green ray from the disruptor disk. Maddrey was now the ruthless tyrant of a strange kingdom.

The reptiles, Craig thought, were about as intelligent as primitive man. They had a grunting language that Maddrey had learned. They hardened copper to make simple weapons and tools. Dwelling in rock caves, they hatched their young from eggs, and flew across the scarlet sea to hunt for food.

They were just advanced enough to feel a superstitious awe for the beings who had come plunging down through the roof of their world. Maddrey had established himself, Craig discovered, as a sort of god.

He exacted tribute from the troglodytes—ornaments of hammered gold, and red pearls that came from the shining sea. He compelled them to build him a rude, leaf-thatched palace, in a walled compound at the edge of the jungle.

So Maddrey reigned, with ray and whip, over his strange kingdom—waiting for Craig to repair the wrecked *Subterrane*.

Many times Craig had wakened, from his uneasy feverish sleep, to find the dark-bearded giant towering over him, the black whip trailing from his immense cruel hands. And Maddrey had stalked, beside the screaming troglodyte, through his delirium.

"Well, Mr. Engineer!"

It seemed to Craig that he had heard that same mocking boast a thousand times—usually accompanied with an expert, agonizing flick of Maddrey's whip.

"Perhaps you hope to get rid of me?" the great voice would boom. "Well, then—repair the *Subterrane!* And I'll go on, with a crew of the trogs. Maybe I'll take the girl—if she can stand the whip so long. But I'll have to leave you behind, Mr. Engineer. We'll see if you can rule the trogs!"

Maddrey was crazy. No doubt of that. And getting crazier, as mad impulse met no restraint. But insanity didn't keep him from being very cunning, and very dangerous.

Craig promised that he would set about repairing the *Subterrane*, as soon as he was able. He made the promise for Ann's sake—after a time when the steaming, fetid jungle wind brought her screams to him, from Maddrey's compound.

In one way only, Craig learned, had Maddrey's mad will been thwarted.

Among the tribal treasures of the troglodytes were great crimson pearls. Maddrey avidly appropriated all that he could discover. And, learning that pearl-bearing mollusks lived in the luminescent sea, he made the creatures build a wooden canoe.

He tried to force them to dredge for the precious shell. But the troglodytes displayed an invincible fear of the scarlet sea. Their few pearls had come from shells washed ashore. Maddrey's whip, and even the deadly ray, failed to make them enter the boat.

At last a time came when Craig was able to stumble out of his hospital hut. He walked swaying up the trail toward Maddrey's high-walled compound, with his reptilian nursemaid flapping and hissing behind him. He hoped to see Ann.

BUT a sentry stopped him at the gate. The thing looked a little like an enormous, scale-covered bird. As tall as Craig, it stood upon the spread talons of one foot, and clutched a long, copper-bladed spear in the other. Its huge eyes, yellow-red and phosphorescent, blinked at him with an alternate malevolence.

And it hissed an angry warning.

The massive wooden gate opened. Maddrey appeared. He was trailing a new whip, which was purple and luminous.

"Maddrey—" Craig gasped hoarsely, "I've got to see Ann."

The mad, icy eyes of Maddrey mocked him.

"You're mistaken, Mr. Engineer," the great voice boomed. "You won't see her till the *Subterrane* is repaired." Maddrey chuckled hoarsely. "But, if you like, you may hear her!"

He drew the shining purple lash through black-gloved fingers.

"I've a new whip, you see," he said thickly. "The trogs are afraid of the medusae that float on the crimson sea. I have found the reason why. The tentacles are covered with thousands of tiny, poisoned hooks. I have braided the new whip from them. The pain—

"But taste it for yourself, Mr. Engineer!"

Lightning-swift, the thin purple lash darted out. Craig flung up his arm, to keep it from his face. The touch was light. It hardly marked the skin. But sheer agony splintered through him. It was blinding, paralyzing. He was drowned in purple pain. It was a tortured eternity before he could move or see or speak.

"Do you like the taste, Mr. Engineer?" Maddrey was booming at him, thickly. "That is what the girl must drink— until you have the *Subterrane* repaired."

He stepped back within. The compound gate creaked shut. The sentry blinked and snarled, and Craig turned trembling back toward the beach. He shuddered, to the knife-like scream that followed him.

CHAPTER FIVE
Madman's Dream

CRAIG began the difficult repair, and time went by. Maddrey had carried away the other auxiliary disk, so that it could not be rewired into a weapon. And he removed the power tubes that were essential to the operation of the main disk. Sometimes he came, with his monstrous retinue, to mock at Craig's helpless toil.

Craig had no measure of the time that passed. Maddrey had taken his watch, and the cave knew neither day nor night. He ate when hunger impelled, the strange foods the monsters brought him. He slept when he had to. And toiled as long as he was able—for the hot, heavy, humid air often brought him the piteous screaming of Ann.

But the long wound on his head had completely healed. He felt that the cave's stern life had toughened him a little. He found hope sometimes to plan against Maddrey's harsh dominion—but the talons of his old fear had never quite released him.

Months, he thought, had gone. The great transformer had been laboriously hoisted, bolted back into place again. His task was almost done, on the day that Ann came.

She came running down the jungle trail, from Maddrey's palisade. Craig heard her eager call, aboard the *Subterrane*, and ran anxiously to meet her. His eyes devoured her tall, sweet-curving loveliness.

All Maddrey's torture, he saw, had not broken her. Time had smoothed many of the marks of the whip from her white body. She had made new clothing for herself, of soft skins.

But the brown leather jacket was ripped across the shoulder, and Craig could see that one of her breasts was beaded with scarlet drops.

"Oh, Weston!" she sobbed. "Weston—we've got to do—*something!*"

Held close in his arms, she shuddered with terror. The bleeding cushion of her breast was hot against Craig's torn shirt. The red drops wet his skin.

"My darling!" He kissed her. "We must—"

"He's insane!" She quivered in his arms. "He's planning terrible things. He's planning to take back an army of the trogs—and attack the world with your disruptor ray. He says he can change the main disk, like the one you rewired."

Holding the girl's hot, pliant body close, Craig tried to repress his own shudder. But he knew what the main disk would be, as a weapon. Frightful instrumentality! Its beam of green annihilation could probe for forty miles. Slice through any fortress! Sink any battleship!

The *Subterrane* would be almost invincible. It could always retreat to safety underground. It could strike unawares, at any point. In the midst of an army, the center of an unwarned city.

"Oh, Weston!" The girl's dark eyes were bright with tears. "I'm so afraid! Can't you run the machine, so that we can get away? Or turn it on Maddrey—somehow?"

Craig's fists were clenched. Quivering with desperation, he looked at the huge helpless bulk of the *Subterrane*, at the margin of the dark-shining sea. He peered toward Maddrey's palisade, at the eldritch jungle's edge.

Hopeless, baffled, he shook his head.

"I'm afraid not, Ann," he muttered. "Maddrey carried away the auxiliary disk. And he got the power tubes too—so I couldn't start the machine, even if I finished the repairs sooner than he expects. Once I tried to slip into the compound. But his monsters are always on guard—"

He bit his lip.

"But, West!" sobbed the girl. "We've got to do something. We must try to get away!" She shuddered and turned pale. "If he takes me again—" she whispered faintly. "That poisoned whip—don't let him take me!"

Craig caught his breath.

"My darling," he promised, "I'll do my best." His shoulders lifted resolutely. "Anyhow," he said, "Maddrey won't attack the Earth. In five minutes I can tear loose the wiring from the disk. I know he can't repair it."

His arm drew hard around her trembling body.

"Then we'll try to get away from him," he breathed. "But I don't know how—"

"Hurry!" sobbed the girl.

FRANTICALLY, Craig labored to undo the work of weeks. He tore wires from their terminals, smashed again the delicate instruments he had rebuilt. Maddrey must not carry out his scheme of mad conquest. Now, he would not.

Ann's frightened voice brought Craig back out of the *Subterrane*. Nerveless, pale with terror, the girl stood by the red water's edge, paralyzed. Her glazed eyes were staring, toward Maddrey's palisade.

"Oh, West!" she breathed faintly. "It's too late!"

For Maddrey came stalking down the trail, from his compound in the phosphorescent jungle. King of the cavern world! He wore a rude gold crown, set with the red malevolent eye of a scarlet pearl.

The mighty barrel of his body was covered with the black-and-yellow fur of some animal the troglodytes had caught in the mysterious land beyond the scarlet sea. His belt was the broad skin of a crimson serpent.

His automatic was thrust in that belt, and a long copper knife. The disruptor disk was slung from his shoulders. Swinging from his black-gloved hand were the purple-shining coils of the poison whip.

Screaming behind him, hopping awkwardly on their taloned feet, spreading green glowing wings to balance themselves, came four of the troglodytes. The heavy wind carried ahead their sharp, sickening stench.

"Well, darling!"

Cold and bright and terrible behind the tangle of black beard, the eyes of Maddrey sought the terror-stricken girl.

"I told you not to leave my palace," his great voice said thickly. "I don't need to tell you, dear, what your punishment will be."

Like a live thing, the purple whip uncoiled itself across the hard black sand. Frozen with terror, the girl uttered a mute, frantic little cry of protest.

Trembling, Craig stepped forward.

"Maddrey—" His voice came low and husky, past the fear that choked him. "You'll have to give up your plans of conquest. Because I have just dismantled the main disk. I've undone all the repairs.

"The *Subterrane* won't move again!"

Behind the black beard, Maddrey went livid with rage.

"You—" His bellow choked. "You'll complete the repairs."

Craig gulped. "I won't do it, Maddrey." His voice was dry with fear. "You can do anything you like. Whip me. Kill me. But I'm through taking orders from you. That's all. Through!"

The cold mad eyes of Maddrey glittered again, craftily.

"Big talk, Mr. Engineer!" Drawing the thin shining length of the whip through black-gloved fingers, he laughed thickly, maliciously. "But I'm not at your mercy. I'm still the king!"

The ice-blue eyes went from Craig to the girl. She shuddered before Maddrey's eyes, and made a dry sob of fear. The whip cracked explosively. Another red drop oozed out of her white, quivering flesh. And she made a dull, hopeless little whimper of agony.

Maddrey coiled the whip, turned back to Craig.

"I'm a scientist, Mr. Engineer," he boasted. "I can compare the two auxiliary disks, and discover what you did— it was merely a change in the wiring. I can learn how to rewire the main disk—into a scourge that will conquer the planet!"

He gestured with the whip at the grotesque monsters standing behind him, blinking huge luminescent eyes.

"The trogs are natural artizans," he boomed. "I'm teaching them modern science. They'll build me a fleet of *Subterranes*. So I don't need you, Mr. Engineer."

He licked his thick lips.

"I'll give you a choice." Maddrey chuckled, and leered at the fear-frozen girl again. "You can complete the repairs, if you like. Or you and the girl can take the canoe the trogs made, and go dive for pearls!"

Craig awayed to a stunning impact of horror.

"Kill us, if you like." His voice was hoarse and flat. "But we won't go out on the sea. You know why. You've seen the things in that red water. Even the trogs are afraid—"

"Take your choice," Maddrey repeated thickly. "Repair the disk. Or dive!"

Craig's fists were clenched.

"I told you, Madrey," He choked. "I'm through!"

But Ann Tancred's quivering fingers clutched his arm.

"We'll go," she whispered faintly. "Tell him we'll go out for pearls."

CHAPTER SIX
Scarlet Pearls

AT the compound's gate, Craig lifted the canoe to his shoulders. It was a frail shell of hardwood. The troglodytes that made it had displayed an amazing skill. Could they really build more *Subterranes*, as Maddrey's mad brain planned?

One of them was watching at the gate. It shifted its balance from one taloned foot to the other, blinked its enormous evilly shining eyes, and hissed at him unpleasantly.

Could Maddrey's flapping reptilian hordes overcome mankind? It was not likely, Craig knew. Maddrey's twisted mind would blunder, somewhere. But there was a nightmare possibility that it *could* happen—that haunted him. Wings of horror, over the world!

Craig carried the canoe down to the beach. Lapping against the black sand, the red water seemed thick and heavy as oil. Its luminescence, he knew, was due to billions of microscopic organisms, perhaps akin to *Noctiluca Scintillons*. But still it seemed to him a sea of blood. He trembled with dread of the monstrous life that dwelt beneath it.

Ann came staggering behind him, laden with paddle and basket and anchor rope. Maddrey stalked behind her. She stumbled once, and the purple whip cracked, and she screamed.

Craig set the canoe down, trembling.

"So you don't like her to be whipped?" Maddrey laughed at his futile anger. "Well, Mr. Engineer, if you want her to know what whipping means—just come back without a pearl!"

Craig snatched the paddle from the girl, started back toward Maddrey. Maddrey reached for his automatic. The troglodytes screamed ominously behind him. Ann caught Craig's arm.

"Come on," she urged. "He'd kill you!"

And Craig turned back. They piled the equipment into the canoe. Ann sat in the bow. He pushed it out on the oily red surface, stepped aboard, dipped the paddle.

"Remember!" Maddrey boomed after them. "A pearl—or the whip!"

With long deep strokes, Craig drove them out across the dully-shining water. The dark, cragged roof sank toward the crimson surface behind them. The jungle became a narrow blur of blue, above the thin black line of the beach.

Suddenly Ann's bare white arm gestured ahead.

"Oh, West!" she cried, huskily. "Let's never go back!"

Craig sat as if frozen, with the paddle lifted. His gray eyes stared for a long time into the vaulted gloom, above the mysterious scarlet infinity of the sea. His lean face lit slowly, to an eager hope.

"There's land!" he whispered at last. "Beyond—somewhere. It can't be so very far. Because the trogs fly across, to hunt."

His eager eyes came back to the girl.

"There might—" His voice shook. "There might even be a way—outside!"

Ann was breathless. "Outside?"

"The living things here," he said slowly, "are akin to those in the world above. They must have come down, through some opening—if we could only find it!"

"But—West," she protested, doubtfully. "Everything here is so different—so terribly strange."

"I know," he said. "Evolution has changed everything here, to live in darkness and humidity and high air-pressure.

The adaptation must have taken ages. And the passage may have been closed a million years ago."

He stared again, into the dark arch of mystery ahead.

"Most caverns are formed by the carbonic acid gas in water, dissolving limestone rock. Underground rivers must flow down into this sea. If we could follow them up, we might find some passage to the surface—"

HE HEARD Ann's muted cry, and saw the terror glaze her eyes.

"See, West!" she gasped. "He won't let us go!"

Looking back, Craig found the dark line of the beach, with the rust-reddened cylinder of the *Subterrane* lying athwart it. Against the luminous jungle, he could see Maddrey's palisade. Green wings were spread above it.

A troglodyte was flapping after them.

Trembling, Craig dipped the paddle again.

"No," he whispered, "Maddrey will never let us go. Because he still wants me to repair the *Subterrane*. He thinks fear will drive me to do it. But I won't!"

He wet his lips, gulped. "Ann—*I mustn't!*"

The soaring reptile overtook them. It wheeled low above the canoe. Each green-shining leathery wing was weirdly splotched with a lurid yellow marking, like a yellow eye. They seemed to blink, as the great wings beat. The fanged beak opened, as the creature dived. It hissed viciously.

Ann shuddered.

"No, West," she whispered, "you mustn't repair the *Subterrane* and let Maddrey lead these things against the world..."

Craig paddled on, beneath the flapping hissing monster, until *Subterrane* and palisade were tiny with distance. He sounded with cord and stone to find a shoal, and at last dropped the weighted basket over the side.

Fighting a silent battle with his fear of the red depths, he prepared to dive. Stripped off the worn remnant of his shirt. Thrust a copper knife into his belt.

Suddenly Ann flung her arms around him clung to him.

"Don't, West!" she sobbed. "You may be—killed! Let's go on—in spite of the monster!"

Craig shook his unkempt head.

"It would follow," he whispered. "More would come. We could never get away. We must wait, for a better chance."

He kissed her cold lips, and dived.

The water was like a thick, shining mist of blood. It stung his opened eyes. He searched along the rocky bottom, amid grotesque sharp-spined phosphorescent creatures.

At last he found a giant shell. A huge, age-old oval, it was black itself, but encrusted with tiny luminescent things. He detached it with a quick slash of the copper knife, lifted it into the basket.

Already his lungs were aching. But he found another great shell. Another. And a fourth. Rotten with time, they crumbled under his fingers. In one he thought he felt the smooth round of a pearl.

Four shells filled the basket, and his lungs were throbbing, bursting. He grasped the rope, heaved himself to the surface. The watching troglodyte dived low again, and screamed.

Craig clung panting to the gunwale, getting back his breath. Beneath the oily crimson surface, something touched his feet. He kicked out, and a needle of agony drove into his knee.

Hastily he tumbled into the boat, and hauled up the basket of shell. Ann took the great black mollusks, as he opened them, to probe the decaying flesh for pearls. His eyes lifted anxiously to her white, frightened face.

"None."

She shook her head and her dark eyes rested sadly upon Craig. Her fingers tossed the last rotting shellfish back into the crimson sea.

"None," she repeated.

Craig's heart constricted with fear.

"I thought—thought I felt one!" he protested anxiously. "Now I must dive again."

"Wait, Weston..."

HER voice was urgent, tense with dread. Her frightened fingers closed hard on his arm. She pointed at the red water beside the canoe. Craig saw a swirl of crimson foam.

Hideous, hairy yellow limbs were fighting for the mollusks they had thrown back!"

"Let's go on!" begged the girl. "On across the sea—"

But Craig jerked his head at the wheeling troglodyte.

"We could never get away."

He kissed Ann's cold tense lips, and dived again.

Three shells were in the basket, when something touched his shoulder with scarlet flame. He twisted to face his attacker. It was a water spider, larger than himself!

In the stinging scarlet water, its body was a glowing yellow moon. Its huge eyes shone purple. Its limbs were hairy, taloned, frightful.

Craig slashed at it desperately. But the dull copper blade slithered harmlessly from the fearful limb that gripped him. He caught the shank in his hands, wrenched with a frantic strength.

The talon came free from his shoulder. Agony shocked him, and a new blinding red was in his eyes. He caught the rope, heaved desperately. With a maddening slowness, he came upward.

He felt the rush of the thing beneath his feet, and it came to the surface almost as quickly as he. Great hairy yellow arms broke the water, groping for him. The sinister purple eyes shone just beneath the surface.

Frantically, Craig scrambled aboard. Panting with pain and terror and exhaustion, with red water streaming down his arms, he hauled desperately at the basket rope.

But a new furious commotion broke the water to scarlet foam. A terrific jerk tore the rope from his fingers. He fell in the bottom of the canoe.

"Weston!" Ann was sobbing. "Oh, Weston—you're hurt!"

Then she shrieked. Hideous yellow arms came over the gunwale. A frightful black talon caught her jacket and tore it half off her.

Craig dragged himself back to his knees, seized the paddle. A swift blow broke that fearful limb. He dipped the paddle, pulled the canoe desperately away. The troglodyte dived on shimmering green wings, hissing insidiously.

"Your shoulder!" Ann was sobbing. "West—your shoulder!"

Craig flung away the red drops that ran down his arm.

"Doesn't matter," he gasped. "No pearl. Can't dive again. Not without basket and rope." His red shoulders Straightened. "So we've got to go on—in spite of the trog!"

A new eager light shone in his eyes.

"Anyhow, we'll try."

Ignoring the blood seeping down from his lacerated shoulder, Craig drove the canoe forward again across the shining scarlet sea, toward the black illimitable mysterious arch ahead.

"I'm glad, Weston!" breathed the girl. "Glad—even if we die!"

Above them, the green-winged troglodyte hissed and screamed its menace.

CHAPTER SEVEN
The River of Terror

FEAR rode the canoe. Craig knew in his heart that it was one grim pursuer that he and the girl could never escape. But he dipped the paddle swiftly, fighting weariness and pain.

"West!" screamed Ann, from the bow. "Behind you!"

Craig felt the dip and swing of the canoe. Twisting, he saw that the troglodyte had dropped upon the stern. Great black talons gripped the gunwales. Shimmering green wings were still half spread, for balance. The toothed beak was hissing.

Craig half-rose in the boat, and brought the paddle over his head with a swinging blow. A green wing lifted, caught it harmlessly. The beak seized the deflected paddle, tore it from his fingers, flung it into the darkly shining water.

Disarmed, Craig trembled.

The huge yellow-red eyes blinked alternately. The creature hitched itself forward. The fanged beak struck and screamed and struck again.

Craig shrank back, chilled with sweat of fear.

"Here!" Ann whispered.

He felt the hilt of the long copper knife in his hand. Surging to his feet on the bottom of the canoe, he lunged. The scaly body was hard beneath the dull blade. The leathery wings folded about him, suffocating with their sickening reek. Black talons raked at him murderously.

The monster swayed with him. They toppled out of the canoe. Craig gasped for breath as they sank in scarlet water. He stabbed, stabbed again and again. Still the wings wrapped him, still fangs and talons slashed.

Abruptly, then, something was ripping at the wings. In the painful, blinding scarlet dimness of the water, he glimpsed hideous yellow limbs. He saw an evil yellow moon, and evil orbs of purple.

The spider had followed.

The troglodyte writhed in agony. The great wings unfolded. Craig drew up his feet, kicked against the scaled body. A hairy yellow limb reached for him. He slashed at it with the copper blade, then fought his way upward.

Ann had retrieved the paddle. She drove the canoe toward him. He clambered shakily aboard, and she paddled away from the increasing confusion in the foaming red water. Craig saw the black, mutilated body of the troglodyte flung clear of the surface, dragged back again by fighting yellow limbs—scores of them.

As soon as he could, Craig relieved Ann. With splinters from the canoe's hard wood, she pinned her torn jacket together again, to cover the curves of her bloodstained breasts.

And they went on across the scarlet sea.

The black roof lifted above them, until it was lost in murky gloom. Now and again they steered away from cragged black walls that rose abruptly from the darkly shining water. However long the cavern might be, Craig supposed, it was never very wide.

Sitting in the bow, Ann kept an apprehensive watch behind. But no green winged troglodyte appeared to follow them. Until at last a confused tremendous roaring came to them across the luminous waters, and then a vague new light was visible against the black and lofty vault ahead.

Presently a new wall of jungle was visible, a barrier higher and more ominous than that upon the shore they had left. Far along it, miles in the distance, a bright pillar of scarlet stood up above the red sea.

The roaring came from that pillar, endlessly.

They reached the shore. Overleaning the dark water, weird plants thrust themselves fifty feet upward. The jungle was a fiat-topped wall of menace. Blood-red tentacles writhed from immense, bell-shaped violet blooms. Tremendous fungi were choked in masses of twisting creepers.

"We could never cut a way through that," Craig muttered apprehensively. "Even if there's nothing to attack—and probably there is!"

CLOUDS of fire drifted above the jungle. Eerie colors shimmered through it—yellow and purple and flaming green. A luminous mist settled toward them. And Ann gasped with pain.

Suddenly they were both slapping furiously at faces and bare arms and the numerous rents in their clothing. For the cloud consisted of minute, luminous insects, whose stings were liquid agony.

Craig drove the canoe back until the torturing swarms diminished. Then they paddled on toward that roaring, enigmatic pillar of red. The low wall of weirdly shining jungle presently became higher. The marshes were broken by lofty cliffs, that shone with blue lichens. Beyond were mysterious, darkly glowing hills.

The roaring had become a crashing, incessant thunder. At last, rounding a dark headland, they saw the crimson fall. Over a sheer precipice, hundreds of feet high, came a long wall of water. A sheet of lambent scarlet, it tumbled into a maelstrom of shining foam.

Craig caught his breath to shout above the din:

"Above the fall—must be a river. We can go up it—toward the Outside! If we can get around the fall!"

He paddled in again, toward the foot of a mossy cliff. They dragged the canoe up upon a narrow scrap of beach, and then climbed inland. The wonder and the terror of this new world awed them to silence.

Far away, beyond a shining purple cloud, the cragged wall of the cave was visible. Ranges Of hills rolled down from it, to their feet. A fantastic world! Everything was luminous.

The soil was covered with a softly glowing, yellow-green moss. And stranger plants scattered it. Here and there thick brown stalks towered out of low dense clumps of greenish fronds. Each stalk bore, a hundred feet above, a swollen sphere of elfin blue.

"Blue moons," Craig whispered. "Growing on stalks!"

He remembered a lecture on animal luminescence. The speaker had described two wonder-chemicals. The protein, *luciferine*. And the enzyme, *luciferase*. The first is oxidized, he recalled, in the presence of the second. The chemical products are *oxy-luciferase* and water. And light is emitted by the most efficient process known to science.

Strange illustration of scientific fact!

Creeping apprehensively, side by side, Craig and Ann came to the summit of the hill. Beyond the forest of moon, winding away like an unimaginable crimson snake, they saw the river.

The river of terror!

Craig shuddered to a cold shock of fear, and drew Ann's trembling body close to his side. The bend of the river spread vast, almost, as a second scarlet sea. Its flatness was alive with dull red light, scattered with floating masses of decaying fungi and patches of greenish scum.

Above it drifted weird-hued clouds of many-colored fire. The farther shore was faintly visible, a gleaming line of metallic blue and frigid violet, radiant with deadly plants.

Far-off, the river came out of another dark arch of mystery. Craig stared for a long time into it, as if trying to see every peril and heartbreak and disaster that might await them there.

Abruptly he shook himself, as if breaking from an unpleasant trance, and caught his breath.

"We may get through alive," he whispered. "We *must!* But there's such a lot to do. We'll have to bring the canoe up through the jungle, and over the hill—we'd never make a mile, without it. But first we must have a fire—a smudge to keep away those insects. And food—"

So began another epic of frightful risk and desperate effort and unmeasured agony. They searched for dry wood, to make a fire by friction. Craig pitted the copper knife against poison dripping yellow fangs, and killed a ten-foot greenish lizard. They dried and smoked its flesh for food, dressed its skin for clothing.

THE dead, heavy air, reeking with the rot of the swamps, was hot and fetid as some unclean monster's breath. Despite the smudge, the stinging insects made rest impossible. Gigantic black spiders swung down from their webs in the forest of moods, to silent and deadly attack.

Exhaustion became a kind of anodyne for fear. A time came even when the continuity of Craig's mind was broken. He toiled in a dull gray haze. He knew only that peril pressed on behind, and awaited them ahead.

Behind, the horror of the troglodytes, and the madness of Maddrey's venomed whip.

Ahead, unguessed danger, guarding the undiscovered passage—if any passage did exist—to the sanity and the sunlight of the world above.

Sometimes, when he had rested, his mind became very vivid. He Saw Ann's slender dark-eyed loveliness, without her rags and her half-healed scars and the fear that was like a shadow over her. It was as though he had never seen her before.

"I love you, Ann," he told her. "And I know we'll find a way!"

Such lucid moments, however, were few.

Craig lived in a haze of exhaustion. For he had little rest. He hacked with the dull copper knife at the teeming river jungle. He dragged the canoe over hot mud that quaked with hideous unseen life beneath.

And the world outside seemed remote beyond the imagination.

A brief elation mounted in him, when at last they pushed the canoe out upon the river. Ann sat in the bow, tending the smudge that held back the swarming midges that looked and felt like clouds of fire.

The shining, hostile jungle wall fell away behind. And the eldritch forest of moons, beneath which they had fought so long. Silence seemed strange, after the endless thunder of the fall. Darkness pressed upon the red waters ahead, hiding both menace and hope.

"We're on the river!" Craig shouted with weak elation, as he paddled. "And water runs downhill. If we go up—and keep on going up—we've got to come to the top of the ground!"

His answer was a raucous, hissing scream.

Ann looked up, and her face went suddenly white. Craig stopped paddling. Trembling, he stared. Two troglodytes flapped low above them. Green flame lined the blackness of their wings, and orange spots winked like monstrous evil eyes.

"Maddrey's beasts!" whispered Ann. "And—see!" Terror choked her. "One of them is going back to tell him where we are!"

Neither of the creatures attacked. But one of them, indeed, with a last vicious hiss, flew back toward the crimson sea. The other still followed—an implacable, green-winged nemesis!

CHAPTER EIGHT
The Bloom of Doom

CRAIG toiled at the paddle. Time lost its meaning. There were no days, no nights. The darkly shining current; the heavy, enervating heat; the tiny, leaking canoe; the slickhandled paddle; their ragged tortured bodies; the tormenting midges; the monster screaming and wheeling above—such things were the only realities.

They lived with but a thin shell of wood between themselves and death. The choking smudge was never out of their nostrils. The scant food that chance brought them they cooked in the smudge-fire. They slept but seldom, half-sitting, cramped. They never left the canoe and the river.

Another troglodyte came at last to relieve the first, and a third to take the place of that, and another, until Craig no longer counted the changes.

"Why do they do it, West?" Ann once whispered fearfully. "Why do they just haunt us? They're getting my nerves." She shuddered. "Almost, I'd rather they attacked!"

Craig's tired eyes lifted to the flapping monster.

"I can think of just one reason," he said slowly. "Maddrey must be following, himself!" Despite himself, the tremor of fear came into his dried, husky voice. "He must send them ahead, to watch us and guide him." Craig looked down at the girl. His gray eyes met her frightened dark ones. Together, they said:

"He won't take us!"

Time there was none. But the scarlet river changed. It narrowed. The opposing current was swifter. The weird life along the banks became different, although no less hostile.

Ann sometimes paddled, while Craig slept. But she could make little gain against the strengthening current, and more often they anchored in shallow water, near the shore. There she had only to watch and tend the smudge.

It was on such a time that Craig came awake, cold and tensed from some intuition of horror. He saw that Ann was asleep, over the smudge. Sickened with an icy, paralyzing dread, he saw—

The bloom!

The plant was drifting toward the canoe, as if some slow eddy moved it through the stagnant shallows. Its broad leaves, yards across, lay flat upon the water. Thick green pads, filled with air-cells, they formed a raft that supported the enormous, luminous bloom.

Amazing, fascinating, was the beauty of that flower.

Yet the first sleep-drugged glimpse of it filled Craig with monstrous dread. Shimmering with a blue that was cold as arctic twilight, the petals formed a wondrous ten-foot bowl of sapphire radiance.

A bowl of hellish fire!

Twin black filaments reached like living whips above the bowl's rim. At their tips hung brilliant little spheres of frigid violet. The whips crawled and wavered. The little globes lifted and fell.

They lifted and fell.

Lifted—fell—

Craig watched them. He followed their slow, monotonous motion. They seemed presently to be returning his gaze. He began to wonder dimly if they were really eyes.

A vague alarm stirred him faintly.

HE WAS getting sleepy again. It must have been the swaying of the spheres that had made Ann sleep at her post.

He tried to turn, to look at her. He was shocked with a cold sudden impact of apprehension, for Ann.

But he couldn't move.

His eyes could not leave the little Violet orbs that rose and fell, waxed and waned, slowly rose and fell.

Then he preceived the perfume. It was sweet, almost insipid. Vaguely, he saw that it had been sprayed toward him. It came in a pinkish, shining cloud, from some unseen source within the giant, bright calyx. He drifted away into the roseate mist of it—

Into shining pinkish cloud-caverns of sleep.

He sighed and closed his eyes. The flower had commanded him to sleep. He was exhausted, from eternal effort with the paddle. It was Ann's duty to keep watch. It was right for him to sleep—

But he heard Ann's sleepy little whimpering sob. A sudden sharp alarm penetrated his deadened mind. He forced his eyes open, against a leaden weight of sleep.

And saw black horror crawling out of the water!

Like slender cruel black snakes, the roots of the plant writhed out from beneath the broad floating leaves, and lifted evil coils into the canoe.

The tentacles were creeping toward Ann.

Craig tried to shout a warning. But that strange perfume had paralyzed him. No sound came from his dry throat. And the cold light of the swaying, hypnotic orbs was suddenly stern.

They looked angry. They were like Maddrey's insane glacial eyes. And Craig was afraid of them. It was fear that stiffened all his body with a paralytic rigor.

The black tentacles writhed about Ann's white, sleeping body. Thin shining coils whipped around her limbs. Black circular suction disks—that looked like ugly serpent-heads— fastened to her soft flesh.

She woke, abruptly.

"Weston! Oh, West—"

The sheer, sobbing horror of her cry sent a ripple of agony through Craig's tense, fear-chilled body. Desperately, with all his will, he fought that strange hypnotic rigor. But he could not break it.

As if clutched in some nightmare, he watched helplessly.

The black tentacles lifted Ann. She screamed again, and struggled frantically. The clinging black coils yielded to her struggles, and yet held fast. The suction disks clung, lifted her out of the canoe.

Nerveless, rigid, drenched with cold sweat of horror, Craig could only watch.

He saw the little horny black finger that opposed the suction disk, at the end of each thin tentacle. Those fingers began to explore Ann's body, moving with a slow horrible undulant motion.

Deliberately, they stripped off her ragged clothing. Curiously, they carressed her long white thighs, all the smooth curves of her body, the full ivory bowls of her breasts.

Slowly, cruelly, the black coils grew tighter about her white, fighting loveliness. Like black wires, they cut into her flesh. Red drops oozed from about the black disks cupped against her long white limbs, her breasts, her throat.

Once more she screamed, with the breath forced from her lungs by that crushing pressure. It was a choked, bubbling, awful cry:

"West—Westo!"

The horror of that appeal, somehow, cleft Craig's bonds of dread. Perhaps the hypnotic attention of those icy violet orbs had momentarily shifted from him. He dragged his eyes from them.

He was free!

Snatching the copper knife that Ami had dropped in the bottom of the canoe, he surged to his feet. She made a last little sob of agony, as those torturing tentacles drew convulsively tighter, about her long nude body.

A black whip struck, snake-like, at Craig.

He ducked under it. Catching up the paddle, he drove the canoe with one deep stroke between those thick floating pads. And he leapt from it, into that great bowl of sapphire flame.

THE shining petals closed upon him. They were like cold, boneless flesh. They were silken-soft. Yet they pressed about him with a crushing, smothering strength. And black filaments whipped about his throat, like garroting wires.

Craig gasped for breath. He kept his arms free of the whipping, clinging tentacles. The copper blade slashed again and again, ripping at the heart of the monster calyx.

The struggles of bright petals and black whips became convulsive, as if with agony. Craig was drenched in a viscid, sickly-sweet liquid. It was like unpleasant blood.

Abruptly the smothering petals opened again. He was flung out into warm red water. Maddened black limbs were beating it to crimson froth. A writhing coil gripped him, dragged him beneath the surface.

Strangling, he clutched it with one hand, hacked at it desperately. Something snatched at his foot—some deadly, unseen denizen of the river. He kicked free of it. The clinging tentacle parted.

Half-drowned, he fought his way upward.

The sentient plant had become a frightful mass of agony and death. Black tentacles were rending the thick green pads. The giant, ice blue bloom had toppled into the water. Swiftly, uncannily, the blue glow died. The petals withered, blackened.

"Ann!" Craig was breathless, hoarse with an awful apprehension. "Ann—Ann!"

The empty canoe was floating away. Bubbles broke out of the frothy crimson water. The dying tentacles had dragged Ann under.

CHAPTER NINE
Flight's End

AGAIN Craig felt the brush of some alert, quick-moving thing beneath the unquiet water. Unseen jaws closed on his ankle, with an agonizing pressure. Once more he was drawn beneath the red-frothing surface.

He doubled himself, slashed down with the copper blade. It raked against an armored body. He kicked out desperately, came free. Back at the surface, gasping for breath, he searched for Ann again.

And still she was gone.

Chilled with apprehension, Craig caught his breath. He dived again. His eyes were open, but he could see only a few feet through the stinging murky crimson. Gripping the knife, he pulled himself down. Down. He felt the foul mud of the bottom.

Then a slender, greenly shining antenna touched him with stinging pain. He glimpsed the hideous, black-armored thing where frightful jaws had caught Ann's naked body. A monstrous, crab-like crustacean.

Huge stalked eyes peered at him, above her feebly struggling limbs. They were crimson moons of evil. Craig swam toward them, stabbing with the copper knife. Green antennae whipped at him, agonizing as Maddrey's venomed lash.

His dull blade failed to penetrate the tough black armor. His breath was gone. Fire was in his lungs. The water was a crushing, oppressive weight. It flowed into his nostrils, stranglingly.

Then a twisting mass of wire-like coils sank down through the dusky redness—black tentacles torn from the dying plant. They touched the hideous dark-armored crab-thing, struck, clung.

Frightful jaws released the nude girl, flashed at Craig. He slashed at the stalked eyes. One evil red moon was severed. The monster let him go, fighting the dying tentacles.

Craig seized Ann's arm, fought toward the surface. They came up, at last. Ann still clung to consciousness. For a little time they floated in the oily red foam, gasping for breath.

Then Craig saw that the canoe's anchor rope had been cut or broken, in the battle. It was drifting out, toward the swift current that swept back toward the crimson sea. He released the girl, overtook it, paddled frantically back to pick up Ann before she was attacked again.

She screamed in the red water, before he could reach her.

"Oh, West—something—"

He drove the canoe to her side, pulled her safely aboard. She was shivering with exhaustion and shock. One ankle was marked by the jaws of the giant crustacean. Her white throat, her back, and her breasts, all were marked with little red circles, from the sucking disks of the deadly flower.

Craig gave her his wet jacket.

"I think we had better paddle upriver a way, before we rest again," he said breathlessly. "To a quieter vicinity."

She saw his little weary grin.

"You aren't angry, Weston?" she whispered. "It's all my fault! I saw the flower coming. But something made me go to sleep."

Craig managed to smile.

"I'm glad," he gasped. "Almost glad it happened. You know, Ann—I wasn't afraid when I dived after you. It's the first time I haven't been afraid."

The troglodyte rose again. Squatting on a snag near the bank, it had watched the struggle in the river, blinking evil yellow-red eyes. It flew low above, as they paddled on, hissing and screaming.

BENEATH those green, ominous wings, Craig and Ann went ahead. They fought an ever-swifter current. It was impossible to advance against it in the middle of the stream. They were forced back into the perilous shallows, in the shadow of the walling, many colored jungle.

Always they were tired, and always tense with an unresting alertness. They were often hungry. Always sleepless, cramped and aching. But they struggled on, beneath the evil wings.

A time came at last when their flapping follower was joined by two others. Looking back across a mighty bend of the dark river, they saw a wheeling swarm of the green-winged troglodytes.

On the water beneath was a little black dot.

Craig bent hard to the paddle, and Ann took turns. But the swarm gained on them. The dot grew larger. At last they could distinguish Maddrey's great bulk, bent over his flashing paddle.

"Maddrey!"

Ann was hoarse with a chilling dread.

"We'll never get away from him—and his whip!"

They had no measure of their flight's duration. But they had eaten and slept innumerable times. Their flesh had been wounded, healed, freshly wounded and healed again, until each of them bore many old scars.

Craig knew that his body had been hardened by his battle with the river. A kind of daring hardihood had been born in him, when he fought the black spiders on the hill of moons, and when he dived under the river for Ann, and on a hundred like occasions.

He had even hoped, sometimes, that fear was gone. But always, listening again to the hissing of the troglodyte above, he had felt that man's grim heritage still clung to him. Now—when he saw that it was Maddrey indeed in the canoe behind—he knew that fear had been only sleeping.

It came upon him with a sickness that left him weak and trembling. Then it touched him with a terrible strength. He dipped the paddle again, and began a desperate race.

Maddrey, with his swarm of monstrous allies, gained steadily. Still he had a madman's strength. But the race was not ended when they reached the second fall.

Ann gasped at the spectacle that marched out of the arch of gloom ahead. A white pillar of water came down out of utter darkness. It made a cloud of snowy spray upon the center of a broad, jungle-rimmed lake. The surface of the lake was queerly mottled, with white froth and dull blood-red luminescence.

The voice of the water was a deafening thunder.

Craig stopped paddling. His eyes were fearful.

"Looks like the end," he shouted to Ann. "It's the end of the river." He peered about, with frantic eyes. "And we can't get through that jungle. We're caught—between Maddrey and the fall!"

"There must be a way!"

Ann's dark, frightened eyes looked at the white booming column that dropped through the roof of the cave. It must fall a thousand sheer feet. No way there...

Then hope stiffened her.

"There!" Her eager cry cleft the voice of the waters. "Beyond the fall—"

Staring through that terrible, thundering curtain, Craig dimly saw the shore beyond. There was a break in the jungle. A mysterious dark slope mounted into black infinity.

"That's the way!" he shouted. "If we can pass the fall—"

The flapping swarm of troglodytes was close behind him. Faintly, above the thunder of the waters, Craig could hear their sinister screaming. Paddling, he could not look back. But Ann's white face was drawn and terrible with fear.

Dimly, above the roaring, he heard Maddrey's voice. Rusty, it seemed, and strange, as if from lack of use. And it held all of the mad violence of an infuriated bull.

"Wire the disk—and you may live!"

CRAIG raced on. He read the warning in the streak of white that abruptly cleft the scarlet water. But there was no escape. Maddrey was too close behind. Craig bent his back, shot the canoe into the deadly current.

"Stop!"

Maddrey's bellow was faint, beneath that tremendous sound, as the whisper of a child.

"Stop—or perish!"

Craig caught his breath, and drove ahead. A great hand flung the bow aside, so swiftly that he could hardly keep them upright. The deadly jungle swept past in a racing blur.

Ahead lay the swift white road of the current, running straight into the fearful, crashing turmoil of white water and smothering mist beneath the fall. Tossing mountains of spray hid all beyond.

Desperately, Craig fought to cross that deadly current.

The roaring drowned all sound of Ann's voice. But he read the words from her pale, frightened lips:

"He came on—he's close behind!"

Fainter than a breath, he heard a troglodyte's scream.

His muscles cracked to the effort of his paddle strokes. Yet all his strength seemed in vain against the terrific force that hurled them toward the fall.

White foam broke over the gunwales. Cold spray drenched them. Violent beyond the meaning of sound, the vibration of crashing tons of water battered and deafened and dazed them.

Ann was bailing frantically. Despite all Craig's efforts, the canoe was swept aside. It spun like a top. He lost all sense of direction.

Snap!

The paddle was a useless stick in his hands. The splintered, smooth-worn handle dropped from nerveless fingers. Craig looked up helplessly, to face the white death of hurtling water.

But that pillar of supernal sound and fury was suddenly behind. Another freakish current had swept them away. One moment of safety!

Craig bent again. Frantically he paddled with his hands, toward the low dark shore. Another mad torrent caught the canoe. A white plume of spray gave him warning of the rock.

He stood up, swayed to grasp Ann's arm.

Crash!

The canoe struck the rock, with a shocking, splintering force. Craig leapt at the impact, lifting Ann. Amid flying fragments of the shattered canoe, they were flung over the rock.

Cold black water swallowed them.

Still clinging to Ann, Craig battled back to the surface. He found himself in the eddy beyond the rock. Behind was the fall, with savage currents racing into the chaos of spray beneath it. Ahead was the dark slope they had glimpsed—

The way, might it be, to the world above?

His frantic feet touched bottom. Ann found her footing, and they waded ashore. Shivering with unaccustomed cold, they looked back. Ann uttered a little sobbing moan of fear.

A long canoe drove out of the mist, attended by a green-winged, monstrous horde.

"Maddrey!" whispered Ann. "He'll never give up!"

They stumbled up the dark slope. It was barren of any luminiferous life. A faint light came up across it, however, from the dully-shining jungle beyond the fall.

Rugged, water-carved rocks grew steeper ahead. The sheer, cragged walls narrowed upon them, and the black roof pressed lower. The way became an appalling, constricted maw of darkness.

"A tunnel?" Still Ann was hopeful. "A passage?"

"Once it was a passage." Craig peered into the blackness, doubtfully. "Once the river flowed through here. But the water has stopped. The passage may be closed—"

Another apprehension turned his glance behind.

HE saw Maddrey's canoe. The black-bearded giant steered it around the menace of the rocks, drove it across the eddy, beached it safely. Maddrey followed them up the slope, with his horde of flapping reptiles.

Craig broke icy fetters of fear. Gasping for breath, he seized Ann's arm. Panting, they stumbled up the slope. Soon their bodies were aching from the unwonted effort of running.

A wall of black granite halted them.

Frantically, they searched to right and left, peered above. But the boulder blocked the way, with a million tons of stone.

"So this is the end!"

Craig's whisper was faint and dry with dread.

"This was the way—once. Until that boulder fell—maybe a million years ago. The river found a new way—down through the roof.

"But we—we're cornered!"

They waited beneath the rock, for Maddrey and his monsters.

CHAPTER TEN
The Man Afraid

BATHED in a weird, flickering green, from the flapping wings of his hideous retainers, Maddrey came plunging up the dark slope. Blackened from exposure, scarred from old wounds, his huge hairy body was still powerful. His bearded face was seamed, haggard. Into his mad blue eyes had come a new feral wildness.

In one great hand he gripped a massive club of black wood, copper-studded. A copper knife gleamed in his broad crimson belt. The shining purple whip was looped at his side. Slung from his shoulders was the heavy rusted mechanism of the disruptor disk.

A hundred feet beneath Craig and Ann, Maddrey paused. Above the hissing screams of his wheeling reptiles, his mighty voice bellowed at them:

"Come back with me. Repair the *Subterrane*. Or die—both of you—by the whip!"

Craig held Ann close to him.

"No, Maddrey," he shouted. "We'll fight to the finish."

Ann sensed a new calm in his voice. She felt the steadiness of his arm. Wonder came into her dark, frightened eyes.

"West?" she breathed softly. "You aren't afraid?"

Craig smiled down at her, briefly. "Something has happened," he whispered. "It was the same, that time I dived. I am afraid, of course—because he may kill us both. But it's different. I'm not afraid—of fear."

The girl made a breathless sob of dread, and he looked back down the rugged slope, at Maddrey. The shaggy, haggard giant had lifted the rust-reddened disruptor disk in both great hands. He was swinging it, threateningly, at the flapping reptiles.

His voice hissed and screamed, in their own strange speech. The monsters squalled and hissed back at him, as if protestingly. But at last a dozen of them came flapping up the slope.

Gripping the copper knife, Craig stepped a little forward. He drew Ann close behind him. Warm against him, her body was quivering with fear.

"Oh, Weston!" she sobbed. "He can't take us back—not after we've come so far!"

The shrieking reptiles dropped upon them. Their acrid, snake-house stench was sickening. Their bright wings whipped up choking dust from the rocks. Half blinded, Craig thrust with the copper blade, slashed and thrust again.

But the monsters evaded his blows. Their dives were always checked, above him. No talon raked him, and he felt no fang. The knife was a feeble weapon, yet the reptiles seemed to fear it.

Then Ann screamed!

Craig wheeled beneath the threatening wings—and horror paralyzed him. For a diving monster had snatched the girl from behind him. It soared up, with her struggling form dangling from its talons.

Breathless with apprehension, forgetting his own defense, Craig stood staring. For Ann's sake, he knew, he would surrender. For her, he would become the slave of Maddrey's madness. He would even repair the *Subterrane*.

Ann fought desperately, against the talons of the monster. It had gripped her by the shoulders. The worn skins of her clothing ripped. Her long-limbed body fell out of them, white and nude.

Craig's heart stopped.

The creature had carried her scores of feet above the rocks. Her naked, helpless body spun in the air, falling. Craig's horror-dazed mind saw her lovely shape broken hideously, mangled.

She screamed once, in the air.

Then the troglodyte dropped her torn garments. It dived after her. A few feet above the rocks, its talons caught her again, by arm and thigh. It checked her fall, lifted her again.

The green flicker of its wings turned her to a statue of living jade. The strange light shimmered on the curves of her slim body, made full jade bowls of her pointed breasts.

The monster carried her down to Maddrey.

It hovered, in the air, with her greenlit body dangling. The purple-glowing serpent of the whip struck again, and dark marks of pain leapt once more across her jade perfection. Blood looked black, against the green.

She sobbed, piteously.

"Let her go!"

CRAIG was amazed at the clear strength of his shout. Clutching the dull copper blade, he went plunging down the slope, toward Maddrey. Against the giant's great mace, against the green flame of the disruption ray, and the horde of troglodytes, the copper knife was a futile weapon. But Craig's old, crippling fear was gone.

Maddrey hissed a command. The winged monster dropped beside him, still clutching the nude, whimpering girl in its talons. Then his great hands leveled the rusty disruptor disk at Craig.

"Stop!" he bellowed. "Or die!"

Craig's leaping body tensed with expectation of that green, dazzling finger of death. Time had been when its threat might have checked him, with shuddering fear. But now he sprang aside, crouched, and ran on.

And Maddrey dropped the disk.

The disruptor weapon was dead, Craig realized elatedly. Useless. The cavern's hot, humid atmosphere must have corroded the terminals. Maddrey's dominion of the troglodytes now lay upon an empty threat.

But nothing was wrong with Maddrey's copper-studded club. Bellowing with rage, he swung it high. Craig darted to meet his lumbering rush.

The club came down. Craig caught it with a stiffened arm. He slashed with the copper blade at the great hairy hand that clutched it. Howling with pain, Maddrey dropped the club.

His bleeding fingers snatched for the purple whip. Viciously it lashed out. Craig slashed again with the copper blade. The glowing, venomed serpent dropped lifeless on the rocks. Maddrey stood with the butt in his red hand.

A slow, stupid bewilderment came over his black-bearded face.

"Make them turn her loose!" Craig gasped.

Maddrey flung away the whipstock, clenched his red empty hands.

"No!" he bellowed. "The trogs can take you!"

He stumbled back from the menace of Craig's copper blade, screaming and hissing in the language of the reptiles. The monsters dropped about him, in a baleful circle. They flapped green wings for balance, and blinked malignant eyes at Craig.

But they didn't attack.

Gripping the knife, Craig advanced suddenly upon the monster that held the naked girl. Croaking and spitting evilly, it released her and retreated. Lovely as an awakened statue of green jade, she ran trembling back to Craig. He gave her his jacket.

"Weston!" Her whisper was electric with hope. "They're afraid of you!"

Gray eyes shining, Craig nodded.

"Yes, they're afraid. They'll never attack mankind."

He stepped confidently toward the glowering giant.

"Maddrey!" His voice was low and even. "I've been afraid of you. I used to obey your orders, because I was afraid. It was fear that drove us up the river. But now I'm not afraid of you, any more.

"I could kill you, Maddrey."

His thumb was testing the copper blade.

"But I'm not even afraid to let you live," he added softly. "You may go back, if you like. And take your monsters with you!"

Maddrey's clenched hands opened. Suddenly he was trembling. Wild, blood shot, his eyes rolled about the circle of hissing, blinking troglodytes.

Maddrey was afraid!

He fell on his knees and began to sob:

"I want to go with you! Please take me with you! The trogs want to keep me. I can never escape them—unless you take me. But they're afraid of you. They would let me go with you."

"What's this?" Craig gasped. "You aren't the master?" Maddrey whimpered, on his knees.

"They found out long ago that the disruptor disk was dead," he whispered. "And they knew that you had built it. That made them set you above me. And they have feared you, since you killed one of them and fed it to the water spiders.

"They want to keep me, for a slave."

THE blinking troglodytes were flapping and hopping closer. Maddrey cowered away from them. His sobbing voice rose to a fear-tortured shriek:

"Don't let them carry me back!"

Craig was touched with pity. He looked at Ann, saw compassion on her white face.

"You may stay with us, Maddrey," he said. "If you like. But the way out is blocked. Perhaps we'll never—"

The ring of troglodytes stalked closer upon Maddrey. They flapped and blinked at him, cackled and hissed and screamed. He flung himself flat on the rocks, shrieking:

"Don't—don't let them—"

The clamoring circle closed upon him. Maddrey's frantic cries changed to the language of the troglodytes. Green wings flapped heavily, and the dread swarm lifted. Maddrey's big body hung limply from great black talons.

So the troglodytes departed.

They glided down toward the scarlet, foam-flecked darkness of the river. They passed the thundering white pillar of the fall. They soared over the flat, hostile wall of shining jungle beyond.

The one that carried Maddrey wearied. Another flew close, and took the burden. They became black motes. They vanished, returning with their human slave to the far-off dwelling-pits beyond the scarlet sea.

Solemnly, Craig drew Ann to him, and kissed her.

"We are free," he told her gravely. "Even if we die here, we won't be afraid again."

Presently they searched once more for some crevice in the ancient rock-fall that blocked the way. They found none. Ann was growing hopeless and depressed again, when Craig led the way back to the rusty disruptor disk that Maddrey had flung away.

"It's dead," she said wearily. "It doesn't work."

"The terminals probably just need cleaning," he told her. "If Maddrey had known—"

He repressed a little shudder.

They carried the disk back down into the glow of the jungle. Craig took it apart, scraped the terminals. He assembled it again, touched the switch. A dazzling lance of emerald stabbed down into the jungle.

The green beam stabbed its uncanny way through the black barrier of granite. They made torches, and packed a little food that they found in Maddrey's canoe. Eargerly, they climbed into the forbidding darkness of the caverns.

For a long time they clambered up through utter, choking blackness. They wandered through endless labyrinthine corridors, where their torches flickered against unimaginable crystal splendor. They forded cold black rivers. They swam the length of an icy lake.

Their food was gone. The last torch went out. They crept blindly ahead, hungry, weary, desperate. They stumbled upon the lip of some unthinkable abyss, and the disruptor disk was lost.

They climbed black boulder-slopes. Climbed vertical ledges. Climbed narrow chimneys. Climbed into an eternal nightmare of weary despair. Climbed and staggered, climbed and rested, climbed and wept. And climbed.

Then came the time when Craig sniffed the long-forgotten aroma of tobacco, and came fumbling in the dark upon the butt of a cigarette. Beyond it, they found a low curb of stone, a smooth, well-trodden trail.

Eagerly, incredulous, they stumbled upward.

Light met them, and magical human voices.

They came upon a tall man in uniform, leading an awed and foot-sore throng.

"Yes, sir," the ranger-guide was informing a perspiring and somewhat apprehensive merchant, "the Carlsbad Cavern is the largest in the world. Just below us is the Big Room. It is 348 feet high, 625 feet wide, and over 4,000 feet long—"

THE ranger's mouth fell open. He staggered back against the merchant. A curious whisper ran through his flock. A fat woman shrieked and fainted. Craig grinned.

"We've been lost in the caves," he said. "Some of them, below, are even larger than the Big Room. We've been lost a long time. We need food and clothing. And Ann is very tired. We've no money, but—"

Ann laughed at him, gaily, saying: "But we will have money!"

She loosened the black shining mass of her hair, and found a little pouch, made from the skin of that great lizard that Craig had killed with the copper knife. She unrolled the pouch. Out poured four splendid moons of scarlet opalescence.

"Pearls!" gasped Craig. "Red pearls! But—*where*—?"

"They were in the shells you dived for," she told him. "I hid them when I found them—so that we couldn't go back to Maddrey's whip!"

Laughing softly, she sank into his arms.

"I'll forgive you, this time," whispered Craig. "But, any more deceit—"

She shuddered deliciously.

The rangers helped them up the trail, into the bright New Mexico sun. Craig asked the date, and learned that it had been four years since the *Subterrane* carried them into the Earth.

THE END

If you've enjoyed this book, you will not want to miss these terrific titles…

ARMCHAIR SCI-FI & HORROR DOUBLE NOVELS, $12.95 each

D-221 **UNDER VENUSIAN FLAGS** by Nelson S. Bond
BLOOD ON MY JETS by Algis Budrys

D-222 **CITIES IN THE AIR** by Edmond Hamilton
THE WAR OF THE PLANETS by Harl Vincent

D-223 **MISTRESS OF MACHINE-AGE MADNESS** by Jack Williamson
THE IMPOSSIBLES by Randall Garrett & Laurence M. Janifer

D-224 **WALL OF FIRE** by Charles Eric Maine
TOO MANY WORLDS by Gerald Vance

D-225 **THE VEILED WOMAN** by Mickey Spillane & Howard Browne
PELLUCIDAR by Edgar Rice Burroughs

D-226 **LOOT OF THE VAMPIRE** by Thorp McClusky
THE MAN WHO MADE MANIACS by Jim Harmon

D-227 **COLOSSUS** by S. J. Byrne
ISLE OF DOOM by Robert Moore Williams

D-228 **RETURN OF CREEGAR** by David Wright O'Brien
EIGHT KEYS TO EDEN by Mark Clifton

D-229 **THE TIMELESS MAN** by Robert Donald Locke
ENEMY OF THE QUA by Dwight V. Swain

D-230 **THE MAN THE TECH-MEN MADE** by Fox B. Holden
A WORLD HE NEVER MADE by Edwin Benson

ARMCHAIR SCIENCE FICTION CLASSICS, $12.95 each

C-77 **THESE ARE MY CHILDREN**
by Rog Phillips

C-78 **STRANGER SUNS**
by George Zebrowski

C-79 **THE SECOND DELUGE**
by Garrett P. Serviss

ARMCHAIR SCI-FI & HORROR GEMS SERIES, $12.95 each

G-27 **SCIENCE FICTION GEMS, Vol. Fourteen**
Robert Moore Williams and others

G-28 **HORROR GEMS, Vol. Fourteen**
Manly Banister and others

YOU CAN SUM IT UP IN TWO WORDS: IM POSSIBLE

First, late-model automobiles began driving themselves…with nobody behind the wheel!

Then, valuables began vanishing into thin air from within the supposed safety of locked rooms…

It was a new kind of crime for sure; and Malone, the Government's expert on "impossibilities," was afraid it meant they were also dealing with a new kind of criminal…one who could disappear at will, walk through walls, and thumb his nose at the police.

And Malone was dead right…

The authors of "Brain Twister," Randall Garrett and Laurence M. Janifer (originally writing together as Mark Phillips), offer up another tale of the wacky world of tomorrow—and of the strange powers of the mind…

Author Portraits

Randall Garrett, 1927-1987

Laurence M. Janifer, 1933-2002

THE
IMPOSSIBLES

By
RANDALL GARRETT & LAURENCE M. JANIFER
(originally writing as Mark Phillips)

ARMCHAIR FICTION
PO Box 4369, Medford, Oregon 97504

For more information about Armchair Books and products, visit our website at…

www.armchairfiction.com

Or email us at…

armchairfiction@yahoo.com

CHAPTER ONE

The sidewalk was as soft as a good bed. Malone lay curled on it, thinking about nothing at all. He was drifting off into a wonderful dream, and he didn't want to interrupt it. There was this girl, a beautiful girl, more wonderful than anything he had ever imagined, with big blue eyes and long blonde hair and a figure that made the average pin-up girl look like a man. And she had her soft white hand on his arm, and she was looking, up at him with trust and devotion and even adoration in her eyes, and her voice was the softest possible whisper of innocence and promise.

"I'd love to go up to your apartment with you, Mr. Malone," she said.

Malone smiled back at her, gently but with complete confidence. "Call me Ken," he said, noticing that he was seven feet tall and superbly muscled. He put his free hand on the girl's warm, soft shoulder and she wriggled with delight.

"All right—Ken," she said. "You know, I've never met anyone like you before. I mean, you're so wonderful and everything."

Malone chuckled modestly, realizing, in passing, how full and rich his voice had become. He felt a weight pressing over his heart, and knew that it was his wallet, stuffed to bursting with thousand-dollar bills.

But was this a time to think of money?

No, Malone told himself. This was the time for adventure, for romance, for love. He looked down at the girl and put his arm around her waist. She snuggled closer.

He led her easily down the long wide street to his car at the end of the block. It stood in godlike solitude, a beautiful red Cadillac capable of going a hundred and ten miles an hour in any gear, equipped with fully automatic steering and braking, and with a stereophonic radio, a hi-fi and a 3-D set installed in both front and back seats. It was a 1972 job, but he meant to trade it in on something even better when the 1973 models came out. In the meantime, he decided, it would do.

He handed the girl in, went round to the other side and slid in under the wheel. There was soft music playing somewhere, and a magnificent sunset appeared ahead of them as Malone pushed a button on the dashboard and the red Cadillac started off down the wide, empty, wonderfully paved street into the sunset, while he... The red Cadillac?

The sidewalk became a little harder, and, Malone suddenly realized that he was lying on it. Something terrible had happened; he knew that right away. He opened his eyes to look for the girl, but the sunset had become much brighter; his head began to pound with the slow regularity of a dead-march, and he closed his eyes again in a hurry.

The sidewalk swayed a little, but he managed to keep his balance on it somehow; and after a couple of minutes it was quiet again. His head hurt. Maybe that was the terrible thing that had happened, but Malone wasn't quite sure. As a matter of fact, he wasn't very sure about anything, and he started to ask himself questions to make certain he was all there.

He didn't feel all there. He felt as if several of his parts had been replaced with second- or even third-hand experimental models, and something had happened to the experiment. It was even hard to think of any questions, but after a while he managed to come up with a few.

What is your name?
Kenneth Malone.
Where do you live?
Washington, D. C.
What is your work?
I work for the FBI.
Then what the hell are you doing on a sidewalk in New York in broad daylight?

He tried to find an answer to that, but there didn't seem to be any, no matter where he looked. The only thing he could think of was the red Cadillac.

And if the red Cadillac had anything to do with anything, Malone didn't know about it.

Very slowly and carefully, he opened his eyes again, one at a time. He discovered that the light was not coming from the gorgeous Hollywood sunset he had dreamed up. As a matter of fact, sunset was several hours in the past, and it never looked very pretty in New York anyhow. It was the middle of the night, and Malone was lying under a convenient street lamp.

He closed his eyes again and waited patiently for his head to go away.

A few minutes passed. It was obvious that his head had settled down for a long stay, and no matter how bad it felt, Malone told himself, it *was* his head, after all. He felt a certain responsibility for it. And he couldn't just leave it lying around somewhere with its eyes closed.

He opened the head's eyes once more, and this time he kept them open. For a long time he stared at the post of the street lamp, considering it, and he finally decided that it looked sturdy enough to support a hundred and sixty-five pounds of FBI man, even with the head added in. He grabbed for the post with both hands and started to pull himself upright, noticing vaguely that his legs had somehow managed to get underneath him.

As soon as he was standing, he wished he'd stayed on the nice horizontal sidewalk. His head was spinning dizzily, and his mind was being sucked down into the whirlpool. He held on to the post grimly and tried to stay conscious.

A long time, possibly two or three seconds, passed. Malone hadn't moved at all when the two cops came along.

One of them was a big man with a brassy voice and a face that looked as if it had been overbaked in a waffle iron. He came up behind Malone and tapped him on the shoulder, but Malone barely felt the touch. Then the cop bellowed into Malone's ear: "What's the matter, buddy?"

Malone appreciated the man's sympathy. It was good to know that you had friends. But he wished, remotely, that the cop and his friend, a shorter and thinner version of the beat patrolman, would go away and leave him in peace. Maybe he could lie down on the sidewalk again and get a couple of hundred years' rest.

Who could tell? "Mallri," he said.

"You're all right?" the big cop said. "That's fine. That's great. So why don't you go home and sleep it off?"

"Sleep?" Malone said. "Home?"

"Wherever you live, buddy," the big cop said. "Come on. Can't stand around on the sidewalk all night."

Malone shook his head, and decided at once never to do it again. He had some kind of rare disease, he realized. His brain was loose, and the inside of his skull was covered with sandpaper. Every time his head moved, the brain jounced against some of the sandpaper.

But the policemen thought he was drunk. That wasn't right. He couldn't let the police get the wrong impression of FBI agents. Now the men would go around telling people that the FBI was always drunk and disorderly.

"Not drunk," he said clearly.

"Sure," the big cop said. "You're fine. Maybe just one too many, huh?"

"No," Malone said. The effort exhausted him, and he had to catch his breath before he could say anything else. But the cops waited patiently. At last he said, "Somebody slugged me."

"Slugged?" the big cop said.

"Right." Malone remembered just in time not to nod his head.

"How about a description, buddy?" the big cop said.

"Didn't see him," Malone said. He let go of the post with one hand, keeping a precarious grip with the other. He stared at his watch. The hands danced back and forth, but he focused on them after a while. It was 1:05. "Happened just—a few minutes ago," he said. "Maybe you can catch him."

The big cop said, "Nobody around here. The place is deserted—except for you, buddy." He paused and then added: "Let's see some identification, huh? Or did he take your wallet?"

Malone thought about getting the wallet, and decided against it. The motions required would be a little tricky, and he wasn't sure he could manage them without letting go of the post entirely. At last he decided to let the cop get his wallet. "Inside coat pocket," he said.

The other policeman blinked and looked up. His face was a studied blank. "Hey, buddy," he said. "You know you got blood on your head?"

"Be damned," the big cop said. "Sam's right. You're bleeding, mister."

"Good," Malone said.

The big cop said, "Huh?"

"I thought maybe my skull was going to explode from high blood pressure," Malone said. It was beginning to be a little easier to talk. "But as long as there's a slow leak, I guess I'm out of danger."

"Get his wallet," Sam said. "I'll watch him."

A hand went into Malone's jacket pocket. It tickled a little bit, but Malone didn't think of objecting. Naturally enough, the hand and Malone's wallet did not make an instantaneous connection. When the hand touched the bulky object strapped near Malone's armpit, it stopped, frozen, and then cautiously snaked the object out.

"What's that, Bill?" Sam said.

Bill looked up with the object in his hand. He seemed a little dazed. "It's a gun," he said.

"My God," Sam said. "The guy's heeled! Watch him! Don't let him get away!"

Malone considered getting away, and decided that he couldn't move. "It's okay," he said.

"Okay, hell," Sam said. "It's a .44 Magnum. What are you doing with a gun, Mac?" He was no longer polite and friendly. "Why [are] you carrying a gun?" he said.

"I'm not carrying it," Malone said tiredly. "Bill is. Your pal."

Bill backed away from Malone, putting the Magnum in his pocket and keeping the FBI agent covered with his own Police Positive. At the same time, he fished out the personal radio every patrolman carried in his uniform, and began calling for a prowl car in a low, somewhat nervous voice.

Sam said, "My God. A gun. He could of shot everybody."

"Get his wallet," Bill said. "He can't hurt you now. I disarmed him."

Malone began to feel slightly dangerous. Maybe he *was* a famous gangster. He wasn't sure. Maybe all this about being an FBI agent was just a figment of his imagination. Blows on the head did funny things. "I'll drill everybody full of holes," he said in a harsh, underworld sort of voice, but it didn't sound very convincing. Sam approached him gently and fished out his wallet with great care, as if Malone were a ticking bomb ready to go off any second.

There was a little silence. Then Sam said, "Give him his gun back, Bill," in a hushed and respectful tone.

"Give him back his gun?" the big cop said. "You gone nuts, Sam?"

Sam shook his head slowly. "Nope," he said. "But we made a terrible mistake. Know who this guy is?"

"He's heeled," Bill said. "That's all I want to know." He put the radio away and gave all his attention to Malone.

"He's FBI," Sam said. "The wallet says so. Badge and everything. And not only that, Bill. He's Kenneth J. Malone."

Well, Malone thought with relief, that settled that. He wasn't a gangster after all. He was just the FBI agent he had always known and loved. Maybe now the cops would do-something about his head and take him away for burial.

"Malone?" Bill said. "You mean the guy who's here about all those red Cadillacs?"

"Sure," Sam said. "So give him his gun back." He looked at Malone. "Listen, Mr. Malone," he said. "We're sorry. We're sorry as hell."

"That's all right," Malone said absently. He moved his head slowly and looked around. His suspicions were confirmed. There wasn't a red Cadillac anywhere in sight, and from the looks of the street there never had been. "It's gone," he said, but the cops weren't listening.

"We better get you to a hospital," Bill said. "As soon as the prowl car gets here, we'll take you right on down to St. Vincent's. Can you tell us what happened? Or is it classified?"

Malone wondered what could be classified about a blow on the head, and decided not to think about it. "I can tell you," he said, "if you'll answer one question for me."

"Sure, Mr. Malone," Bill said. "We'll be glad to help."

"Anything at all," Sam said.

Malone gave them what he hoped was a gracious and condescending smile. "All right, then," he said. "Where the hell am I?"

"In New York," Sam said.

"I know that," Malone said tiredly. "Anywhere in particular, or just sort of all over New York?"

"Ninth Street," Bill said hurriedly. "Near the Village. Is that where you were when they slugged you?"

"I guess so," Malone said. "Sure." He nodded, and immediately remembered that he shouldn't have. He closed his eyes until the pain had softened to agony, and then opened them again. "I was getting pretty tired of sitting around waiting for something to break on this case," he said, "and I couldn't sleep, so I went out for a walk. I ended up in Greenwich Village—which is a hell of a place for a self-respecting man to end up."

"I know just what you mean," Sam said sympathetically. "Bohemians, they call themselves. Crazy people."

"Not the people," Malone said. "The streets. I got sort of lost." Chicago, he reflected, was a long way from the easiest city in the world to get around in. And he supposed you could even get confused in Washington if you tried hard enough. But he knew those cities. He could find his way around in them. Greenwich Village was different.

It was harder to navigate in than the trackless forests of the Amazon. The Village had tracks, all right—thousands of tracks. Only none of them led anywhere in particular.

"Anyhow," Malone said, "I saw this red Cadillac."

The cops looked around hurriedly and then looked back at Malone. Bill started to say, "But there isn't any—"

"I know," Malone said. "It's gone now. That's the trouble."

"You mean somebody got in and drove it away?" Sam said.

"For all I know," Malone said, "it sprouted wings and flew away." He paused. "When I saw it, though—when I saw it, I decided to go over and have a look. Just in case."

"Sure," Bill said. "Makes sense." He stared at his partner as if defying him to prove it didn't make sense. Malone didn't really care.

"There wasn't anybody else on the street," he said, "so I walked over and tried the door. That's all. I didn't even open the car or anything. And I'll swear there was nobody behind me."

"Well," Sam said, "the street was empty when we got here."

"But a guy could have driven off in that red Cadillac before we got here," Bill said.

"Sure," Malone said. "But where did he come from? I figured maybe somebody dropped something by mistake—a safe or something. Because there wasn't anybody behind me."

"There had to be," Bill said.

"Well," Malone said, "there wasn't."

There was a little silence.

"What happened then?" Sam said. "After you tried the door handle, I mean."

"Then?" Malone said. "Then I went out like a light."

A pair of headlights rounded the nearby corner. Bill looked up. "That's the prowl car," he announced, and went over to meet it.

The driver was a solidly built little man with the face of a Pekingese. His partner, a tall man who looked as if he'd have been much more comfortable in a ten-gallon Stetson instead of the regulation blue cap, leaned out at Bill, Sam, and Malone.

"What's the trouble here?" he said in a harsh, high voice.

"No trouble," Bill said, and went over to the car. He began talking to the two cops inside in a low, urgent voice. Meanwhile, Sam got his arm around Malone and began pulling him away from the lamp post.

Malone was a little unwilling to let go, at first. But Sam was stronger than he looked. He convoyed the FBI agent carefully to the rear door of the prowl car, opened it and levered Malone gently to a seat inside, just as Bill said, "So with the cut and all, we figured he ought to go over to St. Vincent's. You people were already on the way, so we didn't bother with ambulances."

The driver snorted. "Next time you want taxi service," he said, "you just call us up. What do you think, a prowl car's an easy life?"

"Easier than doing a beat," Bill said mournfully. "And anyway," he added in a low, penetrating whisper, "the guy's FBI."

"So the FBI's got all kinds of equipment," the driver said. "The latest. Why don't he whistle up a helicopter or a jet?" Then, apparently deciding that further invective would get him nowhere, he settled back in his seat, said, "Aah, forget it," and started the car with a small but perceptible jerk.

Malone decided not to get into the argument. He was tired, and it was late. He rested his head on the back seat and tried to relax, but all he could do was think about red Cadillacs.

He wished he had never even heard of red Cadillacs.

CHAPTER TWO

And it had all started so simply, too. Malone remembered very clearly the first time he had had any indication that red Cadillacs were anything unusual, or special. Before that, he'd viewed them all with slightly wistful eyes: red, blue, green, gray, white, or even black Cadillacs were all the same to him. They spelled luxury and wealth and display, and a lot of other nice things.

Now, he wasn't at all sure what they spelled. Except that it was definitely uncomfortable, and highly baffling.

He'd walked into the offices of Andrew J. Burris, Director of the FBI, just one week ago. It was a beautiful office, pine-paneled and spacious, and it boasted an enormous polished desk. And behind the desk sat Burris himself, looking both tired and somehow a little kindly.

"You sent for me, Chief?" Malone said.

"That's right." Burris nodded. "Malone, you've been working too hard lately."

Now, Malone thought, it was coming. The dismissal he'd always feared. At last Burris had found out that he wasn't the bright, intelligent, fearless, and alert FBI agent he was supposed to be. Burris had discovered that he was nothing more or less than lucky, and that all the "fine jobs" he was supposed to have done were only the result of luck.

Oh, well, Malone thought. Not being an FBI agent wouldn't be so bad. He could always find another job.

Only at the moment he couldn't think of one he liked.

He decided to make one last plea. "I haven't been working so hard, Chief," he said. "Not too hard, anyhow. I'm in great shape. I—"

"I've taken advantage of you, Malone, that's what I've done," Burris said, just as if Malone hadn't spoken at all. "Just because you're the best agent I've got, that's no reason for me to hand you all the tough ones."

"Just because I'm what?" Malone said, feeling slightly faint.

"I've given you the tough ones because you could handle them," Burris said. "But that's no reason to keep loading jobs on you. After that job you did on the Gorelik kidnaping, and the way you wrapped up the Transom counterfeit ring—well, Malone, I think you need a little relaxation."

"Relaxation?" Malone said, feeling just a little bit pleased. Of course, he didn't deserve any of the praise he was getting, he knew. He'd just happened to walk in on the Gorelik kidnapers because his telephone had been out of order. And the Transom ring hadn't been just his job. After all, if other agents hadn't managed to trace the counterfeit bills back to a common area in Cincinnati, he'd never have been able to complete his part of the assignment. But it was nice to be praised, anyhow. Malone felt a twinge of guilt, and told himself sternly to relax and enjoy himself.

"That's what I said," Burris told him. "Relaxation."

"Well," Malone said, "I certainly would like a vacation, that's for sure. I'd like to snooze for a couple of weeks, or maybe go up to Cape Cod for a while. There's a lot of nice scenery up around there. It's restful, sort of, and I could just—"

He stopped. Burris was frowning, and when Andrew J. Burris frowned it was a good idea to look attentive, interested, and alert. "Now, Malone," Burris said sadly, "I wasn't exactly thinking about a vacation. You're not scheduled for one until August, you know."

"Oh, I know, Chief," Malone said. "But I thought—"

"Much as I'd like to," Burris said, "I just can't make an exception; you know that, Malone. I've got to go pretty much by the schedule."

"Yes, sir," Malone said, feeling just a shade disappointed.

"But I do think you deserve a rest," Burris said.

"Well, if I—"

"Here's what I'm going to do," Burris said, and paused. Malone felt a little unsure as to exactly what his chief was talking about, but by now he knew better than to ask a lot of questions. Sooner or later, Burris would probably explain himself. And if he didn't, then there was no use worrying about it. That was just the way Burris acted.

"Suppose I gave you a chance to take it easy for a while," Burris said. "You could catch up on your sleep, see some shows, have a couple of drinks during the evening, take girls out for dinner—you know. Something like that. How would you like it?"

"Well…" Malone said cautiously.

"Good," Burris said. "I knew you would."

Malone opened his mouth, thought briefly and closed it again. After all, it did sound sort of promising, and if there was a catch in it he'd find out about it soon enough.

"It's really just a routine case," Burris said in an offhand tone. "Nothing to it."

"Oh," Malone said.

"There's this red Cadillac," Burris said. "It was stolen from a party in Connecticut, out near Danbury, and it showed up in New York City. Now, the car's crossed a state line."

"That puts it in our jurisdiction," Malone said, feeling obvious.

"Right," Burris said. "Right on the nose."

"But the New York office—"

"Naturally, they're in charge of everything," Burris said. "But I'm sending you out as sort of a special observer. Just keep your eyes open, and nose around and let me know what's happening."

"Keep my eyes and nose what?" Malone said.

"Open," Burris said. "And let me know about it."

Malone tried to picture himself with his eyes and nose open, and decided he didn't look very attractive that way. Well, it was only a figure of speech or something. He didn't have to think about it.

It really made a very ugly picture.

"But why a special observer?" he said after a second. Burris could read the reports from the New York office, and probably get more facts than any single agent could find out just wandering around a strange city. It sounded as if there were something, Malone told himself, just a tiny shade rotten in Denmark. It sounded as if there were going to be something in the nice easy assignment he was getting that would make him wish he'd gone lion hunting in Darkest Africa instead.

And then again, maybe he was wrong. He stood at ease and waited to find out.

"Well," Burris said, "it is just a routine case. Just like I said. But there seems to be something a little bit odd about it."

"I see," Malone said with a sinking feeling.

"Here's what happened," Burris said hurriedly, as if he were afraid Malone was going to change his mind and refuse the assignment. "This red Cadillac I told you about was reported stolen from Danbury. Three days later, it turned up in New York City—parked smack across the street from a precinct police station. Of course it took them a while to wake up, but one of the officers happened to notice the routine report on stolen cars in the area, and he decided to go across the street and check the license number on the car. Then something funny happened."

"Something funny?" Malone asked. He doubted that, whatever it was, it was going to make him laugh. But he kept his face a careful, receptive blank.

"That's right," Burris said. "Now, if you're going to understand what happened, you've got to get the whole picture."

"Sure," Malone said.

"Only that isn't what I mean," Burris added suddenly.

Malone blinked. "*What* isn't what you mean?" he said.

"Understanding what happened," Burris said. "That's the trouble. You won't understand what happened. I don't understand it, and neither does anybody else. So what do you think about it?"

"Think about what?" Malone said.

"About what I've been telling you," Burris snapped. "This car."

Malone took a deep breath. "Well," he said, "this officer went over to check the license plate. It seems like the right thing to do. It's just what I'd have done myself."

"Sure you would," Burris said. "Anybody would. But listen to me."

"All right, Chief," Malone said.

"It was just after dawn—early in the morning." Malone wondered briefly if there were parts of the world where dawn came, say, late in the afternoon, or during the evening sometime, but he said nothing. "The street was deserted," Burris went on. "But it was pretty light out, and the witnesses are willing to swear that there was nobody on that street for a block in either direction. Except them, of course."

"Except who?" Malone said.

"Except the witnesses," Burris said patiently. "Four cops, police officers who were standing on the front steps of the precinct station, talking. They were waiting to go on duty, or anyhow that's what the report said. It's lucky they were there, for whatever reason; they're the only witnesses we've got."

Burris stopped. Malone waited a few seconds and then said, as calmly as he could, "Witnesses to what?"

"To this whole business with Sergeant Jukovsky," Burris said.

The sudden introduction of a completely new name confused Malone for an instant, but he recovered gamely. "Sergeant Jukovsky was the man who investigated the car," he said.

"That's right," Burris said. "Except that he didn't."

Malone sighed.

"Those four officers—the witnesses—they weren't paying much attention to what looked like the routine investigation of a parked car," Burris said. "But here's their testimony. They were standing around talking when this Sergeant Jukovsky came out of the station, spoke to them in passing, and went on across the street. He didn't seem very worried or alarmed about anything."

"Good," Malone said involuntarily. "I mean, go on, Chief," he added.

"Ah," Burris said. "All right. Well. According to Jukovsky, he took a look at the plate and found the numbers checked the listing he had for a stolen Connecticut car. Then he walked around to take a look inside the car. It was empty. Get that, Malone. The car was empty."

"Well," Malone said, "it was parked. I suppose parked cars are usually empty. What's special about this one?"

"Wait and see," Burris said ominously. "Jukovsky swears the car was empty. He tried the doors, and they were all locked but one, the front door on the curb side, the driver's door. So he opened it, and leaned over to have a look at the odometer to check the mileage. And something clobbered him on the back of the head."

"One of the other cops," Malone said.

"One of the—who?" Burris said. "No. Not the cops. Not at all."

"Then something fell on him," Malone said. "Okay. Then whatever fell on him ought to be—"

"Malone," Burris said.

"Yes, Chief?"

"Jukovsky woke up on the sidewalk with the other cops all around him. There was nothing on that sidewalk but Jukovsky. Nothing could have fallen on him; it hadn't landed anywhere, if you see what I mean."

"Sure," Malone said. "But—"

"Whatever it was," Burris said, "they didn't find it. But that isn't the peculiar thing."

"No?"

"No," Burris said slowly. "Now—"

"Wait a minute," Malone said. "They looked on the sidewalk and around there. But did they think to search the car?"

"They didn't get a chance," Burris said. "Anyhow, not then. Not until they got around to picking up the pieces of the car uptown at 125th Street."

Malone closed his eyes. "Where was this precinct?" he said.

"Midtown," Burris said. "In the forties."

"And the pieces of the car were eighty blocks away when they searched it?" Malone said.

Burris nodded.

"All right," Malone said pleasantly. "I give up."

"Well, that's what I'm trying to tell you," Burris said. "According to the witnesses, after Jukovsky fell out of the car, the motor started and the car drove off uptown."

"Oh," Malone said. He thought about that for a minute and decided at last to hazard one little question. It sounded silly—but then, what didn't? "The car just drove off all by itself?" he said.

Burris seemed abashed. "Well, Malone," he said carefully, "that's where the conflicting stories of the eyewitnesses don't agree. You see, two of the cops say there was nobody in the car. Nobody at all. Of any kind. Small or large."

"And the other two?" Malone said.

"The other two swear they saw somebody at the wheel," Burris said, "but they won't say whether it was a man, a woman, a small child, or an anthropoid ape. And they haven't the faintest idea where he, she, or it came from."

"Great," Malone said. He felt a little tired. This trip was beginning to sound less and less like a vacation.

"Those two cops swear there was something—or somebody—driving the car," Burris said. "And that isn't all."

"It isn't?" Malone said.

Burris shook his head. "A couple of the cops jumped into a squad car and started following the red Cadillac. One of these cops saw somebody in the car when it left the curb. The other one didn't. Got that?"

"I've got it," Malone said, "but I don't exactly know what to do with it."

"Just hold on to it," Burris said, "and listen to this. The cops were about two blocks behind at the start, and they couldn't close the gap right away. The Cadillac headed west and climbed up the ramp of the West Side Highway, heading north, out toward Westchester. I'd give a lot to know where they were going, too."

"But they crashed," Malone said, remembering that the pieces were at 125th Street. "So—"

"They didn't crash right away," Burris said. "The prowl car started gaining on the Cadillac slowly. And—now, get this, Malone—both the cops swear there *was* somebody in the driver's seat now."

"Wait a minute," Malone said. "One of these cops didn't see anybody at all in the driver's seat when the car started off."

"Right," Burris said.

"But on the West Side Highway, he did see a driver," Malone said. He thought for a minute. "Hell, it could happen. They took off so fast he could have been confused, or something."

"There's another explanation," Burris said.

"Sure," Malone said cheerfully. "We're all crazy. The whole world is crazy."

"Not that one," Burris said. "I'll tell you when I finish with this thing about the car itself. There isn't much description of whoever or whatever was driving that car on the West Side Highway, by the way. In case you were thinking of asking."

Malone, who hadn't been thinking of asking anything, tried to look clever. Burris regarded him owlishly for a second, and then went on:

"The car was hitting it up at about a hundred and ten by this time, and accelerating all the time. But the souped-up squad car was coming on fast, too, and it was quite a chase. Luckily, there weren't many cars on the road. Somebody could have been killed, Malone."

"Like the driver of the Cadillac," Malone ventured.

Burris looked pained. "Not exactly," he said. "Because the car hit the 125th Street exit like a bomb. It swerved right, just as though it were going to take the exit and head off somewhere, but it was going much too fast by that time. There just wasn't any way to maneuver. The Cadillac hit the embankment, flipped over the edge, and smashed. It caught fire almost at once. Of course the prowl car braked fast and went down the exit after it. But there wasn't anything to do."

"That's what I said," Malone said. "The driver of the Cadillac was killed. In a fire like that—"

"Don't jump to conclusions, Malone," Burris said. "Wait. When the prowl car boys got to the scene, there was no sign of anybody in the car. Nobody at all."

"In the heat of those flames—" Malone began.

"Not enough heat, and not enough time," Burris said. "A human body couldn't have been destroyed in just a few minutes, not that completely. Some of the car's metal was melted, sure; but there would have been traces of anybody who'd been in the car.

Nice, big, easily seen traces. And there weren't any. No corpse, no remains, no nothing."

Malone let that stew in his mind for a few seconds. "But the cops said—"

"Whatever the cops said," Burris snapped, "there was nobody at all in that Cadillac when it went off the embankment."

"Now, wait a minute," Malone said. "Here's a car with a driver who appears and disappears practically at will. Sometimes he's there and sometimes he's not there."

"Ah," Burris said. "That's why I have another explanation."

Malone shifted his feet. Maybe there *was* another explanation. But, he told himself, it would have to be a good one.

"Nobody expects a car to drive itself down a highway," Burris said.

"That's right," Malone said. "That's why it's all impossible."

"So," Burris said, "it would be a natural hallucination—or illusion, anyhow—for somebody to imagine he did see a driver when there wasn't any."

"Okay," Malone said. "There wasn't any driver. So the car couldn't have gone anywhere. So the New York police force is lying to us. It's a good explanation, but it—"

"They aren't lying," Burris said. "Why should they? I'm thinking of something else." He stopped, his eyes bright as he leaned across the desk toward Malone.

"Do I get three guesses?" Malone said.

Burris ignored him. "Frankly," he said, "I've got a hunch that the whole thing was done with remote control. Somewhere in that car was a very cleverly concealed device that was capable of running the Cadillac from a distance."

It did sound plausible, Malone thought. "Did the prowl car boys find any traces of it when they examined the wreckage?" he said.

"Not a thing," Burris said. "But, after all, it could have been melted. The fire did destroy a lot of the Cadillac, and there's just no telling. But I'd give long odds that there must have been some kind of robot device in that car. It's the only answer, isn't it?"

"I suppose so," Malone said.

"Malone," Burns said, his voice filled with Devotion To One's Country In The Face of Great Obstacles, "Malone, I want you to find that device!"

"In the wreck?" Malone said.

Burris sighed and leaned back. "No," he said. "Of course not. Not in the wreck. But the other red Cadillacs—some of them, anyhow—ought to have—"

"What red Cadillacs?" Malone said.

"The other ones that have been stolen. From Connecticut, mostly. One from New Jersey, out near Passaic."

"Have any of the others been moving around without drivers?" Malone said.

"Well," Burris said, "there's been no report of it. But who can tell?" He gestured with both arms. "Anything is possible, Malone."

"Sure," Malone said.

"Now," Burris said, "all of the stolen cars are red 1972 Cadillacs. There's got to be some reason for that. I think they're covering up another car like the one that got smashed: a remote-controlled Cadillac. Or even a self-guiding, automatic, robot-controlled Cadillac."

"They?" Malone said. "Who?"

"Whoever is stealing the cars," Burris said patiently.

"Oh," Malone said. "Sure. But—"

"So get up to New York," Burris said, "keep your eyes open, and nose around. Got it?"

"I have now," Malone said.

"And when that Cadillac is found, Malone, we want to take a look at it. Okay?"

"Yes, sir," Malone said.

*   *   *

Of course there were written reports, too. Burris had handed Malone a sheaf of them—copies of the New York police reports to Burris himself—and Malone, wanting some time to look through them, had taken a train to New York instead of a plane. Besides, the new planes still made him slightly nervous, though he could ride one when he had to. If jet engines had been good enough for the last generation, he thought, they were certainly good enough for him.

But avoidance of the new planes was all the good the train trip did him. The reports contained thousands of words, none of which was either new or, apparently, significant to Malone. Burris, he considered, had given him everything necessary for the job.

Except, of course, a way to make sense out of the whole thing. He considered robot-controlled Cadillacs. What good were they? They might make it easier for the average driver, of course—but that was no reason to cover up for them, hitting policemen over the head and smashing cars and driving a hundred and ten miles an hour on the West Side Highway.

All the same, it was the only explanation Malone had, and he cherished it deeply. He put the papers back in his brief case when the train pulled into Penn Station, handed his suitcases to a redcap and punched the buttons for the waiting room. Now, he thought as he strolled slowly along behind the robot, there was an invention that made sense. And nobody had to get killed for it, or hit over the head or smashed up, had they?

So what was all this nonsense about robot-controlled red Cadillacs?

Driving these unwelcome reflections from his mind, he paused to light a cigarette. He had barely taken the first puff when a familiar voice said, "Hey, buddy, hold the light, will you?"

Malone looked up, blinked and grinned happily. "Boyd!" he said. "What are you doing here? I haven't seen you since—"

"Sure haven't," Boyd said. "I've been out West on a couple of cases. Must be a year since we worked together."

"Just about," Malone said. "But what are you doing in New York? Vacationing?"

"Not exactly," Boyd said. "The chief called it sort of a vacation, but—"

"Oh," Malone said. "You re working with me."

Boyd nodded. "The chief sent me up. When I got back from the West, he suddenly decided you might need a good assistant, so I took the plane down, and got here ahead of you."

"Great," Malone said. "But I want to warn you about the vacation—"

"Never mind," Boyd said; just a shade sadly. "I know. It isn't." He seemed deep in thought, as if he were deciding whether or not to get rid of Anne Boleyn. It was, Malone thought, an unusually apt simile. Boyd, six feet tall and weighing about two hundred and twenty-five pounds, had a large square face and a broad-beamed figure that might have made him a dead ringer for Henry VIII of England even without his Henry-like fringe of beard and his mustache. With them—thanks to the recent FBI rule that agents could wear "facial hair, at the discretion of the director or such board as he may appoint"—the resemblance to the Tudor monarch was uncanny.

But, like his famous double, Boyd didn't stay sad for long. "I thought I'd meet you at the station," he said, cheering up, "and maybe talk over old times for a while, on the way to the hotel, anyhow. So long as there wasn't anything else to do."

"Sure," Malone said. "It's good to see you again. And when did you get pulled out of the Frisco office?"

Boyd grimaced. "You know," he said, "I had a good thing going for me out there. Agent-in-Charge of the entire office. But right after that job we did together—the Queen Elizabeth affair—Burris decided I was too good a man to waste my fragrance on the desert air. Or whatever it is. So he recalled me, assigned me from the home office, and I've been on one case after another ever since."

"You're a home-office agent now?" Malone said.

"I'm a Roving Reporter," Boyd said, and struck a pose. "I'm a General Trouble-shooter and a Mr. Fix-It. Just like you, Hero."

"Thanks," Malone said. "How about the local office here? Seen the boys yet?"

Boyd shook his head. "Not yet," he said. "I was waiting for you to show up. But I did manage hotel rooms—a couple of rooms with a connecting bath over at the Hotel New Yorker. Nice place. You'll like it, Ken."

"I'll love it," Malone said. "Especially that connecting bath. It would have been terrible to have an unconnecting bath. Sort of distracting."

"Okay," Boyd said. "Okay. You know what I mean." He stared down at Malone's hand. "You know you've still got your lighter on?" he added.

Malone looked down at it and shut it off. "You asked me to hold it," he said.

"I didn't mean indefinitely," Boyd said. "Anyhow, how about grabbing a cab and heading on down to the hotel to get your stuff away, before we check in at 69th Street?"

"Good idea," Malone said. "And besides, I could do with a clean shirt. Not to mention a bath."

"Trains get worse and worse," Boyd said absently.

Malone punched the redcap's buttons again, and he and Boyd followed it through the crowded station to the taxi stand. The robot piled the suitcases into the cab, and somehow Malone and Boyd found room for themselves.

"Hotel New Yorker," Boyd said grandly.

The driver swung around to stare at them, blinked, and finally said, "Okay, Mac. You said it." He started with a terrific grinding of gears, drove out of the Penn Station arch and went two blocks.

"Here you are, Mac," he said, stopping the cab.

Malone stared at Boyd with a reproachful expression.

"So how was I to know?" Boyd said.

"I didn't look. If I'd known it was so close we could've walked."

"And saved half a buck," Malone said. "But don't let it bother you—this is expense-account money."

"That's right," Boyd said. He beamed and tipped the driver heavily. The cab drove off and Malone hailed the New Yorker doorman, who equipped them with a robot bellhop and sent them upstairs to their rooms.

Three-quarters of an hour later, Boyd and Malone were in the offices of the Federal Bureau of Investigation, on East 69th Street. There they picked up a lot of nice, new, shiny facts. It was unfortunate, if not particularly surprising, that the facts did not seem to make any sense.

In the first place, only red 1972 Cadillacs seemed to be involved. Anybody who owned such a car was likely to find it missing at any time; there had been a lot of thefts reported, including some that hadn't had time to get into Burris' reports. New Jersey now claimed two victims, and New York had three of its own.

And all the cars weren't turning up in New York, by any means. Some of the New York cars had turned up in New Jersey. Some had turned up in Connecticut—including one of the New Jersey cars. So far, there had been neither thefts nor discoveries in Pennsylvania, but Malone couldn't see why.

There was absolutely no pattern that he, Boyd, or anyone else could find. The list of thefts and recoveries had been fed into an electronic calculator, which had neatly regurgitated them without being in the least helpful. It had remarked that the square of seven was forty-nine, but this was traced to a defect in the mechanism.

Whoever was borrowing the red Caddies exhibited a peculiar combination of burglarious genius and what looked to Malone like outright idiocy. This was plainly impossible.

Unfortunately, it had happened.

Locking the car doors didn't do a bit of good. The thief, or thieves, got in without so much as scratching the lock. This obviously proved that the criminal was either an extremely good lock-pick or else knew where to get duplicate keys.

However, the ignition was invariably shorted across.

This proved neatly that the criminal was not a very good lock-pick, and did not know where to get duplicate keys.

Query: Why work so hard on the doors, and not work at all on the ignition?

That was the first place. The second place was just what had been bothering Malone all along. There didn't seem to be any purpose to the car thefts. They hadn't been sold, or used as getaway cars. True, teenage delinquents sometimes stole cars just to use them joy-riding, or as some sort of prank.

But a car or two every night? How many joy-rides can one gang take? Malone thought. And how long does it take to get tired of the same prank?

And why, Malone asked himself wearily for what was beginning to feel like the ten thousandth time, why only red Cadillacs?

Burris, he told himself, must have been right all along. The red Cadillacs were only a smoke screen for something else. Perhaps it was the robot car, perhaps not; but whatever it was, Burris' general answer was the only one that made any sense at all.

That should have been a comforting thought, Malone reflected. Somehow, though, it wasn't.

After they'd finished with the files and personnel at 69th Street, Malone and Boyd started downtown on what turned out to be a sort of unguided tour of the New York Police Department. They spoke to some of the eyewitnesses, and ended up in Centre Street asking a lot of reasonably useless questions in the Bureau of Motor Vehicles. In general, they spent nearly six hours on the Affair of the Self-Propelled Cadillac, picking up a whole bundle of facts. Some of the facts they had already known. Some were new, but unhelpful.

Somehow, nobody felt much like going out for a night on the town. Instead both agents climbed wearily into bed, thinking morose and disillusioned thoughts.

And, after that, a week passed. It was filled with ennui.

Only one new thing became clear. In spite of the almost identical modus operandi used in all the car thefts, they were obviously the work of a gang rather than a single person. This required the assumption that there was not one insane man at work, but a crew of them, all identically unbalanced.

"But the jobs are just too scattered to be the work of one man," Malone said. "To steal a car in Connecticut and drive it to the Bronx, and then steal another car in Westfield, New Jersey, fifteen minutes later takes more than talent. It takes an outright for-sure magician."

This conclusion, while interesting, was not really helpful. The fact was that Malone needed more clues—or, anyhow, more facts—before he could do anything at all. And there just weren't any new facts around. He spent the week wandering morosely from one place to another sometimes accompanied by Thomas Boyd and sometimes all alone. Time, he knew, was ticking by at its usual rate. But there wasn't a thing he could do about it.

He did try to relax and have some fun, as Burris had suggested. But he didn't seem to be able to get his mind off the case.

Boyd, after the first little while, had no such trouble. He entered the social life of the city with a whoop of joy and disappeared from sight. That was fine for Boyd, Malone reflected, but it did leave Malone himself just a little bit at loose ends.

Not that he begrudged Boyd his fun. It was nice that one of them was enjoying himself, anyway.

It was just that Malone was beginning to get fidgety. He needed to be doing something—even if it was only taking a walk.

So he took a walk and ended up, to his own surprise, downtown near Greenwich Village.

And then he'd been bopped on the head.

CHAPTER THREE

The patrol car pulled up in front of St. Vincent's Hospital, and one of the cops helped Malone into the emergency receiving room. He didn't feel as bad as he had a few minutes before. The motion of the car hadn't helped any, but his head seemed to be knitting a little, and his legs were a little steadier. True, he didn't feel one hundred per cent healthy, but he was beginning to think he might live, after all. And while the doctor was bandaging his head, a spirit of new life began to fill the FBI agent.

He was no longer morose and undirected. He had a purpose in life, and the purpose filled him with cold determination. He was going to find the robot-operated car—or whatever it turned out to be.

The doctor, Malone noticed, was whistling *Greensleeves* under his breath as he worked. That, he supposed, was the influence of the Bohemian folk-singers of Greenwich Village. But he put the noise resolutely out of his mind and concentrated on the red Cadillac.

It was one thing to think about a robot car miles away, doing something or other to somebody you'd never heard of before. That was just theoretical, a case for solution, nothing but an ordinary job.

But when the car stepped up and bopped Malone himself on the head, it became a personal matter. Now Malone had more than a job to contend with. Now he was thinking about revenge.

By God, he told himself, *no car in the world—not even a Cadillac— can get away with beaning Kenneth J. Malone!*

Malone was not quite certain that he agreed with Burris' idea of a self-operating car, but at least it was something to work on. A car that could reach out, crown an investigator, and then drive off humming something innocent under its breath was certainly a unique and dangerous machine within the meaning of the act. Of course, there were problems attendant on this view of things. For one thing, Malone couldn't quite see how the car could have beaned him when he was ten feet away from it. But that was, he told himself uncomfortably, a minor point. He could deal with it when he felt a little better.

The important thing was the car itself. Malone jerked a little under the doctor's calm hands, and swore subvocally.

"Hold still," the doctor said. "Don't go wiggling your head around that way. Just wait quietly until the dermijel sets."

Obediently, Malone froze. There was a crick in his neck, but he decided he could stand it. "My head still hurts," he said accusingly.

"Sure it still hurts," the doctor agreed.

"But you—"

"What did you expect?" the doctor said. "Even an FBI agent isn't immune to blackjacks, you know." He resumed his work on Malone's skull.

"Blackjacks?" Malone said. "What blackjacks?"

"The ones that hit you," the doctor said. "Or the one, anyhow."

Malone blinked. Somehow, though he could manage a fuzzy picture of a car reaching out to hit him, the introduction of a blackjack into this imaginative effort confused things a little. But he resolutely ignored it.

"The bruise is just the right size and shape," the doctor said. "And that cut on your head comes from the seams on the leather casing."

"You're sure?" Malone said doubtfully. It did seem as if a car had a lot more dangerous weapons around, without resorting to blackjacks. If it had really wanted to damage him, why hadn't it hit him with the engine block?

"I'm sure," the doctor said. "I've worked in Emergency in this hospital long enough to recognize a blackjack wound."

That was a disturbing idea, in a way. It gave a new color to Malone's reflection on Greenwich Villagers. Maybe things had changed since he'd heard about them. Maybe the blackjack had supplanted the guitar.

But that wasn't the important thing.

The fact that it had been a blackjack that had hit him *was* important. It was vital, as a matter of fact. Malone knew that perfectly well. It was a key fact in the case he was investigating.

The only trouble was that he didn't see what, if anything, it meant.

The doctor stepped back and regarded Malone's head with something like pride. "There," he said. "You'll be all right now."

"A concussion?"

"Sure," the doctor said. "But it isn't serious. Just take these pills—one every two hours until they're gone—and you'll be rid of any effects within twenty-four hours." He went to a cabinet, fiddled around for a minute, and came back with a small bottle containing six orange pills. They looked very large and threatening.

"Fine," Malone said doubtfully.

"You'll be all right," the doctor said, giving Malone a cheerful, confident grin. "Nothing at all to worry about." He loaded a hypojet and blasted something through the skin of Malone's upper arm. Malone swallowed hard. He knew perfectly well that he hadn't felt a thing but he couldn't quite make himself believe it.

"That'll take care of you for tonight," the doctor said. "Get some sleep and start in on the pills when you wake up, okay?"

"Okay," Malone said. It was going to make waking up something less than a pleasure, but he wanted to get well, didn't he?

Of course he did. If that Cadillac thought it was going to beat him...

"You can stand up now," the doctor said.

"Okay," Malone said, trying it. "Thanks, Doctor. I—"

There was a knock at the door. The doctor jerked his head around.

"Who's that?" he said.

"Me," a bass voice said, unhelpfully.

The emergency-room door opened a crack and a face peered in. It took Malone a second to recognize Bill, the waffle-faced cop who had picked him up next to the lamp post three years or so before. "Long time no see," Malone said at random.

"What?" Bill said, and opened the door wider. He came in and closed it behind him. "It's okay, Doc," he said to the attendant. "I'm a cop."

"Been hurt?" the doctor said.

Bill shook his head. "Not recently," he said. "I came to see this guy." He looked at Malone. "They told me you were still here," he said.

"Who's they?" Malone said.

"Outside," Bill said. "The attendants out there. They said you were still getting stitched up."

"And quite right, too," Malone said solemnly.

"Oh," Bill said. "Sure." He fished in his pockets. "You dropped your notebook, though, and I came to give it back to you." He located the object he was hunting for and brought it out with the triumphant gesture of a man displaying the head of a dragon he had slain. "Here," he said, waving the book.

"Notebook?" Malone said. He stared at it. It was a small looseleaf book bound in cheap black plastic.

"We found it in the gutter," Bill said.

Malone took a tentative step forward and managed not to fall. He stepped back again and looked at Bill scornfully. "I wasn't even in the gutter," he said. "There are limits."

"Sure," Bill said. "But the notebook was, so I brought it along to you. I thought you might need it or something." He handed it over to Malone with a flourish.

It wasn't Malone's notebook. In the first place, he had never owned a notebook that looked anything like that, and in the second place he hadn't had any notebooks on him when he went for his walk. *Mine not to question why*, Malone told himself with a shrug, and flipped the book open.

At once he saw why the cop had mistaken it for his.

It had his name in it.

On the very first page were two names, written out in a careful, semieducated scrawl:

Mr. Kenneth J. Malone, FBI Lt. Peter Lynch, NYPD

The rest of the page was blank. Malone wondered who Lieutenant Lynch was, and made a mental note to find out. Then he wondered what his name was doing in somebody else's notebook. Maybe, he thought, it was a list of people to slug, and the car had made it up. But he hadn't heard of anybody named Lynch being hit on the head by a marauding automobile, and he couldn't quite picture a Cadillac jotting things down in a notebook for future reference. Besides, he had an idea that a Cadillac's handwriting would be more formal, and prettier.

He turned the page. On the next leaf there were more names, eight of them. The first one was written in red pencil and the others were in ordinary black. Malone stared at them:

Mike F. Ramon O. Mario G. Silvo E. Alvarez A. Felipe la B. Juan de los S. Ray del E.

All the names except Mike F. sounded Spanish, or possibly Puerto Rican. Malone wondered who they were. Juvenile delinquents? Other people to slug? Police officers?

Maybe they were all the names of Spanish-speaking Cadillacs.

He blinked and rubbed at his forehead with one hand. His head still hurt, and that was probably why he was getting such strange ideas. It was obvious that, whatever the notebook was, it hadn't been written by an automobile.

He turned the page again.

Here there was a carefully detailed drawing of a car. Malone recognized it as a 1972 Cadillac without any effort at all.

And it had been carefully colored in with red pencil.

Wow, Malone asked himself, *What the hell does that mean?*

He couldn't find an answer. He turned the page, hoping for some more facts that might make some sense out of what he had been seeing, but there was nothing more. All the rest of the pages in the notebook were blank.

He looked up at the cop and the doctor with a bland, blank face. "Thanks a lot," he told Bill. "I thought I'd lost this book. I appreciate it."

"Oh, that's okay, Mr. Malone," Bill said. "Glad to do it."

"You don't know what this means to me," Malone said truthfully.

"No trouble at all," Bill said. "Any time." He gave Malone a nice big smile and turned back to the door. "But I got to get back to my beat," he said. "Listen, I'll see you. And if I can be any help—"

"Sure," Malone said. "I'll let you know. And thanks again."

"Welcome," Bill said, and opened the door. He strode out with the air of a man who has just been decorated with the Silver Star, the Purple Heart and the Congressional Medal of Honor.

Malone tried a few more steps and discovered that he could walk without falling down. He thanked the doctor again.

"Perfectly all right," the doctor said. "Nothing to it. Why, you ought to see some of the cases we get here. There was a guy here the other night with both his legs all mashed up by a—"

"I'll bet," Malone said hurriedly. "Well, I've got to be on my way. Just send the bill to FBI headquarters on 69th Street." He closed the door on the doctor's enthusiastic "Yes, *sir!*" and went on down the hallway and out into the street. At Seventh Avenue and Greenwich Avenue he flagged a cab.

It was a hell of a place to be, Malone thought as the cab drove away. Where but in Greenwich Village did avenues intersect each other without so much as a by-your-leave?

"Hotel New Yorker," he said, giving the whole thing up as a bad job. He put his hat on his head and adjusted it painfully to the proper angle.

And that, he thought, made another little problem. The car had not only hit him on the head, it had removed his hat before doing so, and then replaced it. It had only fallen off when he'd started to get up against the lamp post.

A nice quiet vacation, Malone thought bitterly.

He fumed in silence all the way to the hotel, through the lobby, up in the elevator, and to the door of his room. Then he remembered the notebook.

That was important evidence. He decided to tell Boyd about it right away.

He went into the bathroom and tapped gently on the door to Boyd's connecting room. The door swung open.

Boyd, apparently, was still out painting the town—Malone considered the word *red* and dropped the whole phrase with a sigh. At any rate, his partner was nowhere in the room.

"The hell with it," Malone announced loudly to no one in particular. He went back into his own room, closed the door, and got wearily ready for bed.

*   *   *

Dawn came, and then daylight, and then a lot more daylight. It was streaming in through the windows with careless abandon, filling the room with a lot of bright sunshine and the muggy heat of the city. From the street below, the cheerful noises of traffic and pedestrians floated up and filled Malone's ears.

He got up, turned over in bed, and tried to go back to sleep.

But sleep wouldn't come. After a long time he gave up, and swung himself over the edge of the bed. Standing up was a delicate job, but he managed it, feeling rather proud of himself in a dim, semiconscious sort of way.

He went into the bathroom, brushed his teeth, and then opened the connecting door to Boyd's room softly.

Boyd was home. He lay in a great tangle of bedclothes, snoring hideously and making little motions with his hands and arms like a beached whale. Malone padded over to him and dug him fiercely in the ribs.

"Come on," he said. "Wake up, Tommy-boy."

Boyd's eyes did not open. In a voice as hollow as a zombie's, he said, "My head hurts."

"Can't feel any worse than mine," Malone said cheerily. This, he reflected, was not quite true. Considering everything it had been through recently, his head felt remarkably like its old carefree self. "You'll feel better once you're awake."

"No, I won't," Boyd said simply. He jammed his head under a pillow and began to snore again. It was an awesome sound, like a man strangling to death in chicken fat. Malone sighed and poked at random among the bedclothes.

Boyd swore distantly, and Malone poked him again.

"The sun is up," Malone said, "and all the little pedestrians are chirping. It is time to rise."

Boyd said, "Gah," and withdrew his head from the pillow. Gently, as if he were afraid he were going to fall apart, he rose to a sitting position. When he had arrived at it, he opened his eyes.

"Now," Malone said. "Isn't that better?"

Boyd closed his eyes again. "No," he said.

"Come on," Malone said. "We've got to be up and moving."

"I'm up," Boyd said. His eyes flickered open. "But I can't move," he added. "We had quite a time last night."

"We?" Malone said.

"Me, and a couple of girls, and another guy. Just people I met." Boyd started to stand up and thought better of it. "Just having a good time, that's all."

Malone thought of reading his partner a lecture on the Evils of Drink, and decided against it. Boyd might remember it, and use it against him sometime. Then he realized what had to be done. He went back into his own room, dialed for room service, and ordered a couple of pots of strong black coffee.

By the time a good deal of that was awash in Boyd's intestinal system, he was almost capable of rational, connected conversation. He filled himself to the eyebrows with aspirins and other remedies, and actually succeeded in getting dressed. He seemed quite proud of this feat.

"Okay," Malone said. "Now we have to go downstairs."

"You mean outside?" Boyd said. "Into all that noise?" He winced.

"Bite the bullet," Malone said cheerfully. "Keep a stiff upper lip."

"Nonsense," Boyd said, hunting for his coat with a doleful air. "Have you ever seen anybody with a loose upper lip?"

Malone, busy with his own coat, didn't bother with a reply. He managed somehow to get Boyd downstairs and bundled into a cab. They headed for 69th Street. There he made several phone calls. The first, of course, was to Burris in Washington. After that he got the New York Police Commissioner on the wire and, finding that he needed still more authority, he called the mayor and then, by long-distance to Albany, the governor.

But by noon he had everything straightened out. He had a plan fully worked out in his mind, and he had the authority to go ahead with it. Now, he could make his final call.

"They're completely trustworthy," Burris had told him. "Not only that, but they have a clearance for this kind of special work—we've needed them before."

"Good," Malone said.

"Not only that," Burris told him. "They're damned good men. Maybe among the best in their field."

So Malone made his last call, to the firm of Leibowitz and Hardin, Electronic Engineers.

Then he beckoned to Boyd.

"I don't see what I've been sitting around here for, all this time," his partner complained. "I could have been home sleeping until you needed me."

"I need you now," Malone said. "I want you to take over part of this plan."

Boyd nodded sourly. "Oh, all right," he said.

"Here's what I want," Malone said. "Every red 1972 Cadillac in the area is to be picked up for inspection. I don't care why—make up a reason. A general traffic check. Anything you please. You can work that end of it out with the commissioner; he knows about it and he's willing to go along."

"Great," Boyd said. "Do you have any idea how many cars there are in a city this size?"

"Well, we don't want all of them," Malone said. "Only red 1972 Cadillacs."

"It's still a lot," Boyd said.

"If there were only three," Malone said, "we wouldn't have any problems."

"And wouldn't that be nice?" Boyd said.

"Sure," Malone said, "but it isn't true. Anyhow, I want every one of those cars checked for any oddity, no matter how small. If there's an inch-long scratch on one fender, I want to know about it. If you've got to take the cars apart, then do that."

"Me?" Boyd said. "All by myself?"

"My God, no," Malone said. "Use your head. There'll be a team working with you. Let me explain it. Every nut, every bolt, every inch of those cars has to be examined thoroughly—got it?"

"I've got it," Boyd said, "but I'm damned if I like it. After all, Malone—"

Malone ignored him. "The governor of New York's promised his cooperation," he said, "and he said he'd get in touch with the governors of New Jersey and Connecticut and get cooperation from that angle. So we'll have both state and local police working with us."

"That's a help," Boyd said. "We'll make such a happy team of workmen. Singing as we pull the cars apart through the long day and night and—listen, Malone, when do you want reports on this?"

"Yesterday," Malone said.

Boyd's eyebrows raised, then lowered. "Great," he said dully.

"I don't care how you get the cars," Malone said. "If you've got to, condemn 'em. But get every last one of them. And bring them over to Leibowitz and Hardin for a complete checkup. I'll give you the address."

"Thanks," Boyd said.

"Not at all," Malone said. "Glad to be of help. And don't worry; I'll have other work to do." He paused, and then went on, "I talked to Dr. Isaac Leibowitz—he's the head of the firm out there—and he says—"

"Wait a minute," Boyd said. "What?"

"You mean I don't have to take the cars apart myself? You mean this Leibowitz and Hardin, or whatever it is, will do it for me?"

"Of course," Malone said wearily. "You're not an auto technician or an electronics man. You're an agent of the FBI."

"I was beginning to wonder," Boyd said. "After all."

"Anyhow," Malone said doggedly, "I talked to Leibowitz, and he says he can give a car a complete check in about six hours, normally."

"Six hours?" Boyd stared. "That's going to take forever," he said.

"Well, he can set up a kind of assembly-line process and turn out a car every fifteen minutes. Any better?"

Boyd nodded.

"Good," Malone said. "There can't be so many 1972 red Cadillacs in the area that we can't get through them all at that speed." He thought a minute and then added, "By the way, you might check with the Cadillac dealers around town, and find out just how many have been sold to people living in the area."

"And while I'm doing all that," Boyd said, "what are you going to be doing?"

Malone looked at him and sighed. "I'll worry about that," he said. "Just get started."

"Suppose Leibowitz can't find anything?" Boyd said.

"If Leibowitz can't find it, it's not there," Malone said. "He can find electronic devices anywhere in any car made, he says—even if they're printed circuits hidden under the paint job."

"Pretty good," Boyd said. "But suppose he doesn't?"

"Then they aren't there," Malone said, "and we'll have to think of something else." He considered that. It sounded fine. Only he wished he knew what else there was to think of.

Well, that was just pessimism. Leibowitz would find something, and the case would be over, and he could go back to Washington and rest. In August he was going to have his vacation anyway, and August wasn't very far away.

Malone put a smile carefully on his face and told Boyd, "Get going." He slammed his hat on his head.

Wincing, he took it off and replaced it gently. The bottle of pills was still in his pocket, but he wasn't due for another one just yet.

He had time to go over to the precinct station in the West Eighties first. He headed outside to get another taxi.

CHAPTER FOUR

The door didn't say anything at all except *Lt. P. Lynch*. Malone looked at it for a couple of seconds. He'd asked the desk sergeant for Lynch, shown his credentials and been directed up a set of stairs and around a hall. But he still didn't know what Lynch did, who he was, or what his name was doing in the little black notebook.

Well, he told himself, there was only one way to find out.

He opened the door.

The room was small and dark. It had a single desk in it, and three chairs, and a hatrack. There wasn't any coat or hat on the hatrack, and there was nobody in the chairs. In a fourth chair, behind the desk, sat a huskily built man. He had steel-gray hair, a hard jaw and, Malone noticed with surprise, a faint twinkle in his eye.

"Lieutenant Lynch?" Malone said.

"Right," Lynch said. "What's the trouble?"

"I'm Kenneth J. Malone, FBI." He reached for his wallet and found it. He flipped it open for Lynch, who stared at it for what seemed a long, long time, and then burst into laughter.

"What's so funny?" Malone asked. Lynch laughed some more.

"Oh, come on," Malone said bitterly. "After all, there's no reason to treat an FBI agent like some kind of a—"

"FBI agent?" Lynch said. "Listen, buster, this is the funniest gag I've seen since I came on the force. Really a hell of a funny thing. Who told you to pull it? Jablonski downstairs? Or one of the boys on the beat? I know those beat patrolmen, always on the lookout for a new joke. But this tops 'em all. This is the—"

"You're a disgrace to the Irish," Malone said tartly.

"A what?" Lynch said. "I'm not Irish."

"You talk like an Irishman," Malone said.

"I know it," Lynch said, and shrugged. "Around some precincts, you sort of pick it up. When all the other cops are—hey, listen. How'd we get to talking about me?"

"I said you were a disgrace to the Irish," Malone said.

"I was a—*what?*"

"Disgrace." Malone looked carefully at Lynch. In a fight, he considered, he might get in a lucky punch that would kill Malone. Otherwise, Malone didn't have a thing to worry about except a few months of hospitalization.

Lynch looked as if he were about to get mad, and then he looked down at Malone's wallet again and started to laugh.

"For God's sake," Malone said. "What's so damned funny?"

He grabbed the wallet and turned it toward him. At once, of course, he realized what had happened. He hadn't flipped it open to his badge at all. He'd flipped it open, instead, to a card in the card case:

KNOW ALL MEN BY THESE PRESENTS THAT
Sir Kenneth Malone, Knight, is hereby formally installed with the title of

KNIGHT OF THE BATH

and this card shall signify his right to that title and his high and respected position as officer in and of

THE QUEEN'S OWN FBI

In a very small voice, Malone said, "There's been a terrible mistake."

"Mistake?" Lynch said.

Malone flipped the wallet open to his FBI shield. Lynch gave it a good long examination, peering at it from every angle and holding it up to the light two or three times. He even wet his thumb and rubbed the badge with it. At last he looked up.

"I guess you are the FBI," he said. "But what's with the gag?"

"It isn't a gag," Malone said. "It's just—" He thought of the little old lady in Yucca Flats, the little old lady who had been the prime mover in the last case he and Boyd had worked on together. Without the little old lady, the case might never have been solved; she was an authentic telepath, about the best that had ever been found.

But with her, Boyd and Malone had had enough troubles. Besides being a telepath, she was quite thoroughly insane. She had one fixed delusion: she believed she was Queen Elizabeth I.

She was still at Yucca Flats, along with the other telepaths Malone's investigation had turned up. And she still believed, quite calmly, that she was Good Queen Bess. Malone had been knighted by her during the course of the investigation. This new honor had come to him through the mail; apparently she had decided to ennoble some of her friends still further.

Malone made a mental note to ask Boyd if he'd received one. After all, there couldn't be too many Knights of the Bath. There was no sense in letting *everybody* in.

Then he realized that he was beginning to believe everything again. There had been times, working with the little old lady, when he had been firmly convinced that he was, in fact, the swaggering, ruthless swordsman, Sir Kenneth Malone. And even now...

"Well?" Lynch said.

"It's too long a story," Malone said. "And besides, it's not what I came here about."

Lynch shrugged again. "Okay," he said. "Tell it your way."

"First," Malone said, "what's your job?"

"Me? Precinct Lieutenant."

"Of this precinct?"

Lynch stared. "What else?" he said.

"Who knows?" Malone said. He found the black notebook and passed it across to Lynch. "I'm on this red Cadillac business, you know," he said by way of introduction.

"I've been hearing about it," Lynch said. He picked up the notebook without opening it and held it like a ticking bomb. "And I mean hearing about it," he said. "We haven't had any trouble at all in this precinct."

"I know," Malone said. "I've read the reports."

"Listen, not a single red Cadillac has been stolen from here, or been reported found here. We run a tight precinct here, and let me tell you—"

"I'm sure you do a fine job," Malone said hastily. "But I want you to look at the notebook. The first page."

Lynch opened his mouth, closed it, and then flipped the notebook cover. He stared at the first page for a few seconds. "What's this?" he said at last. "Another gag?"

"No gag, Lieutenant," Malone said.

"It's your name and mine," Lynch said. "What is that supposed to mean?"

Malone shrugged. "Search me," he said. "The notebook was found only a couple of feet away from another car theft, last night." That was the simplest way he could think of to put it. "So

I asked the Commissioner who Peter Lynch was, and he told me it was you."

"And, by God, it is," Lynch said, staring at the notebook. He seemed to be expecting it to rise and strike him.

Malone said, "Have you got any idea who'd be writing about you and me?"

Lynch shook his head. "If I had any ideas I'd feel a lot better," he said.

He wet his finger and turned the notebook page carefully over. When he saw the list of names on the second page he stopped again, and stared. This time he whistled under his breath.

Very cautiously, Malone said, "Something?"

"I'll be damned," Lynch said feelingly.

"What's wrong?" Malone said.

The police lieutenant looked up. "I don't know if it's wrong or what," he said. "It gives me sort of the willies. I know every one of these kids."

Malone took out a pill and swallowed it in a hurry. He felt exactly as if he had been given another concussion, absolutely free and without any obligations. His mouth opened but nothing came out for a long time. At last he managed to say, *"Kids?"*

"That's right," Lynch said. "What did you think?"

Malone shrugged helplessly.

"Every single one of them," Lynch said. "Right from around here."

There was a little silence.

"Who are they?" Malone said carefully.

"They're some kind of kid gang—a social club, or something like that. This first kid—Miguel Fueyo's his full name—is the leader. They call themselves the Silent Spooks."

"The what?" It seemed to Malone that the name was just a little fancy, even for a kid gang.

"The Silent Spooks," Lynch said. "I can't help it. But here they are, every one of them: Fueyo, Ramon Otravez, Mario Grito, Silvo Envoz, Alvarez Altapor, Felipe la Barba, Juan de los Santos, and Ray del Este. Right down the line." He looked up from the notebook with a blank expression on his face. "All of them kids from this neighborhood. The Silent Spooks."

"They know you?" Malone said.

"Sure they do," Lynch said. "They all know me. But do they know you?"

Malone thought. "They could have heard of me," he said at last, trying to be as modest as possible.

"I guess," Lynch said grudgingly. "How old are they?" Malone said.

"Fourteen to seventeen," Lynch said. "Somewhere in there. You know how these kid things run."

"The Silent Spooks," Malone said meditatively. It was a nice name, in a way; you just had to get used to it for a while. When he had been a kid, he'd belonged to a group that called itself the East Division Street Kids. There just wasn't much romance in a name like that. Now the Silent Spooks...

With a wrench, he brought his mind back to the subject at hand. "Do they get into much trouble?" he said.

"Well, no," Lynch said reluctantly. "As a matter of fact, they don't. For a bunch like that, around here, they're pretty well behaved, as far as that goes."

"What do you mean?" Malone said.

Lynch's face took on a delicately unconcerned appearance. "I don't know," he said. "They just don't get into neighborhood trouble. Maybe a scrap now and then—nothing big, though. Or maybe one of them cuts a class at school or argues with his teacher. But there's nothing unusual, and damn little of anything." He frowned.

Malone said, "Something's got to be wrong. What is it?"

"Well," Lynch said, "they do seem to have a hell of a lot of money to spend."

Malone sat down in a chair across the desk, and leaned eagerly toward Lynch. "Money?" he said.

"Money," Lynch said. "New clothes. Cigarettes. Malone, three of them are even supporting their parents. Old Jose Otravez— Ramon's old man—quit his job a couple of months ago, and hasn't worked since. Spends all his time in bars, and never runs out of dough—and don't tell me you can do that on unemployment insurance. Or social security payments."

"Okay," Malone said. "I won't tell you."

"And there's others. All the others, in fact. Mike Fueyo's sister dresses fit to kill, like a high-fashion model. And the Grito kid—"

"Wait a minute," Malone said. "From what you tell me, this isn't just a little extra money. These kids must be rolling in the stuff. Up to their ears in dough."

"Listen," Lynch said sadly, "Those kids spend more than I do. Hell, they do better than that—they spend more than I *earn*." He looked remotely sorry for himself, but not for long. "Every one of those kids spends like a drunken sailor, tossing his money away on all sorts of things."

"Like an expense account," Malone said idly. Lynch looked up. "Sorry," Malone said. "I was thinking about something else."

"I'll bet you were," Lynch said with unconcealed envy.

"No," Malone said. "Really. Listen, I'll check with Internal Revenue on that money. But have you got a list of the kids' addresses?"

"I can get one," Lynch said, and went to the door.

It closed behind him. Malone sat waiting alone for a few minutes, and then Lynch came back. "List'll be here in a minute," he said. He sat down behind his desk and reached for the notebook again. When he turned to the third page his expression changed to one of surprise.

"Be damned," he said. "There does seem to be a connection, doesn't there?" He held up the picture of the red Cadillac for Malone to see.

"Sure does," Malone said. "That's why I want those addresses. If there is a connection, I sure as hell want to find out about it."

Ten minutes later, Malone was walking out of the precinct station with the list of addresses in his pocket. He was heading for his Great Adventure, but he didn't know it. All he was thinking about was the red Cadillacs, and the eight teenagers.

"I'm going to get to the bottom of this if it takes me all summer," he said, muttering to himself.

"That's the spirit," he told himself. "Never say die."

Then, realizing he had just said it, he frowned. Perhaps it hadn't really counted. But then again...

He was on his way down the steps when he hit the girl.

The mutual collision was not catastrophic. On the other hand, it was not exactly minor. It fell somewhere between the two, as an unclassifiable phenomenon of undoubted potency. Malone said, "Oog," with some fervor as the girl collided with his chest and rebounded like a handball striking a wall. Something was happening to her, but Malone had no time to spare to notice just what. He was falling through space, touching a concrete step once in a while, but not long enough to make any real acquaintance with it. It seemed to take him a long time to touch bottom, and when he had, he wondered if *touch* was quite the word.

Bottom certainly was. He had fallen backward and landed directly on his *glutei maximi*, obeying the law regarding equal and opposite reaction and several other laws involving falling bodies.

His first thought was that he was now neatly balanced. His tail had received the same treatment as his head. He wondered if a person could get concussion of the tail bones, and had reached no definite conclusion when, unexpectedly, his eyes focused again.

He was looking at a girl. That was all he saw at first. She had apparently fallen just as he had, bounced once and sat down rather hard. She was now lying flat on her back, making a sound like "rrr" between her teeth.

Malone discovered that he was sitting undignifiedly on the steps. He opened his mouth to say something objectionable, took another look at the girl, and shut it with a snap. This was no ordinary girl.

He smiled at her. She shook her head and sat up, still going "rrr." Then she stopped and said instead, "What do you think—"

"I'm sorry," Malone said in what he hoped was a charming, debonair, and apologetic voice. It was quite a lot to get into one voice, but he tried his very hardest. "I just didn't see—"

"You didn't?" the girl said. She took a long, slow look at him, shook her head again, and then pulled her skirt down carefully. "If you didn't, you must be blind," she said.

Malone noticed with hope that there was no anger in her voice. The last thing in the world he wanted was to get this girl angry at him.

"Oh, no," Malone said. "I'm not blind. Not blind at all." He smiled at her and stood up. His tail throbbed a little, but it didn't

119

seem to be anything really serious. "I'm just polite," he said, and smiled again. His face was beginning to get a little tired, but he retained his last smile as he went over to her, extended a hand and pulled her to her feet.

She was something special. Her hair was long and dark, and fell in soft waves to her shoulders. The shoulders were something all by themselves, but Malone postponed consideration of them for a minute to take a look at her face.

It was heart-shaped and rather thin. She had large brown liquid eyes that could look, Malone imagined, appealing, loving, worshiping—or, like a minute ago, downright furious. Below these features she had a straight lovely nose and a pair of lips which Malone immediately classified as kissable.

Her figure, including the shoulders, was on the slim side, but she was very definitely all there. Malone couldn't think of any parts the Creator had left out, and if there were any he didn't want to hear about them. In an instant, Malone knew that he had met the only great love of his life.

Again.

His mind was whirling, and for a second he didn't know what to do. And then he remembered the Queen's Own FBI. Phrases flowered forth in his mind as if it were a garden packed corner to corner with the most exquisite varieties of blooming idiots.

"My deepest apologies, my dear," Sir Kenneth Malone said gallantly, even managing a small display bow for the occasion. "May I be of any assistance?"

The girl smiled up at him as she came to her feet. The smile was radiant and beautiful and almost loving. Malone felt as if he couldn't stand it. Tingles of the most wonderful kind ran through him, reached his toes and then back the other way, meeting a whole new set going forward.

"You're very nice," the girl said, and the tingles became positive waves of sensation. "Actually, it was all my fault. Please don't apologize, Mr.—" She paused expectantly.

"Me?" Malone said, his gallantry deserting him for the second. But it returned full force before he expected it. "I'm Malone," he said. "Kenneth Joseph Malone." He had always liked the middle name he had inherited from his father, but he never had much opportunity to use it. He made the most of it now, rolling it out with all sorts of subsidiary flourishes. As a matter of fact, he barely restrained himself from putting a "Sir" before his name.

The girl's brown eyes widened just a trifle. Malone felt as if he could have fallen into them and drowned. "Oh, my," she said. "You must be a detective." And then, like the merest afterthought, "My name's Dorothy."

Dorothy. It was a beautiful name. It made Malone feel all choked up inside. He blinked at the girl and tried to look manly and wonderful. It was an effort, but he nearly carried it off.

After a second or two he realized that she had asked him a question. He didn't want to disillusion her in any way, and, after all, an FBI agent was a kind of detective, but he thought it was only fair that she should know the whole truth about him right from the start.

"Not exactly a detective," he said.

"Not exactly?" she said, looking puzzled. She looked positively glorious when puzzled, Malone decided at once.

"That is," he said carefully, "I do detect, but not for the city of New York."

"Oh," she said. "A private eye. Is that right?"

"Well," Malone said, "no." She looked even more puzzled.

Malone hastened to explain before he got to the point where conversation was impossible.

"Federal Bureau of Investigation," he said. After a second he thought of a clarification and added, "FBI."

"Oh," the girl said. *"Oh."*

"But you can call me Ken," Malone said.

"All right—Ken," she said. "And you call me Dorothy."

"Sure," he said. He tried it out. "Dorothy." It felt swell.

"Well," she said after a second.

"Oh," Malone said. "Were you looking for a detective? Because if I can help in any way—"

"Not exactly," Dorothy said. "Just a little routine business. I'll go on in and—"

Malone suddenly found himself talking without having any idea why he'd started, or what he was going to say. At first he said, "Urr," as if the machine were warming up, and this stopped

Dorothy and caused her to give him a rather sharp, baffled stare. Then he found some words and used them hurriedly, before they got away.

"Dorothy," he said, "would you like to take in a show this evening? I think I can get tickets to—well, I guess I could get tickets to almost anything, if I really tried." His expression attempted to leave no doubt that he would really try.

Dorothy appeared to consider for a moment. "Well," she said at last, "how about *The Hot Seat?*"

Malone felt just the way he had several years before when he had bluffed his way into a gigantic pot during a Washington poker game, with only a pair of fours to work with. At the last moment, his bluff had been called.

It had, he realized, been called again. *The Hot Seat* had set some sort of record, not only for Broadway longevity, but for audience frenzy. Getting tickets for it was about the same kind of proposition as buying grass on the moon, and getting them with absolutely no prior notice would require all the wire-pulling Malone could manage. He thought about *The Hot Seat* and wished Dorothy had picked something easy, like arranging for her to meet the Senate.

But he swallowed bravely. "I'll do my best," he said. "Got any second choice?"

"Sure," she said, and laughed. "Pick any one you want. I haven't seen them all, and the ones I have seen are worth seeing again."

"Oh," Malone said.

"I really didn't expect you to get tickets for *The Hot Seat*," she said.

"Nothing," Malone said, "is impossible." He grinned at her. "Meanwhile, where can I pick you up? Your home?"

Dorothy frowned and shook her head. "No," she said. "You see, I'm living with an aunt, and I—well, never mind." She thought for a minute. "I know," she said. "Topp's."

"What?" Malone said.

"Topp's," Dorothy said. "On Forty-second Street, just east of Broadway? It's a restaurant."

"I don't exactly know where it is," Malone said, "but if it's there, I'll find it." He looked gallant and determined. "We can get something to eat there before the show—whatever the show turns out to be."

"Fine," Dorothy said.

"How about making it at six?" Malone said.

She nodded. "Six it is," she said. "Now bye-bye." She touched her forefinger to her lips, and brushed Malone's cheek with the kissed finger.

By the time the new set of tingles had begun to evaporate, she had gone into the police station. Malone heaved a great sigh of passion, and held down a strong impulse to follow her and protect her. He wasn't quite sure what he was going to protect her from, but he felt certain that that would come to him when the time arrived.

Nevertheless, he had work to do, unpleasant as the idea had suddenly begun to seem. He pulled the list of addresses out of his pocket and looked at the first one.

Mike Fueyo.

Mike was the leader of the Silent Spooks, according to Lieutenant Lynch. Logically, therefore, he would be the first one to talk to. Malone tried to think of some good questions, but the best one he could come up with was: "Well, what about all those red Cadillacs?"

Somehow he doubted that this would provide a satisfactory reply.

He checked the address again and started firmly down the street, trying to think of some better questions along the way.

*   *   *

The building was just off Amsterdam Avenue, in the eighties. It had been a shining new development once, but it was beginning to slide downhill now. The metal on the window frames was beginning to look worn, and the brickwork hadn't been cleaned in a long time. Where chain fences had once protected lonely blades of grass, children, mothers, and baby carriages held sway now, and the grass was gone. Instead, the building was pretty well surrounded by a moat of sick-looking brown dirt.

Malone went into the first building and checked the name against the mailboxes there, trying to ignore the combined smells of sour milk, red pepper, and here and there a whiff of unwashed humanity.

It was on the tenth floor: *Fueyo, J.* That, he supposed, would be Mike's widowed mother; Lynch had told him that much about the boy and his family. He found the elevator, which was covered with scribbles ranging from JANEY LOVES MIGUEL to startling obscenities, and rode it upstairs.

Apartment 1004 looked like every other apartment in the building, at least from the outside. Malone pressed the button and waited a second to hear the faint buzzing at the other side of the door. After a minute, he pressed it again.

The door swung open very suddenly, and Malone stepped back.

A short, wrinkled, dark-eyed woman in a print housedress was eying him with deep suspicion. "My daughter is not home," she announced at once.

"I'm not looking for your daughter," Malone said. "I'd like to talk to Mike."

"Mike?" Her expression grew even more suspicious. "You want to talk to Mike?"

"That's right," Malone said.

"Ah," the woman said. "You one of those hoodlum friends he has. I'm right? You can talk to Mike when I am dead and have no control over him. For now, you can just—"

"Wait a minute," Malone said. He pulled out his wallet and flipped it open to show his badge, being very careful that he made the right flip this time. He didn't know exactly how this woman would react to the Queen's Own FBI, but he didn't especially want to find out.

She looked down at the badge without taking the wallet from him. "Hah," she said. "You're cop, eh?" Her eyes left the wallet and examined Malone from head to foot. It was perfectly plain that they didn't like what they saw. "Cop," she said again, as if to herself. It sounded like a curse.

Malone said, "Well, I—"

"You want to ask me stupid questions," she said. "That is what you want to do. I'm right?"

"I only—"

"I know nothing," she said. "Nothing of any kind." She closed her mouth and stood regarding him as if he were a particularly repulsive statue. Malone looked past her into the living room beyond the door.

It was faded now, but it had once been bright and colorful. There was an old rug on the floor, and tables were everywhere. The one bright thing about the room was the assortment of flowers; there were flowers everywhere, in vases, in pots, and even in window boxes. There was also a lot of crockery statuary, mostly faded, chipped, or worn in some way. The room looked to Malone as if its last inhabitant had died ten years before; only the flowers had been renewed. Everything else had not only the appearance of age, but the look of having been cast up as a high-water mark by the sea, which had receded and left only the tangled wreckage.

The woman cleared her throat, and Malone's gaze came back to her. "I can tell you nothing," she said.

"I don't want to talk to you," Malone said again. "I want to talk to Mike."

Her eyes were very cold. "You from the police, and you want to talk to Mike. You make a joke. Only I don't think the joke is very funny."

"Joke?" Malone said. "You mean Mike's not here?"

Her gaze never wavered. "You know he is not," she said. "Ten minutes ago the policemen were taking him away to the police station. How then could he be here?"

"Ten minutes ago?" Malone blinked. Ten minutes ago he had been looking for this apartment. Probably it hadn't taken Lynch's men ten minutes to find it; they weren't strangers in New York. "He was arrested?" Malone said.

"I said so, didn't I?" the woman said. "You must be crazy or else something." Her eyes were still cold points, but Malone suddenly saw a glow behind them, the glow of tears. Mike was her son. She did not seem surprised that the police had taken him away, but she was determined to protect him. He was her son.

Malone's voice was very gentle. "Why did they arrest him?" he said.

The woman shrugged, a single sharp gesture. "You ask me this?" she said.

"I'm not a cop," Malone said. "I'm from the FBI. I don't know anything about why the cops might have arrested Mike."

"FBI?" the woman said.

"It's all right," Malone said, with all the assurance he could muster. "I only want to talk to him."

"Ah," the woman said. Tears were plain in her eyes now, glittering on the surface. "Why they take him away, I do not know. My Mike do nothing. Nothing."

"But didn't they say anything about—"

"They say?" the woman cried. "They say only they have orders from this Lieutenant Lynch. He is lieutenant at police station."

"I know," Malone said gently.

"Lieutenant Lynch wants to ask Mike questions, so police come, take him away." Her English was beginning to lose ground as the tears came closer, as she slowly lost control.

"Lynch asked for him?" Malone said. He frowned. Whatever that meant, he wanted to be there himself. And perhaps he could help the old woman in some way. Anyhow, he would try. She stared up at him stonily. "Look, Mrs. Fueyo," he said. "I'm going down there to talk to Mike right now. And if he hasn't done anything, I'll see that he gets right on home to you. Right away."

Her expression changed a trifle. She did not actually soften, but Malone could feel the gratitude lurking behind her eyes as if it were afraid to come out. She nodded gravely and said nothing at all. He stepped away, and she closed the door without a sound.

He stood staring at the door for a few seconds. Then he turned and punched the elevator button savagely.

There wasn't any time to lose.

He walked back to the precinct station. Knowing the way, it took him about five minutes instead of the fifteen it had taken him to find the Fueyo residence. But he still felt as if time were passing much too fast. He ran up the steps and passed right by the desk sergeant, who apparently recognized him; he said nothing as Malone charged up the stairs and around the hall to Lynch's office.

It was empty.

Malone stared at it and started down the hall again without knowing where he was heading. Halfway to the stairs he met a patrolman.

"Where's Lynch?" he asked.

"The lieutenant?" the patrolman said.

Malone fumed. "Who else?" he said. "Where is he?"

"Got some kid back in the tank, or somewhere," the patrolman said. "Asking him a couple of questions, that's all." He added, "Hey, listen, buddy, what do you want to see the lieutenant for? I mean, you can't just go charging in to—"

Malone was down the stairs before he'd finished. He went, up to the desk.

The desk sergeant looked down. "What's it this time?" he said. "A track meet?"

"I'm in a hurry," Malone said. "Where are the cells? I want to see Lieutenant Lynch."

The desk sergeant nodded. "Okay," he said. "But the lieutenant ain't in any of the cells. He's back in Interrogation with some kid."

"Take me there," Malone said.

"I'll show you, anyway," the sergeant said. "Can't leave the desk on duty." He cleared his throat and gave Malone a set of directions that took him around to the back of the station. He was repeating the directions when Malone left.

There was a door at the end of a corridor at the back of the station. It was a plain wooden door with the numeral *1* stenciled on it. Malone opened it and looked inside.

He was staring into a rather small, rather plain little room. There were absolutely no bright beam lights burning, and there didn't seem to be any rubber hoses around anywhere. There were only four chairs.

Seated in three of the chairs were Lieutenant Lynch and two other police officers. In the fourth chair, facing them, was a young boy.

He didn't look like a tough kid. He had wavy black hair, brown eyes, and what Malone thought looked like a generally friendly appearance. He was slight and wiry, not over five feet five or six.

And he wore an expression that was neither too eager nor hostile. It wasn't just blank, either; Malone finally pinned it down as receptive.

He had the strangest impression that he had seen the boy somewhere before. But he couldn't remember when or where.

Lieutenant Lynch was talking.

"...all we want, Mike, is a little information. We thought you'd be able to help us, if you wanted to. Now, how about it?"

"Sure," Mike Fueyo said. His voice was a little high, but it was well controlled and responsive. "Sure, Lieutenant. I'll help if I can, but I just don't dig what you're giving me. It doesn't make sense."

Lynch stirred a little impatiently, and his voice began to carry a new bite. "I'm talking about Cadillacs," he said. "Red Cadillacs, 1972 models."

"It's a nice car," Mike said.

"What do you know about them?" Lynch said.

"Know about them?" Mike said. "I know they're nice cars. That's about it. What else am I going to know, Lieutenant? Maybe you think I own one of these big red 1972 Caddies. Maybe you think I got that kind of money. Well, listen, Lieutenant. I'd like to help you out, but I'm just not—"

"The Cadillacs," Lynch said, "were—"

"Just a minute, Lieutenant," Malone said. Dead silence fell with great suddenness. Lynch and all the others looked around at Malone, who smiled apologetically. "I don't want to disturb anything," he said. "But I would like to talk to Mike here for a little while."

"Oh," Lynch said sourly. "Sure. Sure."

"I'd like to ask him a couple of questions," Malone said. "Alone."

"Alone." Lynch said. "Oh." But there was nothing for him to do, Malone knew, except bow to the inevitable. "Of course," he said. "Go right ahead."

"You can stand outside the door," Malone said. "He won't get away. And you'd better hold this." Malone, knowing perfectly well that staying armed and alone in a room with a suspect was something you just did not do, unstrapped his .44 Magnum and handed it to the lieutenant.

He left reluctantly with his men. The door closed.

Malone could understand Lynch's attitude. If Malone solved the case, Lynch would not get any credit. Otherwise, it might go down in his personal record. And of course the NYPD would rather wrap the case up themselves; the FBI was treated as a necessary interference. Unfortunately, Malone thought, Lynch had had absolutely no choice. He sighed gently, and turned his attention to Mike Fueyo, who was still sitting in his chair.

"Now, Mike—" he began, and was interrupted.

The door opened. Lieutenant Lynch said, "If you need us, Malone, just yell."

"You'll hear me," Malone promised. The door shut.

He turned back to the boy. "Now, Mike," he began again. "My name is Malone, and I'm with the FBI in Washington. I'd like to ask you a few—"

"Gee, Mr. Malone," Mike broke in eagerly. "I'm glad you're here. I'm really glad about that."

Malone said, "Well, I—"

"These cops here have been giving me a pretty rough deal, you know?" Mike said.

"I'm sure they—" Malone began.

"But I've been looking for you," Mike went on. "See, I wanted to say something to you. Something real important."

Malone leaned forward expectantly. At last he was going to get some information—perhaps the information that would break the whole case wide open. He said, "Yes?"

"Well," Mike began, and stopped.

"You don't have to be afraid of me, Mike," Malone said. "Just tell me whatever's on your mind."

"Sure," Mike said. "It's this."

He took a deep breath. Malone clenched his fists. Now it was coming. Now he would hear the all-important fact. He waited.

Mike stuck out his tongue and blew the longest, loudest, brassiest, and juiciest Bronx cheer that Malone had ever heard.

Then, almost instantly, the room was empty except for Malone himself.

Mike was gone.

There wasn't any place to hide, and there hadn't been any time to hide in. Malone looked around wildly, but he had no doubts at all.

Mike Fueyo had vanished, utterly and instantaneously. He'd gone out like a light.

CHAPTER FIVE

Thirty seconds passed.

During that time, Malone did nothing at all. He just sat there, while a confused montage of pictures tumbled through his head. Sometimes he saw double exposures, and sometimes a couple of pictures overlapped, but it didn't seem to make any difference, because none of the pictures meant anything anyhow.

The reason for that was obvious. He was no longer sane. He had cracked up. At a crucial moment his brain had failed him, and now people would have to come in and cart him away and put him in a strait jacket. It was perfectly obvious to Malone that he was no longer capable of dealing with everyday life. The blow on the head had probably taken final effect, and it had been more serious than the doctor had imagined.

He had always distrusted doctors anyhow.

And now he was suffering from a delayed reaction. He wasn't living in the real world any more. He had gone off to dreamland, where people disappeared when you looked at them. There was no hope for him any more.

It was a nice theory, and it was even comforting in a way. There was only one thing wrong with it.

The room around him didn't look dreamlike at all. It was perfectly solid and real, and it looked just the way it had looked before Mike Fueyo had—well, Malone amended, before whatever had happened had happened. It was a perfectly complete little room, and it had four chairs in it. Malone was sitting in one of the chairs and all the others were empty.

There was absolutely nothing else in the room.

With some regret, Malone abandoned the theory that he had gone mad. This left him with no ideas at all. Because if he hadn't become insane, then what *had* happened?

After another second or two, some ideas began to filter through the daze. Perhaps he'd just blacked out for a minute and the kid had gone out the door. That was possible, wasn't it?

Sure it was. And maybe he had just not seen the kid go. His eyes had failed for a second or two. That could certainly happen after a blow on the head. Malone tried to remember where the sight centers of the brain were. Maybe whoever had hit him had disturbed them, and he'd had a sudden blackout.

Come to think of it, that made pretty good sense. He had blacked out, and Mike had just walked out the door. It had to be the door, of course—the windows were out of the question, since there weren't any windows. And six-inch-wide air-conditioner ducts do not provide reasonable space for an exit, not if you happen to be a human being.

That, Malone told himself, was settled—and a good thing, too. He had begun to worry about it. But now he knew just what had happened, and he felt relieved. He got up from his chair, walked over to the door and opened it.

Lieutenant Lynch nearly fell into the room. He'd obviously had his ear pressed tightly to the door and hadn't expected it to open. The other two cops stood behind him, just about filling the hallway with their broad shoulders.

"Well, well," Malone said.

Lynch recovered his balance and glared at the FBI agent. He said nothing.

"Where is he?" Malone said.

"Where is he?" Lynch repeated, and blinked. "Where's *who*?"

Malone shook his head impatiently. "Fueyo," he said. "The kid. Where did he—"

Lynch's expression was the same as that on the faces of the other two cops: complete and utter bafflement. Malone stopped and stared. It was suddenly very obvious that the lovely theory he had worked out for Mike's disappearance wasn't true in the least. If Mike Fueyo had come out the door, then these cops would know about it. But they obviously knew nothing at all about it.

Therefore, he hadn't come out through the door.

Malone took a deep breath.

"What are you talking about?" Lynch said. "Isn't the kid in there with you? What's happened?"

There was only one thing to do and, straight-faced, Malone went ahead and did it. "Of course not," he snapped, trying to sound impatient and official. "I released him."

"You *what?*"

"Released him," Malone said. He stepped out into the hall and closed the door of the interrogation room firmly behind him. "I got all the information I needed, so I let him go."

"Thanks," Lynch said bitterly. "After all, I was the one who—"

"You called him in for questioning, didn't you, Lieutenant?" Malone said.

"Yes, I did, and I—"

"Well," Malone said, "I questioned him."

There was a little silence. Then Lynch asked, in a strangled voice, "What did he say?"

"Sorry," Malone said at once. "That's classified information." He pushed his way into the corridor, trying to look as if he had fifteen other jobs to accomplish within the next hour. Being an FBI agent was going to help a little, but he still had to look good in order to carry it off.

"But—"

"Thanks for your co-operation, Lieutenant," Malone said. "You've all been very helpful." He smiled at them in what he hoped was a superior manner. "So long," he said, and started walking.

"Wait!" Lynch said. He flung open the door of the interrogation room. There was no doubt that it was empty. "Wait! Malone!"

Malone turned slowly, trying to look calm and in control of the situation. "Yes?" he said.

Lynch looked at him with puzzled, pleading eyes. "Malone, *how* did you release him? We were right here. He didn't come through the door. There isn't any other exit. So how did you get him out?"

There was only one answer to that, and Malone gave it with a quiet, assured air. "I'm terribly sorry, Lieutenant," he said, "but that's classified information, too." He gave the cops a little wave and walked slowly down the corridor. When he reached the stairs he began to speed up and he was out of the precinct station and into a taxicab before any of the cops could have realized what had happened.

He took a deep breath, feeling as if it were the first he'd had in several days. "Breathe air," he told himself. "It's *good* for you." Not that New York had any real air in it. It was mostly carbon fumes and the like. But it was the nearest thing to air that Malone could find at the moment, and he determined to go right on breathing it until something better and cleaner showed up.

But that wasn't important now. As the cab tooled along down Broadway toward 69th Street, Malone closed his eyes and began going over the whole thing in his mind.

Mike Fueyo had vanished.

Of that, Malone told himself, there was no shadow of doubt. No probable, possible shadow of doubt.

No possible doubt (as a matter of fact) whatever.

Dismissing the Grand Inquisitor with a negligent wave of his hand, he concentrated on the main question. It was a good question. Malone could have sat and pondered it admiringly for a long time.

As a matter of fact, that was all he could think of to do, as the cab turned up 70th Street and headed east. He certainly didn't have any answers for it.

But it was a lovely question:

Where does that leave Kenneth J. Malone?

And, possibly even more important: *Where was Miguel Fueyo?*

It was obvious that he'd vanished on purpose. And it hadn't just been something he'd recently discovered. He had known all along that he could pull the trick; if he hadn't known that, he wouldn't have done what he had done beforehand. No seventeen-year-old boy, no matter what he was, would give the FBI the raspberry unless he was pretty sure he could get away with it.

Malone remembered the raspberry and winced slightly. The cab driver called back, "Anything wrong, buddy?"

"Everything," Malone said. "But don't worry about it."

The cab driver shrugged and turned back to the wheel. Malone went back to Mike Fueyo.

The kid could make himself vanish at will.

Invisibility?

Malone thought about that for a while. The fact that it was impossible didn't decide him against it. Everything was impossible; that much was clear. But he didn't think Mike Fueyo had just become invisible. No. There had been the sense of presence actually leaving the room. If Mike had become invisible and stayed, Malone was sure he wouldn't have felt the boy leave.

Mike had not just become invisible. (*And what do I mean, "just"?* Malone asked himself unhappily.) He had gone—elsewhere.

This brought him back full circle to his original question. Where was the boy now? But he ignored it for a minute or two as another, even more difficult query presented itself.

Never mind where, Malone told himself. *How?*

Something was bothering him. Malone realized that it had been bothering him for a long time. At last he managed to locate it and hold it up to the light for inspection.

Dr. O'Connor, the psionics expert at Westinghouse, had mentioned something during Malone's last conversation with him. Dr. O'Connor, who'd invented a telepathy detector, had been discussing further reaches in his field.

"After all," he'd said, "if thoughts can bridge any distance whatever, regardless of other barriers, there is no reason why matter could not do likewise."

"But it doesn't," Malone had said. "Or at least it hasn't so far."

"There's no way to be sure of that," Dr. O'Connor had said sternly. "After all, we have no reports of it—but that means little. Our search has only begun."

"Oh," Malone had said. "Sure."

"Matter, controlled by thought, might bridge distances instantaneously," Dr. O'Connor had said.

And he'd referred to something, some word…

Teleportation.

That was it. Malone sat back. All you had to do, he reflected, was to think yourself somewhere else, and—bing!—you were there. If Malone had been able to do it, it would not only have saved him a lot of time and trouble, but also such things as cab fare and train fare and … oh, a lot of different things.

But he couldn't. And Dr. O'Connor hadn't found anyone else who could, either. As far as Malone knew, nobody could teleport.

Except Mike Fueyo.

The cab stopped in front of FBI headquarters. "You some kind of secret agent?" the cabbie said. "Like on 3-D?"

"Of course not," Malone said pleasantly. "I'm a foreign spy."

"Oh," the cabbie said. "Sure." He took his money with a somewhat puzzled air, while Malone crossed the sidewalk and went into the building.

Everyone was active. Malone pushed his way through arguing knots of men until he reached the small office which he and Boyd had been assigned. He had already decided not to tell Boyd about the disappearing boy. That would only confuse him, and matters were confused enough as they stood. Malone had no proof; he had only his word and the word of a few baffled policemen, all of whom were probably thoroughly confused by now.

Boyd had a job to do, and Malone had decided to let him go on doing it. That, as a matter of fact, was what he was doing when Malone entered the room.

He was sitting at his desk, talking on the telephone. Malone couldn't see the face on the screen, but Boyd was scowling at it fiercely. "Sure," he said. "So some guy makes a fuss. That's what you're there for."

"But he wants to sue the city," a voice said tinnily. "Or somebody, anyhow."

"Let him sue," Boyd said. "We've got authority. Just get that car."

"Look," the voice said. "I—"

"I don't care now," Boyd snapped. "Get it. Then hand it over to the pickup squad and say, 'Mr. Malone wants this car immediately.' They'll know what to do. Got that?"

"Sure, Mr. Boyd," the voice said. "But I don't—"

"Never mind," Boyd said. "Go ahead and get the job done. The United States of America is depending on you." With one last scowl, he hung up and swung around to face Malone. "You gave me a great job," he said. "I really love it, you know that?"

"It's got to be done," Malone said in a noncommittal voice. "How's it going so far?"

Boyd closed his eyes for a second. "Twenty-three red 1972 Cadillacs to date—which isn't bad, I suppose," he said. "And six calls like the one you just heard. All from agents with problems.

What *am* I supposed to do when a guy catches a couple necking in a 1972 red Cadillac?"

"At this time of day?" Malone said.

"New York," Boyd said, and shrugged. "Things are funny here."

Malone nodded. "What did you do about them?" he said.

"Told the agent to take the car and give 'em a pass to a movie," Boyd said.

"Good," Malone said. "Keep that sort of thing in the dark where it belongs." For some reason, this reminded him of Dorothy. He still had to get tickets for a show. But that could wait. "How about the assembly line?" he said.

"Disassembly," Boyd said. "Leibowitz has started it going. He borrowed the use of a big auto repair shop out in Jersey City, and they'll be doing a faster job than we thought." He paused. "But it's been a wonderful day," he said. "One to remember as long as I live. Possibly even until tomorrow. And how have you been doing?"

"Well," Malone said, "I'm not absolutely sure yet."

"That's a nice helpful answer," Boyd said. "In the best traditions of the FBI."

"I can't help it," Malone said. "It's true."

"Well, what the hell have you been doing?" Boyd said. "Drinking? Helling around? Living it up while I sit here and talk to people about Cadillacs?"

"Not exactly," Malone said. "I've been—well, doing more or less what Burris told me to do. Nosing around. Keeping my eyes open. I think—"

The phone chimed. Boyd flipped up the mike and eyed the screen balefully. "Federal Bureau of Investigation," he said crisply. "Who the hell are you?"

A voice on the other end said, "What?" before the image on the screen cleared.

"Federal Bureau of Investigation," Boyd said in a perfectly innocent voice. "Boyd speaking."

"Oh," a voice said. It was a calm, quiet voice. "Hello, Boyd."

The image cleared. Boyd was facing the picture of a man in his middle thirties, a brown-haired man with large, gentle brown eyes and an expression that somehow managed to look both sad and confident. "Hello, Dr. Leibowitz," Boyd said.

"Is Mr. Malone in?" Leibowitz said. "I really wanted to talk to him."

"Sure," Boyd said. "Just a second."

He motioned to Malone, who came around and sat at Boyd's desk as Boyd got up. He nodded to Leibowitz, and the electronics engineer nodded back.

"How's everything coming, Dr. Leibowitz?" Malone said.

Leibowitz shrugged meaningfully. "All right," he said. "I called you to tell you about that, by the way. We've managed to cut the per-car time down somewhat."

"That's wonderful," Malone said.

"It's now down to about four hours per car, and that means we may be able to do even better than running one off the line every fifteen minutes. At the moment, fifteen minutes is about standard, though, with sixteen cars in the line."

"Sure," Malone said softly. "But anything you can do to speed it up—"

"I understand," Leibowitz said. "Of course I'll do anything that I can for you. I have got a small preliminary report, by the way."

"Yes?"

"The first car has just been run off the assembly line," Leibowitz said. "And I'm afraid, Mr. Malone, that there's nothing odd about it at all."

"Well," Malone said, "we can't expect to hit the jackpot with our first try."

"Certainly not," Leibowitz said. "But the second will be off soon. And then the rest. I'm keeping my eye on every one, of course."

"Fine," Malone said, and meant it. Leibowitz was the kind of man who inspired instant and complete trust. Malone was perfectly sure he'd do the job he had started to do. Then an idea struck him. "Has the first car been reassembled yet?" he asked.

"Of course," Leibowitz said. "We took that step into account in our timing. What would you like done with it—and with the other ones, as they come off?"

"Unless you can find something odd about a car, just return it to its owner," Malone said. "Or pass the problem on to the squad men; they'll take care of it." He paused. "If you do find something odd—"

"I'll call you at once, of course," Leibowitz said.

"Good," Malone said. "Incidentally, I did want to ask you something. I don't want you to think I'm doubting your work, or anything like that. Believe me."

"I'm sure you're not," Leibowitz said.

"But," Malone said, "why does it take so long? I'd think it would be fairly easy to spot a robotic or a semi-robotic brain capable of controlling a car."

"It might have been, once," Leibowitz said. "But these days the problems are rather special. Oh, I don't mean we can't do it—we can and we will. But with subminiaturization, Mr. Malone, and semipsionic circuits, a pretty good brain can be hidden beneath a coat of paint."

For no reason at all, Malone suddenly thought of Dorothy again. "A coat of paint?" he said in a disturbed tone.

"Certainly," Leibowitz said, and smiled at him. It was a warm smile that had little or nothing to do with the problem they were talking about. But Malone liked it. It made him feel as if Leibowitz liked him, and approved of him. He grinned back.

"But a coat of paint isn't very much," Malone said.

"It doesn't have to be very much," Leibowitz said. "Not these days. I've often told Emily—that's my wife, Mr. Malone—that I could hide a TV circuit under her lipstick. Not that there would be any use in it; but the techniques are there. Mr. Malone. And if your conjecture is correct, someone is using them."

"Oh," Malone said. "Sure. But you *can* find the circuits, if they're there?"

Leibowitz nodded slowly. "We can, Mr. Malone," he said. "They betray themselves. A microcircuit need not be more than a few microns thick, you see—as far as the conductors and insulators are concerned, at any rate. But the regulators-transistors and such—have to be as big as a pinhead."

"Enormous, huh?" Malone said.

"Well," Leibowitz said, and chuckled, "quite large enough to locate without trouble, at any rate. They're very hard to conceal. And the leads from the brain to the power controls are even easier to find—comparatively speaking, of course."

"Of course," Malone said.

"All the brain does, you see," Leibowitz said, "is control the mechanism that steers the car. But it takes real power to steer—a great deal more than it does to compute the steering."

"I see," Malone, who didn't, said desperately. "In other words, unless something radically new has been developed, you can find the circuits."

"Right," Leibowitz said, grinning. "It would have to be something very new indeed, Mr. Malone. We're up on most of the latest developments here; we've got to be. But I don't want you giving me the credit for this."

"No?" Malone said.

"Oh, no," Leibowitz said. "All I do is work out the general application to theory, as far as actual detection is concerned. It's my partner, Mr. Hardin, who takes care of all the engineering details."

Malone said, "Well, so long as one of you—"

"Sal's a real crackerjack," Leibowitz said enthusiastically. "He had an intuitive feel about these things. It's really amazing to watch him go to work."

"It must be," Malone said politely.

"Oh, it really is," Leibowitz said. "And it's because of Sal that I can make the guarantee I do make: that if there are any unusual circuits in those cars, we can find them."

"Thanks," Malone said. "I'm sure you'll do the job. And we need that information. Don't bother to send along a detailed report, though, unless you find something out of the ordinary."

"Of course, Mr. Malone," Leibowitz said. "I wouldn't have bothered you except for the production speed-up here."

"I understand," Malone said. "It's perfectly all right. I'll be hearing from you, then?"

"Certainly, Mr. Malone," Leibowitz said.

Malone cut the circuit at once and started to turn away, but he never got the chance. It started to chime again at once.

"F.B.I.," Malone said as he flipped up the receiver. He wanted badly to copy Boyd's salutation, but he found that he just didn't have the gall to do it, and said sadly instead, "Malone speaking."

There was no immediate answer from the other party. Instead, the screen slowly cleared, showing Malone the picture of a woman he recognized instantly.

It was Juanita Fueyo, Mike's mother.

Malone stared at her. It seemed to him as if a couple of hours passed while he tried to find his voice. Of course, she'd looked up the FBI number in the phone book, and found him that way. But she was about the last person on earth from whom he'd expected a call.

"Oh, Mr. Malone," she said, "thank you so much. You got my Mike back from the police."

Malone gulped. "I did?" he said. "Well, I—"

"But, Mr. Malone, you must help me again. Because now my Mike says he must not stay at home! He is leaving, he is leaving right away!"

"Leaving?" Malone said.

He thought of a thousand things to do. He could send a squad of men to arrest Mike. And Mike could disappear while they were trying to get hold of him. He could go down himself—and be greeted, if he knew Mike Fueyo, with another giant economy-size raspberry. He could try to plead with Mike on the phone.

And what good would that do?

So, instead, he just sat and stared while Mrs. Fueyo went right on.

"He says he will send me money, but money is nothing compared to my own boy, my own Mike. He says he must go away, Mr. Malone, but I know you can stop him. I know it!"

"Sure," Malone said. "But I—"

"Oh, I knew that you would," Mrs. Fueyo shrieked. She almost came through the screen at him. "You are a great man, Mr. Malone. I will say many prayers for you. Every day I will pray for you in all your work. I will never stop praying for you because you help me." Her voice and face changed abruptly. "Excuse me now," she said. "I must go back to work."

"Well," Malone said, "if I—"

Then she turned back and beamed at him again. "Oh, thank you, Mr. Malone. Thank you with the thanks of a mother. Bring my boy back to me."

And the image faded and died.

Boyd tapped Malone on the shoulder. "I didn't know you were involved in an advice column for the lovelorn," he said.

"I'm not," Malone said sourly.

Boyd sighed. "I'll bite," he said. "Who was that?"

Malone thought of several possible answers and finally chose one. "That," he said, "was my mother-in-law. She worries about me every time I go out on a job with you."

"Very funny," Boyd said. "I am screaming with laughter."

"Just get back to work, Tommy-boy," Malone said, "and leave everything to me."

He hoped he sounded more confident than he felt. Lighting a cigarette—and wishing he were alone in his own room, so that he could smoke a cigar and not have to worry about looking dashing and alert—Malone strolled out of the office with a final wave to Boyd. He was thinking about Mike Fueyo, and he stopped his chain of reasoning just long enough to look in at the office of the Agent-in-Charge, and ask him to pry loose two tickets for *The Hot Seat* for that night.

"My God," the agent said. He was a tall thin man who looked as if he suffered from chronic stomach trouble. "You must be crazy. Are they all like that in Washington?"

"No," Malone said cheerfully. "Some of them are pretty normal. There's this one man—Napoleon, we call him—who keeps insisting that he should have won the battle of Waterloo. But otherwise he's perfectly fine."

He flicked his cigarette in the air and left, grinning. Five steps away the grin disappeared and a frown took its place.

CHAPTER SIX

He walked along 69th Street to Park Avenue without noticing where he was going. Luckily, the streets weren't really crowded, and Malone only had to apologize twice, once for stepping on a man's toe and once for absently toeing a woman's dog. When he reached the corner he headed downtown, humming *Kathleen Mavourneen* under his breath and trying to figure out his next move.

He needed more than one move. He needed a whole series of moves. This was not the usual kind of case. Burris had called it a vacation and, in one way, Malone supposed, Burris was perfectly right. For once there was no question about who had committed the crimes. It was obvious by now that Mike Fueyo and his Silent Spooks had been stealing the Cadillacs.

It was even obvious that Mike—or someone with Mike's talent—had bopped him on the head, and taken the red Cadillac he had been examining. And the same gang probably accounted for the Sergeant Jukovsky affair, too.

Or at least it was reasonable to assume that they did, Malone thought. He could see how it had worked. One of the Silent Spooks was a lot smaller than a grown man, and the two cops who hadn't seen anyone in the parked car just hadn't been able to catch sight of the undersized driver. Of course, there *had* been someone in the car when it had been driving along the West Side Highway. Someone who had teleported himself right out of the car when it had gone over the embankment.

That, of course, meant that there would be no secret machines found in the red Cadillacs Leibowitz and Hardin were examining now. But Malone had already decided to let that phase of things go on. First of all, it was always possible that he was wrong, and that some such machine really did exist. Second, even if they didn't find a machine, they might find something else. Almost anything, he thought, might turn up.

And third, it kept Boyd decently busy, and out of Malone's hair.

That had been an easy solution. And, Malone thought, the problem of who had been taking the red Cadillacs looked just as easy now, if his answers were right. And he was reasonably sure of that.

Unfortunately, he was now left with a new and unusual question: *How do you catch a teleport?*

Malone looked up, jarred to a stop by a man built like a brown bear, with a chunky body and an oval, slightly sloping head and face. He had very short brown hair shot through with gray, and gave Malone a small inquisitive stare and looked away without a word.

Malone mumbled, "Sorry," and looked up at the street sign. He was at 47th Street and Park Avenue. He jerked a hand up to his face, and managed to hook the chunky man by the suit. It fell away, exposing the initials S.M. carefully worked into his shirt. Second Mistake, Malone thought wildly, muttered, "Sorry," again and turned west, feeling fairly grateful to the unfortunate bystander.

He had reminded Malone of one thing. If he wanted to get even a part of his plan past the drawing-board stage, he had to make a call in a hurry.

He found a phone booth in a bar called the Ad Lib, at Madison Avenue. Sternly telling himself that he was stopping there to make a phone call, a business phone call, and not to have a drink, he marched right past the friendly bartender and went into the phone booth, where he made a call to New York Police Commissioner John Henry Fernack.

Fernack's face was that of an old man, but there was no telling how old. The early seventies was one guess, Malone imagined; the late fifties might be another. He looked tough, as if he had spent all of his life trying to persuade other people that he was young enough for the handball tournament. When he saw Malone, his eyebrows lifted slightly, but he didn't say anything.

"Commissioner," Malone said, "I called to ask you to do me a favor."

There was caution hidden in the calm and quiet voice. "Well," Fernack said, "what is it, Malone?"

"Can you have all the robberies for a given period run through the computer?" Malone said. "I need some dope."

"Depends on the given period," Fernack said. "I can't do it for 1774."

"What would I need data on robberies in 1774 for?" Malone said, honestly interested.

"I never question the FBI," Fernack said soberly. "But what dates do you want?"

"The past year, maybe the past year and a half."

"And what data?"

"I want every reported crime that hasn't been solved," Malone said, "and which seems to have been committed by some impossible means. A safe that was robbed without being opened, for instance—that's the kind of thing I mean."

"Every unsolved crime?" Fernack said. "Now, hold your horses, Malone. I'm not at all sure that—"

"Don't worry about a thing, Commissioner," Malone said. "This is confidential."

"You know how I'd feel about this if word ever got out to—"

"I said confidential, John Henry," Malone said, trying to sound friendly and trustworthy. "After all, every place has unsolved crimes. Even the FBI isn't absolutely perfect."

"Oh," Fernack said. "Sure. But confidential, Malone."

"You have my word," Malone said sincerely.

Fernack said, "Well—"

"How fast can you get me the dope?" Malone said.

"I don't exactly know," Fernack said. "The last time anything even remotely like this was run through—departmental survey, but you wouldn't be interested—it took something like eight hours."

"Fine," Malone said. "Eight hours, then. I'll look everything over and if we need a second run-through it won't take too long. I'll let you know as soon as I can about that." He grinned into the phone.

Fernack cleared his throat and asked delicately, "Mind telling me what all this is for?"

Malone offered up a little prayer before answering, and when he did answer it was in his softest and friendliest tones. "I'd rather not say just now, John Henry."

"But, Malone..." Fernack's voice sounded a little strained, and his jaw set just a trifle, "...if you—"

Malone knew perfectly well how Fernack reacted when he didn't get a bit of information he wanted. And this was no time to set off any fireworks in the commissioner's office. "Look, John Henry," he said gently, "I'll tell you as soon as I can. Honest. But this is classified information; it's not my fault."

Fernack said, "But—" and apparently realized that argument was not going to do him any good. "All right, Malone," he said at last. "I'll have it for you as soon as possible."

"Great," Malone said. "Then I'll see you later."

"Sure," Fernack said. He paused, as if he were about to open the controversy just once more. But all he said was "So long, Malone."

Malone breathed a great sigh of relief and flipped the phone off. He stepped out of the booth feeling so proud of himself that he could barely walk. Not only had he managed to calm down Commissioner Fernack, he had also walked right past a bar on the way to the phone. He had performed several acts, he felt, above and beyond the call of duty, and he told himself that he deserved a reward.

Happily, the reward was convenient to hand. He went to the bar and beckoned the bartender over to him. "Bourbon and soda," he said. "And a medal, if possible."

"A what?" the bartender said.

"A medal," Malone said. "For conduct beyond reproach."

The bartender nodded sadly. "Maybe you just ought to go home, Mac," he said. "Sleep it off for a while."

New Yorkers, Malone decided as the bartender went off to get his drink, had no sense of humor. Back in Chicago—where he'd been more or less weaned on gin, and discovered that, unlike his father, he didn't much care for the stuff—and even in Washington, people didn't go around accusing you of drunkenness just because you made some harmless little pleasantry.

Oh, well. Malone drank his drink and went out into the afternoon sunlight.

He considered the itinerary of the magical Miguel Fueyo. He had gone straight home from the police station, apparently, and had then told his mother that he was going to leave home. But he had promised to send her money.

Of course, money was easy for Mike to get. With a shudder, Malone thought he was beginning to realize just *how* easy. Houdini had once boasted that no bank vault could hold him. In Mike Fueyo's case, that was just doubly true. The vault could neither hold him out nor keep him in.

But he was going to leave home.

Malone said, "Hmm," to himself, cleared his throat and tried it again. By now he was at the corner of the block, where he nearly collided with a workman who was busily stowing away a gigantic ladder, a pot of paint, and a brush. Malone looked at the street sign, where the words *Avenue of the Americas* had been painted out, and *Sixth Avenue* hand-lettered in.

"They finally give in," the painter told him. "But do you think they buy new signs? Nah. Cheap. That's all they are. Cheap as pretzels." He gave Malone a friendly push with one end of the ladder and disappeared into the crowd.

Malone didn't have the faintest idea of what he was talking about. And how cheap could a pretzel be, anyhow? Malone didn't remember ever having seen an especially tight-fisted one.

New York, he decided for the fifteenth time, was a strange place.

He walked downtown for a block, still thinking about Mike Fueyo, and absently turned west again. Between Sixth and Seventh, he had another attack of brilliance and began looking for another phone booth.

He found one in a Mexican bar named the Xochitl, across the street from the Church of Saint Mary the Virgin. It was a coincidence that he had landed in another bar, he told himself hopefully, but he didn't quite believe it. To prove it to himself, he headed straight for the phone booths again and put in his call, ignoring the blandishments of several rows of sparkling bottles which he passed on the way.

He dialed the number of Lieutenant Lynch's precinct, and then found himself connected with a new desk sergeant.

"I'm Malone," he said. "I want to talk to Lynch."

"Glad to know you, Malone," the desk sergeant said pleasantly. "Only *Lieutenant* Lynch doesn't want to subscribe to the Irish *Echo*!"

"Damn it," Malone said, "I'm the FBI." He showed his badge.

The desk sergeant took a good long look at it. "Maybe you are, and maybe you aren't," he said at last.

"Does the lieutenant know you?"

"We were kids together," Malone said. "We're brothers. Siamese twins. Put him on the phone."

"Wait a minute," said the desk sergeant. "I'll check."

The screen went blank for two agonizing minutes before it cleared again to show Lynch's face.

"Hello, Mr. Malone," Lynch said formally. "Have you found some new little trick to show up poor stupid policemen? Like, say, making yourself vanish?"

"I'll make the whole damn police force vanish," Malone said, "in a couple of minutes. I called to ask a favor."

"Anything," Lynch said. "Anything within my poor power. Whatever I have is yours. Whither thou goest—"

"Knock it off," Malone said, and then grinned. After all, there was no sense in making an enemy out of Lynch.

Lynch blinked, took a deep breath, and said in an entirely different voice, "Okay, Malone. What's the favor?"

"Do you still have that list of Silent Spooks?" Malone said.

"Sure I do," Lynch said. "Why? I gave you a copy of it."

"I can't do this job," Malone said. "You'll have to.".

"Yes, sir," Lynch said, and saluted.

"Just listen," Malone said. "I want you to check up on every kid on that list."

"What are we supposed to do when we find them?" Lynch said.

"That's the trouble," Malone said. "You won't."

"And why not?"

"I'll lay you ten to one," Malone said, "that every one of them has skipped out. Left home. Without giving a forwarding address."

Lynch nodded slowly. "Ten to one?" he said. "Want to make that a money bet? Or does the FBI frown on gambling?"

"Ten dollars to your one," Malone said. "Okay?"

"Made," Lynch said. "You've got the bet—just for the hell of it, understand."

"Oh, sure," Malone said.

"And where can I call you to collect?"

Malone shook his head. "You can't," he said. "I'll call you."

"I will wait with anxiety," Lynch said. "But it had better be before eight. I get off then."

"If I can make it," Malone said.

"If you can't," Lynch said, "call me at home." He gave Malone the number, and then added, "Whatever information I get, I can keep for my own use this time, can't I?"

"Hell," Malone said, "you've already got all the information you're going to get. I just gave it to you."

"That," Lynch said, "we'll see."

"I'll call to collect my money," Malone said.

"Well talk about it later," Lynch said. "Farewell, old pal."

"Flights of angels," Malone said, "sing thee to thy rest."

Malone replaced the microphone and headed for the door. Halfway there, however, he stopped. He hadn't had any tequila in a long time, and thought he owed it to himself. He felt he'd come out ahead in his exchange with Lynch, and another medal was in order.

Only a small one, though. He told himself that he would order one tequila and quit. Besides, he had to meet Dorothy.

He sat down on one of the tall bar stools. The bartender bustled over and eyed him speculatively.

"*Tequila con limon,*" he said negligently.

"Ah," the bartender said. "*Si, señor.*"

Malone waited with ill-concealed impatience. At last it arrived, Malone took the small glass of tequila in his right hand, with the slice of lemon held firmly between the index and middle fingers of the same hand, the rind facing in toward the glass. On the web between the thumb and forefinger of his left hand he had sprinkled a little salt. Moving adroitly and with dispatch, he downed the tequila, licked off the salt, and bit his teeth into the lemon slice.

It felt better than good; it felt wonderful. He hadn't had such a good time in years.

He had three more before he left the Xochitl.

Then, noticing the time, he moved in a hurry and got out of the bar before temptation overcame him and he started ordering more. It was nearly six o'clock, and he had to meet Dorothy at Topp's.

He hoped he could find it.

He headed downtown toward 42nd Street, turned right and, sure enough, there was a big red sign. It said Topp's. Malone beamed his approval at it. It was just where it ought to be, and he was grateful.

He pushed open the glass door of the place and went in.

The maître d'hôtel was a chunky man with a pleasant face, a receding hairline and, some distance back on his head, dark curly hair. He beamed at Malone as if the FBI agent were a long-lost brother. "Table for one, sir?" he said.

"No," Malone said, peering into the place. It was much bigger than he had expected. "No," he said again. "I guess I'll just have a drink at the bar."

The maître d' smiled and bowed him to a barstool. Malone sat and looked the place over again. His first glance had shown him that Dorothy wasn't there yet, but he saw no harm in making sure. *Always be careful of your facts*, he admonished himself a little fuzzily.

There were a lot of women in the place, but they were all with escorts. Some of them had two escorts, and Malone wondered about them. Were they drunk, or was he? It was obvious that someone was seeing double, but Malone wasn't quite sure who.

He stared at his face in the bar mirror for a few seconds, and ordered a bourbon and soda when a bartender came over and occluded the image. The bartender went away and Malone went on studying himself.

He wasn't bad looking for an FBI agent. He was taller than his father, anyway, and less heavily built. That was one good thing. As a matter of fact, Malone told himself, he was really a pretty good-looking guy.

So why did women keep him waiting?

He heard her voice before he saw her. But she wasn't talking to him.

"Hello, Milty," she said. "How's everything?"

Malone turned around to get a look at Milty. He turned out to be the maître d'. What did he have that Malone didn't have the agent asked himself sourly? Obviously Dorothy was captivated by his charm. Well, that showed him what city girls were like. Butterflies. Social butterflies. Flitting hither and yon with the wind, now drawn to this man, now to that. Once, Malone told himself sadly, he had known this beautiful woman. Now she belonged to someone else.

He felt a little bit sad about it, but he told himself to buck up and learn to live with his tragedy. He drank some more of his bourbon and soda, and then she noticed him.

He heard her say, "Oh. Excuse me, Milty. There's my man." She came over and sat down next to him.

He wanted to ignore her, just to teach her a lesson. But he had already turned around and smiled at her, and she smiled back.

"Hi," she said. "Did you get the tickets?"

Tickets.

Malone knew there was something he'd forgotten, and now he knew what it was. "Oh," he said. "Sure. Just a second. I've got to check up."

"Check up?"

"Friend of mine," Malone improvised hurriedly. "Bringing them." He gave Dorothy a big smile and climbed down off the bar stool. He managed to find a phone booth, and dialed FBI headquarters on 69th Street and blessed several saints when he found that the A-in-C was still there.

"Tickets," Malone said.

The Agent-in-Charge blinked at him. "What tickets?" he said.

"The *Hot Seat* tickets," Malone said. "Did you get 'em?"

"I got 'em," the Agent-in-Charge said sourly. "Had to chase all over town and pull more wires than there are on a grand piano. But they turned up, brother. Two seats. Do you know what a job like that entails?"

"I'm grateful," Malone said. "I'm hysterical with gratitude."

"I'd rather track down a gang of fingerless second-story men than go through that again," the Agent-in-Charge said. He looked as if his stomach trouble had suddenly gotten worse. Malone thought that the A-in-C was considering calling a doctor, and would probably decide to make it the undertaker instead, and save the price of a call.

"I can't express my gratitude," Malone told him. "Where are they? Where do I pick them up?"

"Box office," the A-in-C said sourly. "I tell you, everybody in Washington must be nuts. The things I have to go through—"

"Thanks," Malone said. "Thanks a lot. Thanks a million. If there's ever anything I can do for you, let me know and I'll do it." He hung up and went back to the bar, walking very carefully.

"Well?" Dorothy said. "Where do we go tonight? Joe's hot-dog stand? Or a revival of *The Wild Duck* in a loft on Bleecker Street?"

There was pride in Malone's manner as he stood there on his feet. There was just a touch of hauteur as he said, "We'll see *Hot Seat*."

And he was repaid for all of the Agent-in-Charge's efforts. Dorothy's eyes went wide with appreciation and awe. "My goodness," she said. "A man of his word—and what a tough word, too! Mr. Malone, I congratulate you."

"Nothing," Malone said. "A mere absolute nothing."

"Nothing, the man says," Dorothy muttered. "My goodness. And modest, too. Tell me, how do you do, Mr. Malone?"

"Me?" Malone said. "Very well, so far." He finished his drink. "And you?"

"I work at it," she said cryptically.

"May I have another drink?"

Malone gave her a grin. "Another?" he said. "Have two. Have a dozen."

"And what," she said, "would I do with a dozen drinks? Don't answer. I think I can guess. But let's just take them one at a time, okay?" She signaled to the bartender. "Wally, I'll have a martini. And Mr. Malone will have whatever it is he has, I imagine."

"Bourbon and soda," Malone said, and gave the bartender a grin too, just to make sure he didn't feel left out. The sun was shining (although it was evening outside), and the birds were singing (although, Malone reflected, catching a bird on 42nd Street and Broadway might take a bit of doing), and all was well with the world.

There was only a tiny, nagging, disturbing thought in his mind. It had to do with Mike Fueyo and the Silent Spooks, and a lot of red Cadillacs. But he pushed it resolutely away. It had nothing to do with the evening he was about to spend. Nothing at all.

After all, this *was* supposed to be a vacation, wasn't it?

"Well, Mr. Malone," Dorothy said, when the drinks had arrived.

"Very well indeed," Malone said, raising his. "And just call me Ken. Didn't I tell you that once before?"

"You did," she said. "And I asked you to call me Dorothy. Not Dotty. Try and remember that."

"I will remember it," Malone said, "just as long as ever I live. You don't look the least bit dotty, anyhow. Which is probably more than anybody could say for me." He started to look at himself in the bar mirror again, and decided not to. "By the way," he added, as a sudden thought struck him. "Dotty what?"

"Now," she said. "There you go doing it."

"Doing what?"

"Calling me that name."

"Oh," Malone said. "Make it Dorothy. Dorothy what?" He blinked. "I mean, I know you've got a last name. Dorothy Something. Only it probably isn't Something. What is it?"

"Francis," she said obligingly. "Dorothy Francis. My middle name is Something, in case you ever want to call me by my middle name. Just yell, 'Hey, Something,' and I'll come a-running. Unless I have something else to do. In which case everything will be very simple: I won't come."

"Ah," Malone said doubtfully. "And what do—"

"What do I do?" she said. "A standard question. Number two of a series. I do modeling. Photographic modeling. And that's not all; I also do commercials on 3-D. If I look familiar to you, it's probably because you've seen me on 3-D. Do I look familiar to you?"

"I never watch 3-D," Malone said, crestfallen.

"Fine," Dorothy said unexpectedly. "You have excellent taste."

"Well," Malone said, "it's just that I never seem to get the time—"

"Don't apologize for it," Dorothy said. "I have to appear on it, but I don't have to like it. And now that I've answered your questions, how about answering some of mine."

"Gladly," Malone said. "The inmost secrets of the FBI are yours for the asking."

"Hmm," Dorothy said slowly. "What do you do as an FBI agent, anyhow? Dig up spies?"

"Oh, no," Malone said. "We've got enough trouble with the live ones. We don't go around digging anybody up. Believe me." He paused, feeling dimly that the conversation was beginning to get out of control. "Have I told you that you are the most beautiful woman I've ever met?" he said at last.

"No," Dorothy said. "Not yet, anyway. But I was expecting it."

"You were?" Malone said, disappointed.

"Certainly," Dorothy said. "You've been drinking. As a matter of fact, you've managed to get quite a head start."

Malone hung his head guiltily. "True," he said in a low voice. "Too true. Much too true."

Dorothy nodded, downed her drink and waved to the bartender. "Wally, bring me a double this time."

"A double?"

"Sure," Dorothy said. "I've got to do some fast catching-up on Mr. Malone here."

"Call me Ken," Malone muttered.

"Don't be silly," Dorothy told him. "Wally hardly knows you. He'll call you Mr. Malone and like it."

The bartender went away, and Malone sat on his stool and thought busily for a minute. At last he said, "If you really want to catch up with me..."

"Yes?" Dorothy said.

"Better have a triple," Malone muttered.

Dorothy's eyebrows rose slightly.

"Because I intend to have another one," Malone added. "And even then you'll be just a little behind."

"That sounds sort of sad, in a way," Dorothy said. "Just a little behind. Tell me, is that a compliment or an insult?"

"Both," Malone said instantly. "And an observation, too."

Dorothy nodded. "I can see why you're a Federal cop," she said.

"Really?" Malone said. "I didn't know it showed. Why?"

"You're good at observing," she said. "Like this morning, for instance."

"Ah," Malone said. He searched in his mind for a quotation and found it. "If thine eye offend thee, pluck it out and cast it from thee," he said triumphantly.

"Sounds sort of grisly," Dorothy said.

Malone shrugged. "I can't help it," he said. "That's what it says."

"Well?" Dorothy said. "Did you?"

"Did I what?"

"Pluck your eye out and cast it from you?"

"Didn't have to," Malone said. "Mine eye did not offend me." He blinked and added, "Far from it."

"I guess we'll just have to leave it unplucked," Dorothy said sadly. "It didn't offend me, either."

"Good," Malone said, and the bartender brought drinks.

Malone picked his up and held it in the air. "I propose a toast," he said.

Dorothy picked up her glass. "A toast?"

"An old German toast, as a matter of fact," Malone said.

He fell silent. After a few seconds Dorothy said, "Well? Go ahead."

"Zwieback!" Malone said, bowed carefully to Dorothy and drained his glass with a flourish.

CHAPTER SEVEN

It started a million years ago.

In that distant past, a handful of photons deep in the interior of Sol began their random journey to the photosphere. They had been born as ultrahard gamma radiation, and they were positively bursting with energy, attempting to push their respective ways through the dense nucleonic gas that had been their womb. Within millimicroseconds, they had been swallowed up by the various particles surrounding them—swallowed, and emitted again, as the particles met in violent collision.

And then the process was repeated. After a thousand thousand years, and billions on billions of such repetitions, the handful of photons reached the relatively cool photosphere of the sun. But the long battle had taken some of the drive out of them; over the past million years, even the strongest had become only hard ultraviolet, and the weakest just sputtered out in the form of long radio waves.

But now, at last, they were free! And in the first flush of this newfound freedom, they flung themselves over ninety-three million miles of space, traveling at one hundred and eighty-six thousand miles a second, and making the entire trip in less than eight and one-half minutes.

They struck the earth's ionosphere, and their numbers diminished. The hard ultraviolet was gobbled up by ozone; much of the blue was scattered through the atmosphere. The remainder bore steadily onward.

Down through the air they came, only slightly weakened this time. They hit the glass of a window in the Hotel New Yorker, losing more of their members in the plunge.

And, a few feet from the glass, they ended their million-year epic by illuminating a face.

The face responded to them with something less than pleasure. It was clear that the face did not like being illuminated. The light was very bright, much too bright. It seemed to be searing its way through the face's closed eyelids, right past the optic nerves into the brain-pan itself. The face twisted in a sudden spasm, as if its brain were shriveling with heat. Its owner thoughtfully turned over, and the face sought the seclusion and comparative darkness of a pillow.

Unfortunately, the motion brought the face's owner to complete wakefulness. He did not want to be awake, but he had very little choice in the matter. Even though his face was no longer being illuminated, he could feel other rays of sunlight eating at the back of his head. He put the pillow over his head and felt more comfortable for a space, but this slight relief passed, too.

He thought about mausoleums. Mausoleums were nice, cool, dark places where there was never any sun or heat, and never any reason to wake up. Maybe, he told himself cunningly, if he went to sleep again he would wake up dead, in a mausoleum. That, he thought, would be nice.

Death was nice and pleasant. Unfortunately, he realized, he was not dead. And there was absolutely no chance of his ever getting back to sleep. He finally rolled over again, being very careful to avoid any more poisonous sunlight. Getting up was an even more difficult process, but Malone knew it had to be managed. Somehow he got his feet firmly planted on the floor and sat up.

It had been a remarkable feat, he told himself. He deserved a medal.

That reminded him of the night before. He had been thinking quite a lot about the medals he deserved for various feats. He had even awarded some of them to himself, in the shape of liquid decoctions.

He remembered all that quite well. There were a lot of cloudy things in his mind, but from all the testimony he could gather, he imagined that he'd had quite a time the night before. Quite a wonderful time, as a matter of fact.

Not that that reflection did anything for him now. As he opened his eyes, one at a time, he thought of Boyd. Once, long ago, ages and ages ago, he had had to wake Boyd up, and he recalled how rough he had been about it. That had been unforgivable.

He made a mental note to apologize to Boyd the next time he saw him—if he could ever see again. Now, he knew how Boyd had felt. And it was terrible.

Still sitting on the bed, he told himself that, in spite of everything, he was lucky. To judge by his vague memories, he'd had quite a time the night before, and if the hangover was payment for it, then he was willing to accept the payment. Almost. Because it had really been a terrific time. The only nagging thought in his mind was that there had been something vital he'd forgotten.

"Tickets," he said aloud, and was surprised that his voice was audible. As a matter of fact, it was too audible; the noise made him wince slightly. He shifted his position very quietly.

And he hadn't forgotten the tickets. No. He distinctly remembered going to see *The Hot Seat*, and finding seats, and actually sitting through the show with Dorothy at his side. He couldn't honestly say that he remembered much of the show itself, but that couldn't be the important thing he'd forgotten. By no means.

He had heard that it was a good show, though. Sometime, he reminded himself, he would have to get tickets and actually see it.

He checked through the evening. Drinks. Dinner ... he had had dinner, hadn't he? Yes, he had. He recalled a broiled sea bass looking up at him with mournful eyes. He couldn't have dreamed anything like that.

And then the theater, and after that some more drinks ... and so on, and so on, and so on, right to his arrival back in his hotel room, at four-thirty in the morning, on a bright, boiled cloud.

He even remembered arguing with Dorothy about taking her home. She'd won that round by ducking into a subway entrance, and he had turned around after she'd left him and headed for home. Had he taken a taxi?

Yes, Malone decided, he had. He even remembered that.

Then what had he forgotten?

He had met Dorothy, he told himself, starting all over again in an effort to locate the gaps, at six o'clock, right after phoning...

"My God!" Malone said, and winced. He looked at his watch. It was ten o'clock in the morning. He had completely forgotten to call Fernack and Lynch.

Hangover or no hangover, Malone told himself grimly, there was work to be done. Somehow, he managed to get to his feet and start moving.

He checked Boyd's room after a while. But his partner wasn't home. *Probably at work already*, Malone thought, *while I lie here useless and helpless*. He thought of the Sermon on the Evils of Alcohol, and decided he'd better read it to himself instead of delivering it to Boyd.

But he didn't waste any time with it. By ten-fifteen he was showered and shaved, his teeth were brushed, and he was dressed. He felt, he estimated, about fifteen hundred per cent better. That was still lousy, but it wasn't quite as bad as it had been. He could move around and talk and even think a little, if he was careful about it. Before he left, he took a look at himself in the mirror.

Well, he told himself, that was nice.

It hardly showed at all. He looked tired, to be sure, but that was almost normal. The eyes weren't bloodshot red, and didn't seem to bug out at all, although Malone would have sworn that they were bleeding all over his face. His head was its normal size, as near as he remembered; it was not swollen visibly, or pulsing like a jellyfish at every move.

He looked even better than he felt.

He started for the door, and then stopped himself. There was no need to go out so early; he could start work right in his own hotel room and not even have to worry about the streets of New York, the cars or the pedestrians for a while.

He thought wistfully about a hair of the hound, decided against it with great firmness, and sat down to the phone.

He dialed a number, and the face of Commissioner Fernack appeared almost at once. Malone forced himself to smile cheerfully, reasonably sure that he was going to crack something as he did it. "Hello, John Henry," he said in what he hoped was a good imitation of a happy, carefree voice. "And how are you this lovely morning?"

"Me?" Fernack said sourly. "I'm in great shape. Tiptop. Dancing in the goddamn daisies. Malone, how did you—"

"Any news for me?" Malone said.

Fernack waited a long time before he answered, and when he did his voice was dangerously soft and calm. "Malone," he said, "when you asked for this survey, just what kind of news did you expect to get?"

"A godawful lot of impossible crimes," Malone said frankly. "How did I do, John Henry?"

"You did damn well," Fernack said. "Too damn well. Listen, Malone, how could you know about anything like this?"

Malone blinked. "Well," he said, "we have our sources. Confidential. Top secret. I'm sure you understand, Commissioner." Hurriedly, he added, "What does the breakdown look like?"

"It looks like hell," Fernack said. "About eight months ago, according to the computer, there was a terrific upswing in certain kinds of crime. And since then it's been pretty steady, right at the top of the swing. Hasn't moved down hardly at all."

"Great," Malone said.

Fernack stared. "What?" he said.

"I mean—" Malone stopped, thought of an answer and tried it. "I mean, that checks out my guess. My information. Sources."

Fernack seemed to weigh risks in his mind. "Malone, I know you're FBI," he said at last. "But this sounds pretty fishy to me. Pretty strange."

"You have no idea how strange," Malone said truthfully.

"I'm beginning to," Fernack said. "And if I ever find out that you had anything to do with this—"

"Me?"

"And don't look innocent," Fernack said. "It doesn't succeed in looking anything but horrible. You remind me of a convicted murderer trying to steal thirty cents from the prison chaplain."

"What would I have to do with all these crimes?" Malone said. "And what kind of crimes were they, anyway?"

"What you'd have to do with them," Fernack said, "is an unanswered question. And so long as it remains unanswered, Malone, you're safe. But when I come up with enough facts to answer it—"

"Don't be silly, Commissioner," Malone said. "How about those crimes? What kind were they?"

"Burglaries," Fernack said. "And I have a hunch you know that well enough. Most of them were just burglaries—locked barrooms, for instance, early in the morning. There's never any sign of tampering with the locks, no sign of breaking and entering, no sign of any alarms being tampered with in any way. But the money's gone from the cash register, and all of the liquor is gone too."

Malone stared. "*All* the liquor?" he said in a dazed voice.

"Well," Fernack said, "all of it that's in plain sight, anyway. Except for the open bottles. Disappeared. Gone. Without a trace. And most of the time the extra stock's gone too, from the basement or wherever they happen to keep it."

"That's a lot of liquor," Malone said.

"A hell of a lot," Fernack said. "Some of the bars have gone broke, not being insured against the losses."

The thought of thousands of bottles of liquor—millions of bottles—went through Malone's mind like an ice pick. He could almost see them, handle them, taste them. "Hair of the dog," he muttered. "What hair. What a dog."

"What did you say, Malone?"

"Nothing," Malone said hastily. "Nothing at all." After a second another query occurred to him. "You mean to tell me that only bars were robbed? Nothing else?"

"Oh, no," Fernack said. "Bars are only part of it. Malone, why are you asking me to tell you this?"

"Because I want to know," Malone said patiently.

"I still think—" Fernack began, and then said, "Never mind. But it hasn't been only bars. Supermarkets. Homes. Cleaning and tailoring shops. Jewelers. Hell, Malone, you name it and it's been hit."

Malone tried valiantly to resist temptation, but he was not at his best, and he lost. "All right," he said. "I will name it. Here's a list of places that haven't even been touched by the rising crime wave. Banks, for one."

"Malone!"

"Safes that have been locked, for another," Malone went on. "Homes with wall safes, though that's not quite accurate. The homes may have been robbed, but the safes won't have been touched."

"Malone, how much do you know?" Fernack said. "My God, man—"

"I'll make a general rule for you," Malone said. "Any place that fits the following description is safe: it's got a secure lock on it, and it's too small for a human being to get into."

Fernack opened his mouth, shut it, and stared downward, obviously scanning some papers lying on the desk in front of him. Malone waited patiently for the explosion, but it never came.

Instead, Fernack said, "You know, Malone, you remind me of an old friend of mine."

"Really?" Malone said pleasantly.

"You certainly do," Fernack said. "There's just one small difference. You're an FBI man, and he's a crook. If that's a difference."

"It is," Malone said. "And on behalf of the FBI, I resent the allegation. And, as a matter of fact, defy the allegator. But that's neither here nor there," he continued. "If that's the difference, what are the similarities?"

Fernack drew in a deep, hissing breath, and when he spoke his voice was as calm and quiet as a coiled cobra. "The both of you come up with the goddamnedest answers to things. Things I never knew about or even cared about before. Things I wish I'd never heard of. Things that don't have any explanation. And—" He stopped, his face dark in the screen. Malone wondered what color it was going to turn, and decided on purple as a good choice.

"Well?" Malone said at last.

"And you're always so goddamned right it makes me sick," Fernack finished flatly. He rubbed a hand through his hair and stared into the screen at Malone. "How did you know all this stuff?" he said.

Malone waited one full second, while Fernack got darker and darker on the screen. When he judged that the color was right, he said quietly, "I'm prescient. And thanks a lot, John Henry; just send the reports to me personally, at 69th Street. By messenger. So long."

He cut the circuit just as Fernack started: "Now, Malone—"

With a satisfied, somewhat sheepish smile, Malone dialed another number. This time a desk sergeant told him politely that Lynch wasn't at the precinct, and wouldn't arrive until noon.

Malone had Lynch's home number. He dialed it.

It was a long wait before the lieutenant answered, and he didn't look much like a police officer when his face finally showed up on the screen. His hair was uncombed and he was unshaven. His eyes were slightly bleary, but he was definitely awake.

"Oh," Malone said. "Hello."

"Hi, there," Lynch said with enormous cheerfulness. "Old buddy-boy. Old pal. Old friend."

"What's wrong?" Malone said.

"Wrong?" Lynch said. "Nothing. Nothing. Nothing at all. I just wanted to thank you for not waking me up last night. I only waited for your call until midnight. Then I decided I just wasn't very important to you. You obviously had much bigger things on your mind."

"As a matter of fact," Malone said, speculatively eying Lynch's figure, dressed in a pair of trousers and a T-shirt, "you're right."

"That's what I thought," Lynch said. "And I decided that, since you were so terribly busy, it could wait until I woke up. Or even until I got down to the station. How about it, *buddy-boy*?"

"Listen, Lynch," Malone said, "we made a bet. Ten to one. I just want to know if I can come down to collect or not."

There was a second of silence.

"All right," Lynch said at last, looking crestfallen. "I owe you a buck. Every last one of those kids has skipped out on us."

"Good," Malone said. He wondered briefly just what was good about it, and decided he'd rather have lost the money to Lynch. But facts, he reflected, were facts. Thoroughly nasty facts.

"I spent all night tracing them," Lynch said. "Got nowhere. Nowhere at all. Malone, how did you know—"

"Classified," Malone said. "Very classified. But you're sure they're all gone? Vanished?"

Lynch's face reddened. "Sure I'm sure," he said. "Every last one of them is gone. And what more do you want me to do about it?" He paused, then added, "What do you expect, Malone? Miracles?"

Malone shook his head gently. "No," he said. "I—"

"Oh, never mind," Lynch said. "But I—"

"Look, Malone," Lynch said, "there's a guy who wants to talk to you."

"One of the Silent Spooks?" Malone said hopefully.

Lynch shook his head and made a growling noise. "Don't be silly," he said. "It's just that this guy might have some information, but he won't say anything to me about it. He's a social worker or something like that."

"Social worker?" Malone said. "He works with the kids, right?"

"I guess," Lynch said. "His name's Kettleman. Albert Kettleman."

Malone nodded. "Okay," he said. "I'll be right over."

"Hey," Lynch said, "hold on. He's not here now. What do you think this is—my house or a reception center?"

161

"Sorry," Malone said wearily. "Where and when?"

"How about three o'clock at the precinct station?" Lynch said. "I can have him there by then, and you can get together and talk." He paused. "Nobody likes the cops," he said. "People hear the FBI's mixed up in this, and they figure the cops are all second-stringers or something."

"Sorry to hear it," Malone said.

"I'll bet you are," Lynch told him bitterly.

Malone shrugged. "Anyway," he said, "I'll see you at three, right?"

"Right," Lynch said, and Malone flipped off.

He sat there for a few seconds, grinning quietly. His brain throbbed like an overheated motor, but he didn't really mind any more. His theory had been justified, and that was the most important thing.

The Silent Spooks were all teleports.

Eight of them—eight kids on the loose, stealing everything they could lay their hands on, and completely safe. How could you catch a boy who just disappeared when you started for him? No wonder their names hadn't appeared on the police blotter, Malone thought.

Spooks didn't get into trouble. They didn't have to.

They could get into any place big enough to hold them, take what they wanted and just disappear. They'd been doing it for about eight months, according to the figures Malone had received from Fernack; maybe teleportative ability didn't develop until you were around fourteen or fifteen.

But it had developed in these kids—and they were using it in the most obvious way. They had a sure method of getting away from the cops, and a sure method of taking anything they wanted. No wonder they had so much money.

Malone got up, feeling slightly dazed, and left the hotel room.

CHAPTER EIGHT

By three o'clock, he was again among the living. Maybe his occupations had had something to do with it; he'd spent about four hours supervising Operation Dismemberment, and then listening to the reports on the dismantled Cadillacs. It was nice, peaceful, unimportant work, but there just wasn't anything else to do. FBI work was ninety-five per cent marking time, anyway. Malone felt grateful that there was any action at all in what he was doing.

Dr. Leibowitz had found all sort of things in the commandeered Caddies—everything from guns and narcotics to pornographic pictures in lots of three hundred, for shipment into New York City from the suburbs where the processing plant probably was. Of course, there had been personal effects, too—maps and lucky dolls and, just once, a single crutch.

Malone wondered about that for quite a while. Who'd just walk off and leave one crutch in a car? But people did things like that all the time, he finally told himself heavily. There wasn't any explanation for it, and there probably never would be.

But in spite of the majestic assortment of valuables found in the cars, there was no sign of anything remotely resembling an electro-psionic brain. Dr. Leibowitz had found just about everything—except what he was looking for.

At a quarter to three, Malone gave up. The search wasn't quite finished, but he'd heard enough to last him for a long time. He grabbed a cab downstairs and went over to Lynch's office to meet Kettleman.

The "social worker or something" was a large, balding man about six feet tall. Malone estimated his weight as close to two hundred and fifty pounds, and he looked every pound of it; his face was round without being chubby, and his body was stocky and hard. He wore black-rimmed glasses, and he was going bald in front. His face was like a mask; it was held in a gentle, almost eager expression that Malone would have sworn had nothing to do with the way Kettleman felt underneath.

Lynch performed the introductions, escorted the two of them to one of the interrogation rooms at the rear of the station, and left them there, with, "If either of you guys comes up with anything, let me know," for a parting shot.

Kettleman blinked slowly behind his glasses. "Mr. Malone," he said, "I understand that the FBI is interested in one of the—ah—adolescent social groups with which I work."

"Well, the Silent Spooks," Malone said. "That's right."

"The Spooks," Kettleman said. His voice was rather higher than Malone would have expected, oddly breathy without much depth to it. "My, yes. I did want to talk to somebody about it, and I thought you might be the man."

"I'll be interested in anything you have to say," Malone said diplomatically. He was beginning to doubt whether he'd get any real information out of Kettleman. But it was impossible to tell. He sat back in a hard wooden chair and tried to look fascinated.

"Well," Kettleman said tentatively, "the boys themselves have sort of a word for it. They'd say that there was something oddball about the Spooks. Do you understand? Not just the fact that they never drink liquor, but—"

"Something strange," Malone said. "Is that what you mean?"

"Ah," Kettleman said. "*Strange.* Of course." He acted, Malone thought, as if he had never heard the word before, and was both pleased and startled by its sound. "Perhaps I had better explain my position a little more clearly," he said. "That will give you an idea of just where I 'fit into' this picture."

"Whatever you think best," Malone said, resigning himself to a very dull hour. He tried to picture Kettleman in the midst of a gang of juvenile delinquents. It was very hard to do.

"I'm a social worker," Kettleman said, "working on an individual basis with these—social groups that the adolescents have formed. It's my job to make friends with them, become accepted by them, and try to turn their hostile impulses toward society into more useful, more acceptable channels."

"I see," Malone said, feeling that something was expected of him. "That's fine."

"Oh, we don't expect praise, we social workers," Kettleman said instantly. "The worth of a good job well done, that's enough for us." He smiled. The effect was a little unsettling, as if a hippopotamus had begun to laugh like a hyena. "But to continue, Mr. Malone," he said.

"Of course," Malone said. "Certainly."

"I've worked with many of the organizations in this neighborhood," Kettleman said. "And I've been quite successful in getting to know them, and in being accepted by them. Of course, the major part of my job is more difficult, but—well, I'm sure that's enough about my own background. That isn't what you're interested in, now, is it?"

He looked penitent. Malone said, "It's all right. I don't mind." He shifted positions on the hard chair.

"Well, then," Kettleman said, with the air of a man suddenly getting down to business. He leaned forward eagerly, his eyes big and bright behind the lenses. "There's something very peculiar about those boys," he said in a whisper.

"Really?" Malone said.

"Very peculiar indeed," Kettleman said. "My, yes. All of the other social groups are afraid of them."

"Big, huh?" Malone said. "Big strong boys who—"

"Oh, my, no," Kettleman said. "My goodness, no. All of the Spooks are rather slight, as a matter of fact. They've got *something*, but it isn't strength."

"My goodness," Malone said tiredly.

"I doubt if—in the language of my own groups—any one of the Spooks could punch his way out of a paper bag," Kettleman said. "It's more than that."

"Frankly," Malone said, "I'm inclined to agree with you. But what is this something that frightens everyone else?"

Kettleman leaned even closer. "I'm not sure," he said softly. "I can't say for certain, Mr. Malone. I've only heard rumors."

"Well," Malone said, "rumors might—"

"Rumors are a very powerful force among my groups, Mr. Malone," Kettleman said. "I've learned, over the years, to keep my ear to the ground, as it were, and pay very close attention to rumors."

"I'm sure," Malone said patiently. "But what did this particular rumor say?"

"Well," Kettleman said, and stopped. "Well," he said again. And at last he gulped and got it out. "Magicians, Mr. Malone. They say the Spooks are magicians—that they can come and go at will. Make themselves invisible. All sorts of things. Of course, I don't believe that, but—"

"Oh, it's quite true," Malone said, solemn faced.

"It's what?"

"Perfectly true," Malone said. "We know all that."

"Oh, my," Kettleman said. His face took on a whitish cast. "Oh, my goodness," he said. "Isn't that—isn't that amazing." He swallowed hard. "True all the time," he said.

"Magicians. I—"

"You see, this information isn't new to us," Malone said.

"Oh," Kettleman said. "No. Of course not. My. It's—rather disconcerting to think about, isn't it?"

"There," Malone said, "I agree with you."

Kettleman fell silent. Malone offered him a cigarette, but the social worker refused with a pale smile, and Malone lit one for himself. He took a couple of puffs in the silence, and then Kettleman said, "Well, Mr. Malone, Lieutenant Lynch did say that I was to tell you everything I could about these boys."

"I'm sure we all appreciate that," Malone said at random, wondering exactly what he meant.

"There is—well, there is one more thing," Kettleman said. "Ordinarily, of course, I wouldn't say anything about this to anyone. In my line of work, Mr. Malone, you learn the need for confidence. For being able to keep one's word."

"Certainly," Malone said, wondering what startling new fact was on its way now.

"And we certainly try to keep the confidence of the boys," Kettleman said maddeningly. "We wouldn't betray them to the police in any way unless it were absolutely necessary."

"Betray them? Mr. Kettleman," Malone said, "just what are you trying to tell me?"

"It's about their meeting place," Kettleman said. "Oh, my. I'm not at all sure I ought to tell you this." He wrung his pale fat hands together and looked at Malone appealingly.

"Now, now," Malone said, feeling foolish. "It's perfectly all right. We don't want to hurt the Spooks. Not any more than we have to. You can tell me, Mr. Kettleman."

"Oh," Kettleman said. "Well, the Spooks do have a sort of secret meeting place, you know. And they meet there."

He stopped. Malone said, "Where is it?"

"Oh, it's a big empty warehouse," Kettleman said. "I really feel terrible about this. They're meeting there tonight sometime, or that's what the rumors say. I shouldn't be telling you—"

"Of course you should," Malone said, trying to sound reassuring. "Don't worry about a thing, Mr. Kettleman. Tonight?"

"That's right," Kettleman said eagerly. He grinned, and then looked morosely down at his hands.

"Do you know where this warehouse is?" Malone said. "If any of the other little social groups use it—"

"Oh, no, they don't," Kettleman said. "That's what makes it so funny. You see, the warehouse is deserted, but it's kept in good repair; there are bars on the windows, and it's protected by all sorts of alarm systems and things like that. So none of the others can use it. Only the Spooks. You can't get in without a key, not at all."

"But do the Spooks—" Malone began.

"Oh, no," Kettleman moaned. "They don't have a key. At least, that's what the other groups say. The Spooks just—just melt borough the walls, or something like that."

"Mr. Kettleman," Malone said, "where is this warehouse?"

"I shouldn't be telling you this," Kettleman said.

Malone sighed. "Please, Mr. Kettleman. You know we're working for the good of those boys, don't you?"

"Well, I—"

"Sure we are," Malone said. "So you can tell me."

Kettleman blinked behind his glasses, and moaned a little. Malone waited with his hands tense in his lap. At last Kettleman said, "It's on West Street, near Chambers. That's downtown." He gave Malone an address. "That's where it is," he said. "But you won't do anything to the boys, will you? They're basically good boys. No matter what. And they—"

"Don't worry about it, Mr. Kettleman," Malone said. "We'll take care of the Spooks."

"Oh," Kettleman said. "Yes. Sure."

He got up. Malone said, "There's just one more thing, Mr. Kettleman."

"Yes?" The big man's voice had reached the high, breathy pitch of a fife.

"Do you have any idea what time the Spooks usually meet?"

"Well, now," Kettleman said, "I don't really know. You see, the reason I wanted to tell you all this was because Lieutenant Lynch was checking up on all those boys yesterday, and I thought..." He stopped and cleared his throat, and when he began again his voice had dropped almost to a whisper. "Well, Mr. Malone, I thought, after all, that since he was asking me questions—you know, questions about where the Spooks were, and all of that—since he was asking me questions…"

"Yes?" Malone said.

"I thought perhaps I ought to tell you about them," Kettleman said. "Where they were, and all of that."

Malone stood up. "Mr. Kettleman," he said in his most official voice, "I want you to know that the FBI appreciates what you've done. Your information will probably be very helpful to us, and the FBI certainly commends you for being public-spirited enough to come to us and tell us what you know." He thought for a second, and then added, "In the name of the FBI, Mr. Kettleman—well done!"

Kettleman stared, smiled, and gulped. "My goodness," he said. "Well." He smiled again, a little more broadly. "One has one's duty, you know. My, yes. Duty." He nodded to Malone.

"Of course," Malone said, going to the door and opening it. "Thanks again, Mr. Kettleman."

Kettleman saw the open door and headed for it blindly. As he left he flashed one last smile after Malone, who sighed, shut the door, and leaned against it for a second.

The things an FBI agent had to go through!

When he had recovered, he opened the door again and peered carefully down the hallway to make sure Kettleman had gone. Then he left the interrogation room and went down the hall, past the desk sergeant, and up the stairs to Lieutenant Lynch's office. He was still breathing a little hard when he opened Lynch's door, and Lynch didn't seem to be expecting him at all. He was very busy with a veritable snow flurry of papers, and he looked as if he had been involved with them steadily ever since he had left Malone and Kettleman alone downstairs.

"Well," Malone said. "Hello there, Lieutenant."

Lynch looked up, his face a mask of surprise. "Oh," he said. "It's you. Through with Kettleman?"

"I'm through," Malone said. "As if you didn't know." He looked at Lynch for a long minute, and then said, "Lieutenant…"

Lynch had gone right back to his papers. He looked up again with a bland expression. "Yes?"

"Lieutenant, how reliable is Kettleman?" Malone said.

Lynch shrugged. "He's always been pretty good with the kids, if that's what you mean. You know these social workers—I've never got much information out of him. He feels it's his duty to the kids—I don't know. Some such thing. Why do you ask?"

"Well," Malone said, "what he told me. Was he kidding me? Or does he know what he's talking about? Was what he said reasonably accurate?"

"How would I know?" Lynch said. "After all, you were down there alone, weren't you? I was up here working. If you'll tell me what he said, maybe I'll be able to tell you whether or not I think he was kidding."

Malone placed both his palms on the lieutenant's desk, mashing a couple of piles of papers. He leaned forward slowly, his eyes on Lynch's bland, innocent face. "Now look, Lynch," he said. "I like you. I really do. You're a good cop. You get things done."

"Well, thanks," Lynch said. "But I don't see what this has to do with—"

"I just don't want you trying to kid your buddy-boy," Malone said.

"Kid you?" Lynch said. "I don't get it."

"Come on, now," Malone said. "I know that room was bugged, just as well as you do. It was the sensible thing for you to pull, and you pulled it. You've got the whole thing recorded, haven't you?"

"Me?" Lynch said. "Why would I—"

"Oh, cut it out," Malone said impatiently. "Let's not play games, okay?"

There was a second of silence.

"All right," Lynch said. "So I recorded the conversation. Kill me. Crucify me. I'm stealing FBI secrets. I'm a spy secretly working for a foreign power. Take me out and electrocute me."

"I don't want to fight you," Malone said wearily. "So you've got the stuff recorded. That's your business."

"My business?"

"Sure," Malone said cheerfully. "As long as you don't try to use it."

169

"Now, Malone—" Lynch began.

"This is touchy stuff," Malone said. "We're going to have to take a lot of care in handling it. And I don't want you throwing raids all over the place and mixing everything up."

"Malone, I—"

"Eventually," Malone said, "I'm going to need your help with these kids. But for right now, I want to handle this my way, without any interference."

"I wouldn't think of—"

"You wanted information," Malone said. "Fine. That's all right with me. You got the information, and that's okay too. But if you try to use it before I say the word, I'll—I'll talk to good old Uncle John Henry Fernack. And he'll help me out; he'll give you a refresher course on How To Be A Beat Cop. In Kew Gardens. It's nice and lonely out there now, Lynch, You'd love it."

"Malone," Lynch said tiredly.

"Don't give me any arguments," Malone said. "I don't want any arguments."

"I won't argue with you, Malone," Lynch said. "I've been trying to tell you something."

Malone stepped away from the desk. "All right," he said. "Go ahead."

Lynch took a deep breath. "Malone, I'm not trying to queer your pitch," he said. "If I were going to pull a raid, here's what I'd have to do: get my own cops together, then call the precinct that covers that old warehouse. We don't cover the warehouse from here, Malone, and we'd need the responsible precinct's aid in anything we did down there."

Malone said, "Well, all I—"

"Not only that," Lynch said. "I'd have to call Safe and Loft, and get them in on it. A warehouse raid would probably be their baby first of all. That means it takes this precinct, the warehouse precinct, and the Safe and Loft Squad, all together, to raid that warehouse. Malone, would I pull a raid at this stage, if I had to go through all that, without knowing what the hell I was going to find down there?"

"Oh," Malone said.

"If those kids can just appear and disappear at will," Lynch said, "I'm not going to pull a raid on them, and end up looking like a damn fool, until I've got some way of making sure they're there when the raid goes through."

Malone coughed gently. "Okay," he said at last. "Sorry."

"There's only one thing I want," Lynch said. "I want to be able to move as soon as possible."

"Well, sure," Malone said apologetically.

"And that means I'm going to have to be informed," Lynch said. "I want to know what's going on, as fast as possible."

Malone nodded gently. "Sure," he said. "I'll tell you everything that happens—as soon as I know myself. But right now, I haven't got a thing for you. All I have is a kind of theory, and it's pretty screwy."

He stopped. Lynch looked up at him. "How screwy can it get?" he said. "The facts are nutty enough."

"You have absolutely no idea," Malone assured him. "I'm not even saying a word about this, not until I prove it out one way or another. I'm not even thinking about it—not until it stops sounding so nutty to me."

"Okay, Malone," Lynch said. "I can see a piece of it, if no more. The Fueyo kid vanishes mysteriously—never mind all that about you getting him out of the interrogation room by some kind of confidential method. There isn't any confidential method. I know that better than you do."

"I had to say something, didn't I?" Malone asked apologetically.

"So the kid disappears," Lynch said, brushing Malone's question away with a wave of his hand. "So now I hear all this stuff from Kettleman. And it begins to add up. The kids can disappear somehow, and reappear some place else. Walk through walls?" He shrugged. "How should I know? But they can sure as hell do something like it."

"Something," Malone said. "Like I said, it sounds screwy."

"I don't like it," Lynch said.

Malone nodded. "Nobody likes it," he said. "But keep it under your hat. I'll give you everything I have—whenever I have anything. And by the way—"

"Yes?" Lynch said.

"Thanks for giving me and Kettleman a chance to talk," Malone said. "Even if you had reasons of your own."

"Oh," Lynch said. "You mean the recording."

"I was a little suspicious," Malone said. "I didn't think you'd give Kettleman to me without getting *something* for yourself."

"Would you?" Lynch said.

Malone shrugged. "I'm not crazy either," he said.

Lynch picked up a handful of papers. "I've got all this work to do," he said. "So I'll see you later."

"Okay," Malone said.

"And if you need my help, buddy-boy," Lynch said, "just yell. Right?"

"I'll yell," Malone said. "Don't worry about that. I'll yell loud enough to get myself heard in Space Station One."

CHAPTER NINE

The afternoon was bright and sunny, but it didn't match Malone's mood. He got a cab outside the precinct station and headed for 69th Street, dining off his nails en route. When he hit the FBI headquarters, he called Washington and got Burris on the line.

He made a full report to the FBI chief, including his wild theory and everything else that had happened. "And there was this notebook," he said, and reached into his jacket pocket for it.

The pocket was empty.

"What notebook?" Burris said.

Malone tried to remember if he'd left the book in his room. He couldn't quite recall. "This book I picked up," he said, and described it. "I'll send it on, or bring it in when the case is over."

"All right," Burris said.

Malone went on with his description of what had happened. When he'd finished, Burris heaved a great sigh.

"My goodness," he said. "Last year it was telepathic spies, and this year it's teleporting thieves. Malone, I hate to think about next year."

"I wish you hadn't said that," Malone said sadly.

Burris blinked. "Why?" he said.

"Oh, just because," Malone said. "I haven't even had time to think about next year yet. But I'll think about it now."

"Well, maybe it won't be so bad," Burris said.

Malone shook his head. "No, Chief," he said. "You're wrong. It'll be worse."

"This is bad enough," Burris said.

"It's a great vacation," Malone said.

"Please," Burris said. "Did I have any idea—"

"Yes," Malone said.

Burris' eyes closed. "All right, Malone," he said after a little pause. "Let's get back to the report. At least it explains the red Cadillac business. Sergeant Jukovsky was hit by a boy who vanished. Vanished. My God."

"I was hit by a boy who vanished, too," Malone said bitterly. "But of course I'm just an FBI agent. Expendable. Nobody cares about—"

"Don't say that, Malone," Burris said. "You're one of my most valuable agents."

Malone tried to stop himself from beaming, but he couldn't. "Well, Chief," he began, "I—"

"Vanishing boys," Burris muttered. "What are you going to do with them, Malone?"

"I was hoping you might have some suggestion," Malone said.

"Me?"

"Well," Malone said, "I suppose I'll figure it out. When I catch them. But I did want something from you, Chief."

"Anything, Malone," Burris said. "Anything at all."

"I want you to get hold of Dr. O'Connor, out at Yucca Flats, if you can. He's the best psionics man Westinghouse has right now, and I might need him."

"If you say so," Burris said doubtfully.

"Well," Malone said, "these kids are teleports. And maybe there's some way to stop a teleport. Give him a good hard kick in the psi, for instance."

"In the what?"

"Never mind," Malone said savagely. "But if I'm going to get any information on what makes teleports tick, I'm going to have to get it from Dr. O'Connor. Right?"

"Right," Burris said.

"So get in touch with Dr. O'Connor," Malone said.

"I'll have him call you," Burris said. "Meanwhile—well, meanwhile just carry on, Malone. I've got every confidence in you."

"Thanks," Malone growled.

"If anybody can crack a case like this," Burris said, "it's you."

"I suppose it had better be," Malone said, and rang off.

Then he started to think. The notebook wasn't in his pockets. He checked every one, even the jacket pocket where he usually kept a handkerchief and nothing else. It wasn't anywhere on his person.

Had he left it in his room?

He thought about that for several minutes, and finally decided that he hadn't. He hadn't taken it out of his pocket, for one thing, and if it had fallen to the ground he couldn't have helped seeing it. Of course he'd put his wallet, keys, change, and other such items on the dresser, and then replaced them in his pockets in the morning. But he could remember how they'd looked on the dresser.

The notebook hadn't been there among them.

Now that he came to think of it, when had he seen the notebook last? He'd shown it to Lieutenant Lynch during the afternoon, and then he'd put it back in his pocket, and he hadn't looked for it again.

So it had to be somewhere in one of the bars he'd visited, or at the theater where he and Dorothy had seen *The Hot Seat*.

Proud of himself for this careful and complete job of deduction, he strolled out and, giving Boyd and the Agent-in-Charge one small smile each, to remember him by, he went into the sunlight, trying to decide which place to check first.

He settled on the theater because it was most probable. After all, people were always losing things in theaters. Besides, if he started at the theater, and found the notebook there, he could then go on to a bar to celebrate. If he found the notebook in a bar, he didn't much relish the idea of going on to an empty theater in the middle of the afternoon to celebrate.

Shaking his head over this flimsy structure of logic, he headed down to *The Hot Seat*. He banged on the lobby doors for a while without any good result, and finally leaned against one of the side doors, which opened. Malone fell through, recovered his balance, and found himself facing an old bewhiskered man with a dustpan, a broom, and a surprised expression.

"I'm looking for a notebook," Malone said.

"Try a stationery store, youngster," the old man said. "I thought I'd heard 'em all, but—"

"No," Malone said. "You don't understand."

"I don't got to understand," the old man said. "That's what's so restful about this here job. I just got to sweep up. I don't got to understand nothing. Good-bye."

"I'm looking for a notebook I lost here last night," Malone said desperately.

"Oh," the old man said. "Lost and Found. That's different. You come with me."

The old man led Malone in silence to a cave deep in the bowels of the theater, where he went behind a little desk, took up a pencil as if it were a club, held it poised over a sheet of grimy paper, and said, "Name?"

Malone said, "I just want to find a notebook."

"Got to give me your name, youngster," the old man said solemnly. "It's the rules here."

Malone sighed. "Kenneth Malone," he said. "And my address is—"

The old man, fiercely scribbling, looked up. "Wait a minute, can't you?" he said. "I ain't through 'Kenneth' yet." He wrote on, and finally said, "Address?"

"Hotel New Yorker," Malone said. "In Manhattan?" the old man said. "That's right," Malone said wearily.

"Ah," the old man said. "Tourist, ain't you? Tourists is always losing things. Once it was a big dog. Don't know yet how a dog got into this here theater. Had to feed it for four days before somebody showed up to claim it. Fierce-looking animal. Part bloodhound, part water spaniel."

Fascinated in spite of himself, Malone said, "That's impossible."

"Nothing's impossible," the old man said. "Work for a theater long enough and you find that out. Part bloodhound, I said, and part water spaniel. Should have seen that dog before you start talking about impossibilities. Hell of a strange-looking beast. And then there was the time—"

"About the notebook," Malone said.

"Notebook?" the old man said.

"I lost a notebook," Malone said. "I was hoping that—"

"Description?" the old man said, and poised his pencil again.

Malone heaved a great sigh. "Black plastic," he said. "About so big." He made motions with his hands. "No names or initials on it. But the first page had my name written on it, along with Lieutenant Peter Lynch."

"Who's he?" the old man said.

"He's a cop," Malone said.

"My, my," the old man said. "Valuable notebook, with a cop's name in it and all. You a cop, youngster?"

Malone shook his head.

"Too bad," the old man said obscurely. "I like cops." He stood up. "You said black plastic? Black?"

"That's right," Malone said. "Do you have it here?"

"Got no notebooks at all here, youngster," the old man said. "Empty billfold, three hats, a couple of coats, and some pencils. And an umbrella. No dogs tonight, youngster, *and* no notebooks."

"Oh," Malone said. "Well—wait a minute."

"What is it, youngster?" the old man said. "I'm busy this time of day. Got to sweep and clean. Got work to do. Not like you tourists."

With difficulty, Malone leashed his temper. "Why did I have to describe the notebook?" he said. "You haven't got any notebooks at all."

"That's right," the old man said cheerfully.

"But you made me describe—"

"That's the rules," the old man said. "And I ain't about to go against the rules. Not for no tourist." He put the pencil down and rose. "Wish you were a cop," he said. "I never met a cop. They don't lose things like people do."

Making a mental note to call up later and talk to the manager, if the notebook hadn't turned up in the meantime, Malone went off to find the bars he had stopped in before the theater.

Saving Topp's for last, he started at the Ad Lib, where a surprised bald-headed man told him they hadn't found a notebook anywhere in the bar for something like six weeks. "Now if you'd been looking for umbrellas," he said, "we could have accommodated you. Got over ten umbrellas downstairs, waiting for their owners. I wonder why people lose so many umbrellas?"

"Maybe they hate rain," Malone said.

"I don't know," the bald man said. "I'm sort of a psychologist—you know, a judge of people. I think it's an unconscious protest against the fetters of a society which is slowly strangling them by—"

Malone said good-bye in a hurry and left. His next stop was the Xochitl, the Mexican bar on 46th Street. He greeted the bartender warmly.

"Ah," the bartender told him. "You come back. We look for you."

"Look for me?" Malone said. "You mean you found my notebook?"

"Notesbook?" the bartender said.

"A little black plastic book," Malone said, making motions, "about so big. And it—"

"Not find," the bartender said. "You lose him?"

"Sure I lost him," Malone said. "I mean *it*. Would I be looking for it if I hadn't lost it?"

"Who knows?" the bartender said, and shrugged.

"But you said you were looking for me," Malone said. "What about?"

"Oh," the bartender said. "I only say that. Make customer feel good, think we miss him. Customers like, so we do. What your name?"

"Pizarro," Malone said disgustedly, and went away.

The last stop was Topp's. Well, he had to find the notebook there. It was the only place the notebook could be. That was logic, and Malone was proud of it. He walked into Topp's, trying to remember the bartender's name, and found it just as he walked into the bar.

"Hello, Wally," he said gaily.

The bartender stared at him. "I'm not Wally," he said. "Wally's the night barman. My name's Ray."

"Oh," Malone said, feeling deflated. "Well, I've come about a notebook."

"Yes, sir?" Ray said.

"I lost the notebook here yesterday evening, between six and eight. If you'll just take me to the Lost and Found—"

"One moment, sir," Ray said, and left him standing at the bar, all alone.

In a few seconds he was back. "I didn't see the notebook myself, sir," he said. "But if Wally picked it up, he'd have turned it over to the maître d'. Perhaps you'd like to check with him."

"Sure," Malone said. The daytime maître d' turned out to be a shortish, heavy-set man with large blue eyes, a silver mane, and a thin, pencil-line mustache. He was addressed, for no reason Malone was able to discover, as BeeBee.

Ray introduced them. "This gentleman wants to know about a notebook," he told BeeBee.

"Notebook?" BeeBee said.

Malone explained at length. BeeBee nodded in an understanding fashion for some moments and, when Malone had finished, disappeared in search of the Lost and Found. He came back rather quickly, with the disturbing news that no notebook was anywhere in the place.

"It's got to be here," Malone said.

"Well," BeeBee said, "it isn't. Maybe you left it some place else. Maybe it's home now."

"It isn't," Malone said. "And I've tried every place else."

"New York's a big city, Mr. Malone," BeeBee said.

Malone sighed. "I've tried every place I've been. The notebook couldn't be somewhere I haven't been. A rolling stone follows its owner." He thought about that. It didn't seem to mean anything, but maybe it had. There was no way to tell for sure.

He went back to the bar to think things over and figure out his next move. A bourbon and soda while thinking seemed the obvious order, and Ray bustled off to get it.

Had he left the notebook on the street somewhere, just dropping it by accident? Malone couldn't quite see that happening. It was, of course, possible; but the possibility was so remote that he decided to try and think of everything else first. There was Dorothy, for instance.

Had he got stewed enough so that he'd showed Dorothy the notebook?

He didn't remember doing it, and he didn't quite see why he would have. Most of the evening was more or less clear in his mind; he hadn't apparently, forgotten any other details, either.

All the same, it was an idea. He decided to give the girl a call and find out for sure. Maybe she remembered something that would help him, anyway.

He took the drink from Ray and slid off the bar stool. Two steps away, he remembered one more little fact.

He didn't have her number, and he didn't know anything about where she lived, except that it could be reached by subway. That, Malone told himself morosely, limited things nicely to the five boroughs of New York.

And she said she was living with her aunt. Would she have a phone listing under her own name? Or would the listing be under her aunt's name, which he also didn't know?

At any rate, he could check listings under Dorothy Francis, he told himself.

He did so.

There were lots and lots of people named Dorothy Francis, in Manhattan and in all the other boroughs.

Malone went back to the bar to think some more. He was on his second bourbon and soda, still thinking but without any new ideas, when BeeBee tapped him gently on the shoulder.

"Pardon me," the maître d' said, "but are you English?"

"Am I what?" Malone said, spilling a little of his drink on the bar.

"Are you English?" BeeBee said.

"Oh," Malone said. "No. Irish. Very Irish."

"That's nice," BeeBee said.

Malone stared at him. "I think it's fine," he said, "but I'd love to know why you asked me."

"Well," BeeBee said, "I knew you couldn't be American. Not after the phone call. You don't have to hide your nationality here; we're quite accustomed to foreign visitors. And we don't have special prices for tourists."

Malone waited two breaths. "Will you please tell me," he said slowly, "what it is you're talking about?"

"Certainly," BeeBee said with aplomb. "There's a call for you in the upstairs booth. A long-distance call, personal."

"Oh," Malone said. "Who'd know I was—" He stopped, thinking hard. There was no way for anybody in the world to know he was in Topp's. Therefore, nobody could be calling him. "They've got the wrong name," he said decisively.

"Oh, no," BeeBee said. "I heard them quite distinctly. You *are* Sir Kenneth Malone, aren't you?"

Malone gaped for one long second, and then his mind caught up with the facts. "Oh," he said. "Sure." He raced upstairs to the phone booth, said, "This is Sir Kenneth Malone," into the blank screen, and waited.

After a while an operator said, "Person-to-person call, Sir Kenneth, from Yucca Flats. Will you take this call?"

"I'll take it," Malone said. A face appeared on the screen, and Malone knew he was right. He knew exactly how he'd been located, and by whom.

Looking only at the face in the screen, it might have been thought that the woman who appeared there was somebody's grandmother, kindly, red-cheeked, and twinkle-eyed. Perhaps that wasn't the only stereotype; she could have been an old-maid schoolteacher, one of the kindly schoolteachers who taught, once upon a time that never was, in the little red schoolhouses of the dim past. The face positively radiated kindliness, and friendship, and peace.

But if the face was the face of a sentimental dream, the garb was the garb of royalty. Somebody's grandmother was on her way to a costume party. She wore the full court costume of the days of

Queen Elizabeth I, complete with brocaded velvet gown, wide ruff collar, and bejeweled skullcap.

She was, Malone knew, completely insane.

Like all the other telepaths Malone and the rest of the FBI had found during their work in uncovering a telepathic spy, she had been located in an insane asylum. Months of extensive psychotherapy, including all the newest techniques and some so old that psychiatrists were a little afraid to use them, had done absolutely nothing to shake the firm conviction in the mind of Miss Rose Thompson.

She was, she insisted, Elizabeth Tudor, rightful Queen of England.

She claimed she was immortal, which was not true. She also claimed to be a telepath. This was perfectly accurate. It had been her help that had enabled Malone to find the telepathic spy, and a grateful government had rewarded her.

It had given her a special expense allotment for life, covering the clothing she wore, and the style in which she lived. Rooms had been set aside for her at Yucca Flats, and she held court there, sometimes being treated by psychiatrists and sometimes helping Dr. Thomas O'Connor in his experiments and in the development of new psionic machines.

She was probably the happiest psychopath on Earth.

Malone stared at her. For a second he could think of nothing to say but, "My God." He said it.

"Not at all, Sir Kenneth," the little old lady said. "Your Queen."

Malone took a deep breath. "Good afternoon, Your Majesty," he said.

"Good afternoon, Sir Kenneth," she said, and waited. After a second Malone figured out what she was waiting for.

He inclined his head in as courtly a bow as he could manage over a visiphone. "I am deeply honored," he said, "that Your Majesty has called on me. Is there any way in which I might be of service?"

"Oh, goodness me, no," said the little old lady. "I don't need a thing. They do one very well here in Yucca Flats. You must come out soon and see my new throne room. I've had the decorations done by—but I can see you're not interested in that, Sir Kenneth."

"But—" Malone realized it was useless to argue with the old lady. She was telepathic, and knew exactly what he was thinking. That, after all, was how he had been located; she had mentally "hunted" for him until she found him.

But why?

"I'll tell you why, Sir Kenneth," the little old lady said. "I'm worried about you."

"Worried? About me, Your Majesty?"

"Certainly," the little old lady said, inclining her head just the proper number of degrees, and raising it again. "You, Sir Kenneth, and that silly little notebook you lost. You've been stewing about it for the last hour."

It was obvious that, for reasons of her own, the Queen had seen fit to look into Malone's mind. She'd found him worrying, and called him about it. It was, Malone thought, sweet of her in a way. But it was also just a bit disconcerting.

He was perfectly well aware that the Queen could read his mind at any distance. But unless something reminded him of the fact, he didn't have to think about it.

And he didn't like to think about it.

"Don't be disturbed," the Queen said. "Please. I only want to help you, Sir Kenneth; you know that."

"Well, of course I do," Malone said. "But—"

"Heavens to Betsy," she said. "Sir Kenneth, what kind of a detective are you?"

"What?" Malone said, and added at once, "Your Majesty." He knew perfectly well, of course, that Miss Thompson was not Queen Elizabeth I—and he knew that Miss Thompson knew what he thought.

But she didn't mind. Politeness, she held, was the act of being pleasant on the surface, no matter what a person really thought. People were polite to their bosses, she pointed out, even though they were perfectly sure that they could do a better job than the bosses were doing.

So she insisted on the surface pretense that Malone was going through, treating her like a Queen.

The psychiatrists had called her delusion a beautifully rationalized one. As far as Malone was concerned, it made more sense than most of real life.

"That's very nice of you, Sir Kenneth," the Queen said. "But I ask you again, what kind of detective are you? Haven't you got any common sense at all?"

Malone hated to admit it, but he had always had just that suspicion. After all, he wasn't a very good detective. He was just lucky. His luck had enabled him to break a lot of tough cases. But some day people would find out, and then—

"Well," the Queen said, "at the very least you ought to *act* like a detective." She sniffed audibly. "Sir Kenneth, I'm ashamed that a member of my own FBI can't do any better than you're doing now."

Malone blinked into the screen. He did feel ashamed in a vague sort of way, and he was willing to admit it. But he did feel, wistfully, that it would be nice to know just what he was being ashamed of. "Have I been missing something?" he said.

"Outside of the obvious," the Queen said, "that you've been missing your notebook—or rather Mike Fueyo's notebook—"

"Yes?" Malone said.

"You certainly have," the Queen said. "Don't you see what happened to that notebook? You've been missing the only possible explanation."

"But there isn't any," Malone said. "Unless Miss Francis has it."

Her Majesty gave him a bright smile. "There!" she said.

"There, what?" Malone said.

"I knew you could do it," the Queen said. "All you had to do was apply your intelligence, and you'd come up with just the fact you needed."

"What fact?" Malone said.

"That Miss Francis has your notebook," the Queen said. "You just told me."

"All right," Malone said, and stopped and took a deep breath. "My God," he said after a pause. "What is that supposed to mean? Did I give it to her after all?"

"No," the Queen said.

"Did I lose it, and did she pick it up?"

"No," the Queen said.

"My God," Malone said again. "All right. I give up. Is this Twenty Questions?"

"Sir Kenneth!" the Queen said. "What a way to talk to your Queen!"

Malone took another breath. "I'm very sorry," he muttered. "But—"

"Yes, I know," the Queen said sympathetically. "You're upset. But you didn't give Miss Francis the notebook, and she didn't find it after you'd lost it."

"Then—" Malone stared. "She stole it. She stole it from me."

"I imagine she took it right from your jacket pocket," the Queen said. "Now, if you'd only wear proper clothing, and a proper pouch at your belt—"

"I'd be stared at," Malone said. "In court clothing."

"No one in New York would stare at you," the Queen said. "They'd think it was what they call an advertising stunt."

"Anyhow," Malone said, "I wasn't wearing court clothing. So that made it easy for her to steal the notebook. But why, for God's sake? Why?"

"Because," the Queen said, "she needed it."

"Needed it?" Malone shrieked.

"Please, Sir Kenneth," the Queen said. "Don't talk to your Sovereign in that manner. And I do wish you'd stop thinking of that girl as Dorothy Francis. She isn't at all, you know."

"No," Malone said. "I don't know. If she isn't Dorothy Francis, who in hell is she?"

"Don't swear, Sir Kenneth," the Queen said. "She's Dorothea Francisca Fueyo, if you want to know."

Malone gulped. "Then she's—"

"That's right," the Queen said. "She's little Miguel Fueyo's older sister."

CHAPTER TEN

Malone put in a great deal of time, he imagined, just staring at the face of the little old lady on the screen. At last he spoke. "My God," he said. "Her name is Fueyo. I'll be damned."

"I've told you," the Queen said with some asperity, "not to swear, Sir Kenneth."

"I know," Malone said. "But—"

"You're excited," the Queen said. "You're stunned. Goodness, you don't need to tell me that, Sir Kenneth. I know."

"But she's—" Malone discovered that he couldn't talk. He swallowed a couple of times and then went on. "She's Mike Fueyo's sister."

"That's exactly right, Sir Kenneth," the Queen said. "That's just what I told you."

"Then she swiped the book to protect her little brother," Malone said. "Oh, boy."

"Exactly, Sir Kenneth," the Queen said.

"And she doesn't care about me at all," Malone said. "I mean, she only went out with me because I was me. Malone. And she wanted the notebook. That was all there was to it." He added an expletive. The Queen frowned, but said nothing about it.

"I wouldn't say that if I were you," she went on. "Quite the contrary. She does like you, you know. And she thinks you're a very nice person." The Queen beamed. "You are, you know," she said.

"Oh," Malone said uncomfortably. "Sure."

"You don't have to think that she merely went out with you because of her brother's notebook," the Queen said. "But she does have a strong sense of loyalty—and he is—her younger brother, after all."

"He sure is," Malone said. "He's a great kid, little Mike."

"You see," the Queen continued imperturbably, "Mike told her about losing the notebook the other night—when he struck you."

"When he struck me," Malone said. "Oh, yes. He struck me, all right."

"He guessed that you must have it when you started asking questions about the Silent Spooks, you see," the Queen said. "That was the only way you could have found out about him—unless you were telepathic. Which, of course, you're not."

"No," Malone said.

"Now, understand me," the Queen said. "I do not think that his striking you was a very nice act."

"I don't either," Malone said. "It hurt like—it hurt quite a lot."

"Certainly," the Queen said. "But he didn't hurt the car any, and he didn't want to. He just wanted to ride around in it for a while."

"He likes red Cadillacs," Malone said.

"Oh, yes," the Queen said. "He thinks they're wonderful."

"Good for him," Malone said sourly.

"Well, now," the Queen said. "You just go right on over to her house. Of course she doesn't live with an aunt."

"No," Malone said. "She lives with Mike and his mother."

"Why not?" the Queen said. "She's part of the family."

Malone nodded silently.

"She'll give you the book, Sir Kenneth. I just know that she will. And I want you to be very nice to her when you ask for it. She's a very nice girl, you know."

"She's a swell girl," Malone said morosely. "And I'll—hey. Wait a minute."

"Yes, Sir Kenneth?"

"How come you can read her thoughts?" Malone said. "And Mike's? I thought you had to know somebody pretty well before you could read them at a distance like this. Do you? Know them, I mean."

"Oh, no," the Queen said. "But I can read *you*, of course." Malone could see that the Queen was trying very hard not to look proud of herself. "And last night," she went on, "you two were— well, Sir Kenneth, you had a real *rapport* with each other. My goodness, yes."

"Well," Malone said, "we—"

"Don't explain, Sir Kenneth," the Queen said. "It really isn't necessary; I thought it was very sweet. And, in any case, I can pick her up now. Because of that rapport. Not quite as well as I can pick you up, but enough to get the strong surface thoughts."

"Oh," Malone said. "But Mike—"

"I can't pick him up at all, this far away," the Queen said. "There is just a faint touch of him, though, through the girl. But all I know about him is what she thinks." She smiled gently. "He's a nice boy, basically," she said.

"Sure he is," Malone said. "He's got a nice blackjack, too— basically." He grimaced. "Were you reading my mind all last night?" he said.

"Well," the Queen said, "no. Toward morning you were getting so fuzzy I just didn't bother."

"I can understand that," Malone said. "I nearly didn't bother myself."

The queen nodded. "But toward afternoon," she said, "I didn't have anything to do, so I just listened in. You do have such a nice mind, Sir Kenneth. So refreshing and different. Especially when you're in love."

Malone blushed quietly.

"Oh, I know," the Queen said. "You'd much rather think of yourself as a sort of apprentice lecher, a kind of cynical Don Juan, but—"

"I know," Malone said. "Don't tell me about it. All right?"

"Of course, Sir Kenneth," the Queen said, "if you wish it."

"Basically, I'm a nice boy," Malone said. "Sure I am." He paused. "Do you have any more pertinent information, Your Majesty?"

"Not right now," the Queen admitted. "But if I do, I'll let you know." She giggled. "You know, I had to argue awfully hard with Dr. Hatterer to get to use the telephone," she said.

"I'll bet," Malone said.

"But I did manage," she said, and winked. "I won't have that sort of trouble again."

Malone wondered briefly what dark secret Dr. Hatterer had, that Her Majesty had discovered in his mind and used to blackmail him with. At last he decided that it was probably none of his business, and didn't matter too much anyway.

"Quite right, Sir Kenneth," the Queen said. "And good bye for now."

"Good-bye, Your Majesty," Malone said. He bowed again, and flipped off the phone. Bowing in a phone booth wasn't the easiest thing in the world to do, he thought to himself. But somehow he had managed it.

He reached into his pocket, half-convinced for a moment that it was an Elizabethan belt-pouch. Talks with Her Majesty always had that effect; after a time, Malone came to believe in the strange, bright world. But he shook off the lingering effects of her psychosis, fished out some coins and thought for a minute.

So Dorothy—Dorothea—had lifted the notebook. That was some help, certainly. It let him know something more about the enemy he was facing. But it wasn't really a lot of help.

What did he do now?

Her Majesty had suggested going to the Fueyo house, collaring the girl (but treating her nicely, Malone reminded himself) and demanding the book back. She'd even said he would get the book back, and since she knew some of what went on in Dorothea Fueyo's mind, she was probably right.

But what good was that going to do him?

He knew everything that was in the book. Getting it back was something that could wait. It didn't sound particularly profitable, and it didn't even sound like fun.

What he needed was a next move. He thought for a minute, dropped the coins into the phone and dialed the number of the Police Commissioner's office. After a brief argument with a secretary, he had Fernack on the phone. And this time, Malone told himself, he was going to be polite.

If possible.

"Good afternoon, John Henry," he said sunnily, when the commissioner's face was finally on the screen. "Can you get me some more information?"

Fernack stared at him sourly. "Depends," he said.

"On what?" Malone said, telling himself he wasn't going to get irritated, and knowing perfectly well that he was lying.

"On what kind of information you want," Fernack said.

"Well," Malone said, "there's a warehouse I want to know some more about. Who the owner is, for one thing, and—"

Fernack nodded. "I've got it," he said. He fished around on his desk, and brought up a sheet of paper. He held it up to the screen while Malone copied off the name and address. "Lieutenant Lynch told me all about it."

"Lynch?" Malone said. "But he—"

"Lynch works for me, Malone," Fernack said. "Remember that."

"But he said he'd—"

"He said he wouldn't do anything, and he won't," Fernack said. "He just reported it to me for my action. He knew I was working with you, Malone. And I am his boss, remember."

"Great," Malone said. "Now, John Henry—"

"Hold it, Malone," Fernack said. "I'd like a little information too, you know. I'd like to know just what the hell is going on, if it isn't too much trouble."

"It's not that, John Henry," Malone said earnestly. "Really. It's just that I—"

"All this about vanishing boys," Fernack said. "Disappearing into thin air. All this nonsense."

"It isn't nonsense," Malone said.

"All right," Fernack said indulgently. "Boys disappear every day like that. Sure they do." He leaned toward the screen and his voice was as hard as his face. "Malone, are these kids mixed up with those impossible robberies you had me looking up?"

"Well," Malone said, "I think so. But I doubt if you could prove it."

Fernack's face had begun its slow climb toward purple again. "Malone," he said, "if you're suppressing evidence, even if you are the FBI, I'll—"

"I'm not suppressing any evidence," Malone said. "I don't think *you* could prove a connection. I don't think *I* could prove a connection. I don't think *anybody* could—not right now."

Fernack leaned back, apparently mollified.

"John Henry," Malone said, "I want to ask you to keep your hands off this case. To let me handle it my way."

Fernack nodded absently. "Sure, Malone," he said.

"What?"

"I said sure," Fernack said. "Isn't that what you wanted?"

"Well, yes," Malone said, "but—"

Fernack leaned all the way back in his chair, his face a mask of disappointment and frustration. "Malone," he said, "I wish I'd never heard of this case. I wish I'd been retired or died before it ever came up. I've been a police officer in New York for a long time, and I wish this case had waited a few more years to happen."

He stopped. Malone leaned against the back wall of the phone booth and lit a cigarette.

"Andy Burris called me less than half an hour ago," Fernack said.

"Oh," Malone said.

"That's right," Fernack said. "Good old Burris of the FBI. And he told me this was a National Security case. National Security! It's your baby, Malone, because Burris wants it that way." He snorted. "So don't worry about me," he said. "I'm just here to co-operate. The patriotic, loyal, dumb slave of a grateful government."

Malone blew out a plume of smoke. "You know, John Henry," he said, "you might have made a good FBI man yourself. You've got the right attitude."

"Never mind the jokes," Fernack said bitterly.

"Okay," Malone said. "But tell me, did you actually make arrangements for me to get into that warehouse? I suppose you know that's what I want."

"I guessed that much," Fernack said. "I haven't made any arrangements yet, but I will. I'll have Safe and Loft get the keys, and a full set of floor plans to the place. Will that do, Your Majesty?"

Malone choked on his smoke and shot a quick look over his shoulder. There was nothing there but the wall of the booth. Queen Elizabeth I was nowhere in evidence. Then he realized that Fernack had been talking to him.

"Don't *do* that," he said.

"What?" Fernack said.

Malone realized in one awful second how strange the explanation was going to sound. Could he say that he thought he'd been mistaken for an old friend of his, Elizabeth Tudor? Could he say that he'd just had a call from her?

In the end he merely said, "Nothing," and let it go at that.

"Well, anyhow," Fernack said, "do you want anything else?"

"Not right now," Malone said. "I'll let you know, though. And thanks, John Henry. No matter why you're doing this, thanks."

"I don't deserve 'em," Fernack muttered. "I hope you get caught in some kind of deadfall and have to come screaming to the cops."

That, Malone reflected, was the second time a cop had suggested his yelling if he got into trouble. Hadn't the police force ever heard of telephones?

He said good-bye and flipped off.

Then he stared at the screen for a little while, as his cigarette burned down between his fingers. At last he put the cigarette out and went downstairs again to the bar.

If he had to do some heavy thinking, he told himself, there was absolutely no reason why he couldn't enjoy himself a little while doing it.

The evening rush had begun, and Malone found himself a stool simply by slipping into one while a drinker's back was turned. Once ensconced, he huddled himself up like an old drunk, thus effectively cutting himself off from interruptions, and lit another cigarette. Ray was down at the other end of the bar, chatting with a red-headed woman and her pale, bald escort. Malone sighed and set himself to the job of serious, constructive thinking.

How, he asked himself, *do you go about catching a person who can vanish away like so much smoke?*

Well, Malone could think of one solution, but it was pretty bloody.

Nailing the kids to a wall would probably work, but he couldn't say much else for it. There had to be another way out. For some reason, Malone just couldn't see himself with a mouthful of nails, a hammer, and a teen-ager.

It sounded just a little too messy.

Then, of course, there were handcuffs.

That sounded a little better. The trouble was that Malone simply didn't have enough information, and knew it. Obviously, the kids could carry stuff with them when they teleported; the stuff they stole proved that. And their clothes, Malone added. Apparently the kids didn't arrive at wherever they went stark staring naked.

But how close to a teleport did the things he carried have to be?

In other words, Malone thought, if you put handcuffs on a teleport, would the handcuffs vanish when the teleport did? And did that include the part of the cuff you were holding?

What happened if you snapped half the cuff around your own wrist first? Did you go along with the teleport? Or did your wrist go, while you stayed behind and wondered how long it would take to bleed to death?

Or what?

All the questions were intriguing ones. Malone sighed, wishing he knew the answer to even one of them.

It was somewhat comforting to think that he'd managed to progress a little, anyway. The kids hadn't meant anybody to find out about them; but Malone had found out about them, and alerted all the cops in town, as well as the rest of the FBI. He knew just who they were, and where they lived, and how they performed the "miracles" they performed.

Anyhow, he knew something about that last item.

He even knew who had his notebook.

He tabled that thought, and went back to feeling victorious. Within a few seconds, the sense of achievement was gone, and futility had come in its place. After all, he still didn't know how to catch the kids, did he?

No.

He thought about handcuffs some more and then gave up. He'd just have to try it and see how it worked. And if the teleports took his wrist away he'd—he'd go after them and make them give it back.

Sure he would.

That reminded him of the notebook again, and since the thing was being so persistent, he decided he might as well pay some attention to it.

Dorothea had the notebook. Malone tried to see himself barging in on her and asking for it, and he didn't care for the picture at all—no matter how Good Queen Bess felt about it.

After all, she thought Mike Fueyo was basically a nice kid.

So what did she know?

He closed his eyes. There he was, in the Fueyo apartment, talking to Dorothea.

"Dorothea," he muttered. "You filched my notebook."

That didn't sound very effective. And besides, it wasn't really his notebook. He tried again.

"Dorothea, you pinched your brother's notebook."

Now, for some reason, it sounded like something covered by the Vice Squad. It sounded terrible. But there were other ways of saying the same thing.

"Dorothea," he muttered, "you borrowed your brother's notebook."

That was too patronizing. Malone told himself that he sounded like a character straight out of 3-D screens, and settled himself gamely for another try.

"Dorothea, you *have* your brother's notebook."

To which the obvious answer was, "Yes, I do, and so what?"

Or possibly, "How do you know?"

And Malone thought about answering that one. "Queen Elizabeth told me," was the literal truth, but somehow it didn't sound like it. And he couldn't find another answer to give the girl.

"Dorothea," he said, and a voice from nowhere added:

"Will you have another drink?"

"Damn it," Malone exploded, "that's not the question. Drinks have nothing to do with notebooks. It's notebooks I'm after. Can't you understand..." Belatedly, he looked up.

There was Ray, the barman. "Oh," he said.

"I just came over," Ray said. "And I figured if you couldn't find your notebook, maybe you'd like a drink. So long as you're here."

"Ray," Malone said with feeling, "you are an eminently reasonable fellow. I accept your solution. Nay, more. I endorse your solution. Wholeheartedly."

Ray went off to mix, and Malone stared after him happily. This was really a nice place, he reflected; almost as nice as the City Hall Bar in Chicago, where he'd gone long ago with his father.

But he tore his mind away from the happy past, and concentrated instead on the miserable present. He decided for the last time that he was not going to ask Dorothea for the book—not just yet, anyhow. After all, it wasn't as if he needed the book; he knew his own name, and he knew Lynch's name, and he knew the names on the second page. And he didn't see any particular need for a picture of a red Cadillac, no matter how nicely colored it was.

So, he asked himself, why embarrass everybody by trying to get it back?

Of course, it *was* technically a crime to pick pockets, and that went double or triple for the pockets of FBI agents. But Malone told himself that he didn't feel like pressing charges, anyhow. And Dorothy probably didn't make a habit of pocket-picking.

He sighed and glanced at his watch. It was fifteen minutes of six.

Now he knew what his next move was going to be.

He was going to go back to his hotel and change his clothes.

That is, he amended, as soon as he finished the drink that Ray was setting up in front of him.

CHAPTER ELEVEN

By the time Malone reached the Hotel New Yorker it was six-twenty. Malone hadn't reckoned with New York's rush-hour traffic, and, after seeing it, he still didn't believe it. Finding a cab had been impossible, and he had started for the subway, hoping that he wouldn't get lost and end up somewhere in Brooklyn.

But one look at the shrieking mob trying to sardine itself into the Seventh Avenue subway entrance had convinced him it was better to walk. Bucking the street crowds was bad enough. Bucking the subway crowds was something Malone didn't even want to think about.

He let himself into his room, and was taking off his shoes with a grateful sigh when there was a rap on the door of the bathroom that connected his room with Boyd's. Malone padded over to the door, his shoes in one hand. "Tom?" he said.

"You are expecting maybe Titus Moody?" Boyd called.

"Okay," Malone said. "Come on in."

Boyd pushed open the door. He was stripped to the waist, a state of dress which showed the largest expanse of chest Malone had ever seen, and he was carrying the small scissors which he used to trim his Henry VIII beard. He stabbed the scissors toward Malone, who shuffled back hurriedly.

"Listen," Boyd said. "Did you call the office after you left this afternoon?"

"No," Malone admitted. "Why? What happened?"

"There was a call for you," Boyd said. "Long distance, just before I left at five. I came on back to the hotel and waited until I heard you come in. Thought you might want to know about it."

"I do, I guess," Malone said. "Who from?" Looking at Boyd, a modern-day Henry VIII, the association was too obvious to be missed. Malone thought of Good Queen Bess, and wondered why she was calling him again.

And—more surprising—why she'd called him at FBI headquarters, when she must have known that he wasn't there.

"Dr. O'Connor," Boyd said.

"Oh," Malone said, somewhat relieved. "At Yucca Flats."

Boyd nodded. "Right," he said.

"You're to call operator nine."

"Thanks." Malone went over to the phone, remembered his shoes and put them down carefully on the floor. "Anything else of importance?" he asked.

"On the Cadillacs," Boyd said. "We've got a final report now. Leibowitz and Hardin finally finished checking the last of them; there weren't quite as many as we were afraid there were going to be. Red isn't a very popular color around here."

"Good," Malone said.

"And there isn't a doggone thing on any of 'em," Boyd said. "Oh, we cleared up a lot of small-time crime, one thing and another, but that's about all. No such thing as an electro-psionic brain to be found anywhere in the lot. Leibowitz says he's willing to swear to it."

Malone sighed. "I didn't think he'd find one," he said.

"You didn't?"

"No," Malone said.

Boyd stabbed at him with the scissors again. "Then why did you cause all that trouble?" he said.

"Because I thought we might find electro-psionic brains," Malone said wearily. "Or one, anyhow."

"But you just said—"

Malone picked up the phone, got long distance, and motioned Boyd to silence in one sweeping series of moves. The long-distance operator said, "Yes, sir? May we help you?"

"Give me operator nine," Malone said.

There was a buzz, a click, and a new voice which said, "Operator ni-yun. May we help you?"

"All nine of you?" Malone muttered. "Never mind. This is Kenneth Malone. I've got a call from Dr. Thomas O'Connor at Yucca Flats. Please connect me."

There was another buzz, a click and an ungodly howl which was followed by the voice of operator ni-yun saying, "We are connecting you. There will be a slight delay. We are sor-ree."

Malone waited. At last there was another small howl, and the screen lit up. Dr. O'Connor's face, as stern and ascetic as ever, stared through at Malone.

"I understand you called me," Malone said.

"Ah, yes," Dr. O'Connor said. "It's very good to see you again, Mr. Malone." He gave Malone a smile good for exchange at your corner grocery; worth, one icicle.

"It's good to see you too," Malone lied.

"Mr. Burris explained to me what it was that you wanted to talk to me about," O'Connor said, "Am I to understand that you have actually found a teleport?"

"Unless my theories are away off," Malone said, "I've done a lot better than that. I've found eight of them."

"Eight." Dr. O'Connor's smile grew perceptibly warmer. It now stood at about thirty-four degrees Fahrenheit. "That is really excellent, Mr. Malone. You have done a fine job."

"Thanks," Malone muttered. He wished that O'Connor didn't make him feel quite so much like a first-year law student talking to an egomaniacal professor.

"When can you deliver them?" O'Connor said.

"Well," Malone said carefully, "that depends." O'Connor seemed to view the teleports as pieces of equipment, he thought. "I can't deliver them until I catch them," he said. "And that's why I wanted to talk to you."

"Some slight delay," Dr. O'Connor said, "will be quite understandable." His face left no doubt that he didn't like the necessity of understanding anything that was going to keep him and the eight teleports apart for even thirty seconds longer, now that he knew about them.

"You see," Malone said, "they're kids. Juvenile delinquents, or something like that. But they are teleports, that's for sure."

"I see," Dr. O'Connor said.

"So we've got to nab them," Malone said. "And for that I need all the information I can get."

Dr. O'Connor nodded slowly. "I'll be happy," he said, "to give you any information I can provide."

Malone took a deep breath, and plunged. "How does this teleportation bit work, anyhow?" he said.

"You've asked a very delicate question," Dr. O'Connor said. "Actually, we can't be quite positive." His expression showed just how little he wanted to make this admission. "However," he went on, brightening, "there is some evidence which seems to show that it is basically the same process as psychokinesis. And we do have quite a bit of empirical data on psychokinesis." He scribbled something on a sheet of paper and said, "For instance, there's this." He held the paper up to the screen so that Malone could read it.

It said:

$$(m*d)/(f*t**2) = 1/k$$

Malone looked at it for some seconds. At last he said, "It's very pretty. What the hell is it?"

"This," Dr. O'Connor said, in a condescending tone of voice that meant, You should have known all along, but you're just hopeless, "is the basic formula for the phenomenon, where m is the mass in grams, d is the distance in centimeters, f is the force in dynes, and t is the time in seconds. K is a constant whose value is not yet known, and the numeral 1 is unity."

Malone said, "Hmm," and stared at the equation again. Somehow, the explanation was not very helpful. The numeral 1 was unity. He understood that much, all right, but it didn't seem to do him any good.

"As you can see," Dr. O'Connor went on, "the greater the force, and the longer time it is applied, the greater distance any given mass can be moved. Or, contrariwise, the more mass, the greater mass, that is, the easier it is to move it any given distance. This is, as you undoubtedly understand, not at all in contradistinction to physical phenomena."

"Ah," Malone said, feeling that something was expected of him, but not being quite sure what.

Dr. O'Connor frowned. "I must admit," he said, "that the uncertainty as to the constant k, and the lack of any real knowledge as to just what kind of force is being applied, have held up our work so far." Then his face smoothed out. "Of course, when we have the teleports to work with, we may derive a full set of laws which—"

"Never mind that now," Malone said.

"But our work is most important, Mr. Malone," Dr. O'Connor said with a motion of his eyebrows. "As I'm sure you must understand."

"Oh," Malone said, feeling if he'd been caught without his homework, "of course. But if you don't mind—"

"Yes, Mr. Malone?" Dr. O'Connor said smoothly.

"What I want to know," Malone said, "is this. What are the limitations of this—uh—phenomenon?"

Dr. O'Connor brightened up thoroughly. "Well, theoretically," he said, "there do not appear to be any limitations. However, practical limitations do exist. If the process is at all parallel with psychokinesis, or with levitation…" He stared at Malone, as if daring him to say that it wasn't, "…if that parallel exists, then the subject is mentally limited by his own physical strength."

Malone said, "What?"

"Try and be patient, Mr. Malone," O'Connor said calmly. "Please. As I was saying, the subject is limited by his own physical strength. In other words, he cannot move psionically any subject larger than he can lift physically. This appears to be a psychological limitation which—"

"Oh," Malone said. "You mean he couldn't carry off a building, or anything like that?"

"Of course not," Dr. O'Connor said. "Nor, as a matter of fact, could he carry off anything that was securely bolted down. I hope you follow me."

"I think so," Malone said. "But look here. Suppose you handcuffed him to, say, a radiator, or a jail cell bar."

"Yes?"

"Could he get *away*?"

Dr. O'Connor appeared to consider this with some care. "Well," he said at last, "he certainly couldn't take the radiator with him, or the cell bar. If that's what you mean." He hesitated, looked slightly shamefaced, and then went on: "But you must realize that we lack any really extensive data on this phenomenon."

"Of course," Malone said.

"That's why I'm so very anxious to get those subjects," Dr. O'Connor said.

"Dr. O'Connor," Malone said earnestly, "that's just what I had in mind from the start. I've been going to a lot of extra trouble to make sure that those kids don't get killed or end up in reform schools or something, just so you could work with them."

"I appreciate that, Mr. Malone," O'Connor said gravely.

Malone felt as if someone had given him a gold star. Fighting down the emotion, he went on: "I know right now that I can catch one or two of them. But I don't know for sure that I can hold one for more than a fraction of a second."

"I see your problem," Dr. O'Connor said. "Believe me, Mr. Malone. I do see your problem."

"And is there a way out?" Malone said. "I mean a way I can hold on to them for—"

"At present," Dr. O'Connor said heavily, "I have no suggestions. I lack data."

"Oh, fine," Malone said. "We need the kids to get the data, and we need the data to get the kids." He sighed. "Hooray for our side," he added.

"There does appear to be something of a dilemma here," Dr. O'Connor admitted sadly.

"Dilemma is putting it mildly," Malone said.

Dr. O'Connor opened his mouth, shut it, opened it again and said, "I agree."

"Well," Malone said, "maybe one of us will think of something. If anything does occur to you, let me know at once."

"I certainly will," Dr. O'Connor said. "Believe me, Mr. Malone, I want you to capture those kids just as badly as you want to capture them yourself."

"I'll try," Malone said at random. He flipped off and turned with a sense of relief back to Boyd. But it looked as if Henry VIII had been hit on the head with a cow, or something equally weighty. Boyd looked glassy-eyed and slightly stunned.

"What's the matter with you?" Malone said. "Sick?"

"I'm not sick," Boyd said carefully. "At least I don't think I'm sick. It's hard to tell."

"What's wrong?"

"Teleporting!" Boyd said. "Juvenile delinquents!"

Malone felt a sudden twinge in the area of his conscience. He realized that he had told Boyd nothing at all about what had been going on since the discovery of the notebook two nights ago. He filled his partner in rapidly, while Boyd stood in front of the mirror and rather shakily attempted to trim his beard.

"That's why I had the car search continue," Malone said. "I was fairly sure the fault wasn't in the cars, but the boys. But I had to make absolutely sure."

Boyd said, "Oh," chopped a small section out of the center of his beard and added, "Damn. My hand's shaky."

"Well," Malone said, "that's the story."

"It's a hell of a story," Boyd said. "And I don't want you to think I don't believe it. Because I don't."

"It's true," Malone said.

"That doesn't affect me," Boyd said. "I'll go along with the gag. But enough is enough. Vanishing teenagers. Ridiculous."

"Just so you go along with me," Malone said.

"Oh, I'll go along," Boyd said. "This is my vacation too, isn't it? What's the next move, Mastermind?"

"We're going down to that warehouse," Malone said decisively. "I've got a hunch the kids have been hiding there ever since they left their homes yesterday."

"Malone," Boyd said. "What?"

"You mean we're going down to the warehouse *tonight*?" Boyd said.

Malone nodded.

"I might have known," Boyd said. "I might have known!"

"Tom," Malone said. "What's wrong?"

"Oh, nothing," Boyd said. "Nothing at all. Everything's fine and dandy. I think I'm going to commit suicide, but don't let that bother you."

"What happened?" Malone said.

Boyd stared at him. "You happened," he said. "You and the teen-agers and the bloody damn warehouse happened. Three days' work—ruined."

Malone scratched his head, found out that his head still hurt and put his hand down again. "What work?" he said.

"For three days," Boyd said, "I've been taking this blonde chick all over New York. Wining her. Dining her. Spending money as if I were Burris himself, instead of the common or garden variety of FBI agent. Night clubs. Theaters. Bars. The works. Malone, we were getting along famously. It was wonderful."

"And tonight—" Malone said.

"Tonight," Boyd said, "was supposed to be the night. The big night. The payoff. We've got a date for dinner—T-bone steak, two inches thick, with mushrooms. At her apartment, Malone. She will probably—"

"You'll have to break it," Malone said sympathetically. "Too bad, but it can't be helped now. You can pick up a sandwich before you go."

"A sandwich," Boyd said with great dignity, "is not my idea of something to eat."

"Look, Tom—" Malone began.

"All right, all right," Boyd said tiredly. "Duty is duty. I'll go call her."

"Fine," Malone said. "And meanwhile, I'll get us a little insurance."

"Insurance?"

"John Henry Fernack," Malone said, "and his Safe and Loft Squad."

CHAPTER TWELVE

The warehouse was locked up tight, all right, Malone thought. In the dim light that surrounded the neighborhood, it stood like a single stone block, alone near the waterfront. There were other buildings nearby, but they seemed smaller; the warehouse loomed over Malone and Boyd threateningly. They stood in a shadow-blacked alley just across the street, watching the big building nervously, studying it for weak points and escape areas.

Boyd whispered softly, "Do you think they have a look-out?"

Malone's voice was equally low. "We'll have to assume they've got at least one kid posted," he said. "But they can't be watching all the time. Remember, they can't do everything."

"They don't have to," Boyd said. "They do quite enough for me. Do you realize that, right now, I could be—"

"Break it up," Malone said. He took a small handset from his pocket and pressed the stud. "Lynch?" he whispered.

A tinny voice came from the earpiece. "Here, Malone."

"Have you got them located yet?" Malone said.

"Not yet," Lynch's voice replied. "We're working on a triangulation now. Just hold on for a minute or so. I'll let you know as soon as we've got results."

The police squads—Lynch and his men, the warehouse precinct men, and the Safe and Loft Squad—had set up a careful cordon around the area, and were now hard at work trying to determine two things.

First, they had to know whether there was anybody in the building at all.

Second, they had to be able to locate anyone in the building with precision.

The silence of the downtown warehouse district helped. They had several specially designed, highly sensitive directional microphones aimed at the building from carefully selected spots around the area, trying to pick up the muffled sounds of speech or motion within the warehouse. The watchmen in buildings nearby had been warned off for the time being so that their footsteps wouldn't occlude any results.

Malone waited, feeling nervous and cold. Finally Lynch's voice came through again. "We're getting something, all right," he said. "There are obviously several people in there. You were right, Malone."

"Thanks," Malone said. "How about that fix?"

"Hold it a second," Lynch said. Wind swept off the river at Malone and Boyd. Malone closed his eyes and shivered. He could smell fish and iodine and waste, the odor of the Hudson as it passes the city. Across the river lights sparkled warmly. Here there was nothing but darkness.

A long time passed, perhaps ten seconds.

Then Lynch's voice was back. "Sergeant McNulty says they're on the top floor, Malone," he said. "Can't tell how many for sure. But they're talking and moving around."

"It's a shame these things won't pick up the actual words at a distance," Malone said.

"Just a general feeling of noise is all we get," Lynch said. "But it does some good."

"Sure," Malone said. "Now listen carefully. Boyd and I are going in. Alone."

Lynch's voice whispered, "Right."

"If those mikes pick up any unusual ruckus—any sharp increase in the noise level—come running," Malone said. "Otherwise, just sit still and wait for my signal. Got that?"

"Check," Lynch said.

Malone pocketed the radiophone. "Okay, Tom," he whispered. "This is it."

"Right," Boyd muttered. "Let's move in."

"Wait a minute," Malone said. He took his goggles and brought them down over his eyes, adjusting the helmet on his head. Boyd did the same. Malone flicked on the infrared flashlight he held in his hand.

"Okay?" he whispered. "Check," Boyd said.

Thanks to the goggles, both of them could see the normally invisible beams of the infrared flashlight. They'd equipped themselves to move in darkness without betraying themselves, and they'd be able to see where a person without equipment would be blind.

Malone stayed well within the shadows as he moved silently around to the alley behind the warehouse, and then to a narrow passageway that led to the building next door. Boyd followed a few feet behind him along the carefully planned route.

Malone unlocked the small door that led into the ground floor of the building adjoining. As he did so, he heard a sound behind him and called, "Tom?"

"Hey, Malone," Boyd whispered. "It's—"

Before there was any outcry, Malone rushed back. Boyd was struggling with a figure in the dimness. Malone grabbed the figure and clamped his hand over its mouth. It bit him. He swore in a low voice, and clamped the hand over the mouth again.

It hadn't taken him more than half a second to realize what, whoever it was who struggled in his arms, it wasn't a boy.

"Shut up!" Malone hissed in her ear. "I won't hurt you."

The struggle stopped immediately. Malone gently eased his hand off the girl's mouth. She turned and looked at him.

"Kenneth Malone," she said, "you look like a man from Mars."

"Dorothea!" Malone gasped. "What are you doing here? Looking for your brother?"

"Never mind that," she said. "You play too rough. I'm going home to Mother."

"Answer me!" Malone said.

"All right," Dorothea said. "You must know anyhow, since you're here.... Yes, I'm looking for that fatheaded brother of mine. But now I suppose it's too late. He'll—he'll go to prison."

Her voice broke. Malone found his shoulder suddenly occupied by a crying face.

"No," he said quickly. "No. Please. He won't."

"Really?"

Boyd whispered: "Malone, what is this? It's a hell of a place for a date. And I—"

"Oh, shut up," Malone told him in a kindly fashion. He turned back to Dorothea. "I promise he won't," he said. "If I can just talk to your brother, make him listen to reason, I think we can get him and the others off. Believe me."

"But you—"

"Please," Malone said. "Believe me."

"Oh, Ken," Dorothea said, raising her head. "Do you mean it?"

"Sure I mean it," Malone said. "What have I been saying? The Government needs these kids."

"The Government?"

"It's nothing to worry about," Malone said. "Just go on home now, and I'll call you tomorrow. Late tonight, if I can. All right?"

"No," Dorothea said. "It's not all right. Not at all."

"But—"

Boyd hissed, "Malone!"

Malone ignored him. He had a bigger fight on his hands. "I'm not going home," Dorothea announced. "I'm going in there with you. After all," she added, "I can talk more sense into Mike's head than you can."

"Now look," Malone began.

Dorothea grinned in the darkness. "If you don't take me along," she said quietly, "I'll scream and warn them."

Malone surrendered at once. He had no doubt at all that Dorothea meant what she said. And, after all, the girl might really be some use to them. And there probably wouldn't be much danger.

Of course there wouldn't, he thought. He was going to see to that.

"All right," he said. "Come along. Stick close to us, and don't worry about the darkness. We can see, even if you can't, so let us guide you. And for heaven's sake be quiet!"

Boyd whispered, "Malone, what's going on?"

"She's coming with us," Malone said, pointing to Dorothea.

Boyd shrugged. "Malone," he said, "who do you think you are? The Pied Piper of Hamelin?"

Malone wheeled and went ahead. Opening the door, he played his I-R flashlight on the room inside and he, Boyd, and Dorothea trailed in, going through rooms piled with huge boxes. They went up an iron stairway to the second floor, and so on up to the roof.

They moved quickly across the roof to the wall of the warehouse, which was two stories higher than the building they were on. Of course there were no windows in the warehouse wall facing them, except on the top story.

But there was a single, heavy, fireproof emergency exit. It would have taken power machinery or explosive to open that door from the outside without a key, although from the inside it would open easily. Fortunately, Malone had a key.

He took it out and stepped aside. "Give that lock the works," he whispered to Boyd.

Boyd took a lubricant gun from his pocket and fired three silent shots of special oil into the lock. Then he shot the hinges, and the cracks around the door.

They waited for a minute or two while the oil, forced in under pressure, did its work. Then Malone fitted the key carefully into the lock and turned it, slowly and delicately.

The door swung open in silence. Malone slipped inside, followed by Boyd and Dorothea Fueyo.

Infrared equipment went on again, and the eerie illumination spread over their surroundings. Malone tapped Boyd on the shoulder, and jerked his thumb toward the back stairs. This was plainly no time for talk.

From the floor above, they could hear the murmur of youthful voices.

They started for the stairway. Fortunately, the building was of the steel-and-concrete type; there were no wooden floors to creak and groan beneath their feet.

At the bottom of the stairs, they paused. Voices came down the stairwell clearly, even words being defined in the silence.

"...and quit harping on whose fault it was." Malone recognized Mike Fueyo's voice. "That FBI guy was onto us, and we had to pull out; you know that. We always figured we'd have to pull out some day. So why not now?"

"Yeah," another voice said. "But you didn't have to go and vanish right under that Fed's nose. You been beating it into our heads not to do that sort of stuff ever since we first found out we could make this vanishing bit. And then you go and do it in front of a Fed. Sure, you got a big bang out of it, but is it smart? I ask you—"

"Yeah?" Mike said. "Listen, Silvo, they never would've got onto us if it hadn't been for your stupid tricks. Slugging a cop on the dome. Cracking up a car. You and your bug for speed!"

Malone blinked. Then it hadn't been Miguel Fueyo who'd hit Sergeant Jukovsky, but Silvo. Malone tried to remember the list of Silent Spooks. Silvo Envoz—that was his name.

"You slugged the FBI guy, Mike," Silvo said. "And now you got us all on the run. That's your fault, Mike. I want to see my old lady."

"I had to slug him," Mike said. "Listen, all Ramon's stuff was in that Cadillac. What would've happened if he'd found all that stuff?"

"So what happened anyway?" a third voice said (That was probably Ramon Otravez, Malone thought.) "He found your stupid notebook, didn't he? He went yelling to the cops, didn't he? We're running, ain't we? So what's the difference?"

"Shut up!" Mike roared.

"You ain't telling me to shut up!"

"Me either," Silvo yelled. "You think you're a great big big-shot! You think you're king of the world!"

"Who figured out the Vanish?" Mike screamed. "You'd all be a bunch of bums if I hadn't showed you that! And you know it! You'd all—"

"Don't give us that," Silvo said. "We'd have been able to do it, same as you. Like you said, anybody who's got talent could do it. There were guys you tried to teach—"

"Sure," said a fourth voice. "Listen, Fueyo, you're so bright— so why don't you try teaching it to somebody who don't have the talent?"

"Yeah," said voice number five. "You think you could teach that flashy sister of yours the Vanish?"

"You shut up about my sister, Phil!" Mike screamed.

"So what's so great about her?"

"She got that book back from the Fed," Mike said. "That's what. It's enough!"

"Hell," a voice said, "any dame with a little—"

"Shut your goddamn face before I shut it for you!"

Malone couldn't tell who was yelling what at who after a minute. They all seemed unhappy about being on the run from the police, and they were all tired of being cooped up in a warehouse under Mike's orders. Mike was the only person they could take it out on—and Mike was under heavy attack.

Two of the boys, surprisingly, seemed to side with him. The other five were trying to outshout them. Malone wondered if it would become a fight, and then realized that these kids could hardly fight each other when the one who was losing could always fade out.

He leaned over and whispered to Dorothea and Boyd, "Let's sneak up there while the argument's going on."

"But—" Boyd began.

"Less chance of their noticing us," Malone explained, and Started forward.

They tiptoed up the stairs and got behind a pile of crates in the shadows, while invective roared around them. This floor was lit by a single small bulb hanging from a socket in the ceiling. The windows were hung with heavy blankets to keep the light from shining out.

The kids didn't notice anything except each other. Malone took a couple of deep breaths and began to look around.

All things considered, he thought, the kids had fixed the place up pretty nicely. The unused warehouse had practically been made over into an apartment. There were chairs, beds, tables, and everything else in the line of furnishings for which the kids could conceivably have any use. There were even some floor lamps scattered around, but they weren't plugged in. Malone guessed that a job would have to be done on the warehouse wiring to get the floor lamps in operation, and the kids just hadn't got around to it yet.

By now the boys were practically standing toe-to-toe, ripping air-blueing epithets at each other. Not a single hand was lifted.

Malone stared at them for a second, then turned to Dorothea. "We'll wait till they calm down a little," he whispered. "Then you go out and talk to them. Tell them we won't hurt them or lock them up or anything. All we want to do is talk to them for awhile."

"All right," she whispered back.

"They can vanish any time they want to," Malone said, "so there's no reason for them not to listen to—"

He stopped suddenly, listening. Over the shouting, screaming, and cursing of the kids, he heard motion on the floor below.

Cops?

It couldn't be, he told himself. But when he took out his radiophone, his hands were shaking a little.

Lynch's voice was already coming over it when Malone thumbed it on.

"...so hang on, Malone! I repeat: We heard the ruckus, and we're coming in! We're on our way! Hang on, Malone!"

The voice stopped. There was a click.

Malone stared at the handset, fascinated and horrified. He swallowed. "No, Lynch!" he whispered, afraid to talk any louder for fear the kids would hear him. "No! Don't come up. Go away. Repeat: Go away! Stay away, Lynch!"

It was no use. The radiophone was dead.

Lynch, apparently thinking Malone's set had been smashed in the fight, or else that Malone was unconscious, had shut his own receiver off.

There was absolutely nothing that Malone could do.

The kids were still yelling at the top of their voices, but the thundering of heavy, flat feet galumphing up from the lower depths couldn't be ignored for long. All the boys noticed it at about the same time. They jerked their heads round to face the stairway. Malone and his compatriots crouched lower behind the boxes.

Mike Fueyo was the first to speak. "Don't vanish yet," he snapped. "Let's see who it is."

The internal dissent among the Silent Spooks disappeared as if it had never been, as they faced a common foe. Once again they fell naturally under Fueyo's leadership. "If it's cops," he said, "we'll give 'em the grasshopper play we worked out. We'll show 'em."

"They can't fool with us," another boy said. "Sure. The grasshopper play."

It was cops, all right. Lieutenant Lynch ran up the stairs waving his billy in a heroic fashion, followed by a horde of blue-clad officers.

"Where's Malone?" Lynch shouted as he came through the doorway.

"Where's your what?" Mike yelled back, and the fight was on.

Later, Malone thought that he should have been surprised, but he wasn't. There wasn't any time to be surprised. The kids didn't disappear.

They spread out over the floor of the room easily and lightly, and the cops charged them in a great blundering mass.

Naturally, the kids winked out one by one—and re-formed in the center of the cops' muddle. Malone saw one cop raise his billy and swing it at Mike. Mike watched it come down and vanished at the last instant. The cop's billy descended on the head of another cop, standing just behind where Mike had been.

The second cop, blinded by the blow on his head, swung back and hit the first cop. Meanwhile, Mike was somewhere else.

Malone stayed crouched behind the boxes. Dorothea stood up and shouted, "Mike! Mike! We just want to talk to you!"

Unfortunately, the police were making such a racket that this could not be heard more than a foot or so from the speaker. Lynch himself charged into the mass, swinging his billy and his free fist, and laying others out one after the other. Pretty soon the floor was littered with cops. Lynch was doing yeoman duty, but it was hard to tell what side he was on.

The vanishing trick Mike had worked out was being used by all of the kids. Cops were hitting other cops, Lynch was hitting everybody, and the kids were winking on and off all over the loft. It was a scene of tremendous noise and carnage.

Malone suddenly sprang to his feet and charged into the melee, shouting at the top of his lungs and swinging both fists. The first person he saw was one of the teen-agers, and he charged him with abandon.

He should, he reflected, have known better. The kid disappeared. Malone caromed off the stomach of a policeman, received a blow on the shoulder from his billy, and rebounded into the arms of a surprised police officer at the edge of the battle.

"Who're you?" the officer gasped.

"Malone," Malone said.

"You on our side?"

"How about you?" Malone said.

"I'm a lieutenant here," the officer said. "In charge of the warehouse precinct. I—"

Malone and the lieutenant stepped nimbly aside as another cop careened by them, waving his billy helplessly. They looked away as the crash came. The cop had fallen over a table, and now lay with his legs in the air, supported by the overturned table, blissfully unconscious.

"We seem," Malone said, "to be in an area of some activity. Let's move."

They shifted away a few feet. Malone looked into the foray and saw Boyd at work, roaring and going after the kids. One of them had established a kind of game with him. He appeared just in front of Boyd, who rushed at him, arms outstretched. As Boyd almost reached him, the kid disappeared, and reappeared again just behind Boyd. He tapped the FBI agent gently on the shoulder; Boyd turned and the process was repeated.

Boyd seemed to be getting winded.

"Damn kids," the lieutenant muttered suddenly, and dashed back into the fray. Malone looked around, saw Mike Fueyo flickering in and out at the edges, and headed for him.

A cop swung at Mike, missed, and hit Malone on the arm. Malone swore. The cop backed off, looking in a bewildered fashion for his victim, who was nowhere in sight. Then Malone caught sight of him, at the other edge of the fight. He started to work his way around.

He tried to avoid blows, but it wasn't always possible. A reeling cop caught his lapel and tore it, and Lynch, indefatigable in battle, managed to graze his chin with a blow meant for one of the disappearing boys. Other cops were battling each other, going after the kids and clutching empty air, cursing and screaming unheard orders in the fracas.

Malone ducked past Lynch, rubbed at his chin and looked for Mike. In the tangle of bodies it was getting hard to see. There was the sound of breaking ceramics as a floor lamp went over, and then a table followed it, but Malone avoided both. He looked for Mike Fueyo.

A cop clutched him around the middle, out of nowhere, said, "Sorry, buddy. Who the hell are you?" and dove back into the mass of bodies. Malone caught his breath and forged onward.

There was Mike, at the edge of the fight, watching everything coolly. No cop was near him. In the dim light the place looked like a scene from hell, a special hell for policemen.

Malone wove through battling hordes to the edge, and came out a few feet away from Mike Fueyo.

Fueyo didn't see him. He was looking at Boyd instead—still stumbling back and forth as the teen-ager baiting him winked on and off in front of him and behind him. He was laughing.

Malone came up silently from behind. The trip seemed to take hours. He was being very quiet, although he was reasonably sure that even if he yelled he wouldn't be heard. But he didn't want to take the slightest chance.

He sprang on Mike, and attached the handcuffs to his wrist and to Mike's wrist within ten seconds.

"Ha!" he said involuntarily. "Now come with me!"

THE IMPOSSIBLES

He gave his end of the handcuffs a tremendous yank.

He started to stagger, trailing an empty cuff behind him, flailing his arms wildly. Ahead of him he could see a big cop with an upraised billy. Malone tried to alter his course, but it was too late. He skidded helplessly into the cop, who jerked round and swung the billy automatically. Malone said: "Ugh," as he caught the blow on the cheekbone, bounced off the cop and kept going.

He careened past a blur of figures, trying to avoid hard surfaces and other human beings. But there was—

Oh, no, Malone thought. Lynch.

Lynch was ready to swing. His fist was cocked, and he was heading for one of the teen-agers with murder in his eye. Malone knew their paths were going to intersect. "Watch out," he yelled. "Watch out, it's me! Stop me! Somebody stop me!" He went completely unheard.

Lynch swung and missed, hitting a cop who had been hiding behind the teen-ager. The cop went down to join the wounded, and Lynch roared like a bull and swung around, looking for more enemies.

That was when Malone hit him.

Long afterward, he remembered Lynch's hat sailing through the air, and landing in the center of a struggling mass of policemen. He remembered Lynch saying, "So there you are!" and swinging before he looked.

He remembered the blow on the chin.

And then he remembered falling, and falling, and falling. Somewhere there was a voice: "Where the hell are they? They've disappeared for good."

And then, for long seconds, nothing.

He woke up with a headache, but it wasn't too bad. Surprisingly, not much time had passed; he got up and dusted off his trousers, looking around at the battlefield. Wounded and groaning cops were lying all over. The room was a shambles; the walking wounded—which comprised the rest of the force—were stumbling around in a slow, hopeless sort of fashion.

Lynch was standing next to him. "Malone," he said, "I'm sorry. I hit you, didn't I?"

"Uh-huh," Malone said. "You seemed to be hitting every body."

"I was *trying* for the kids," Lynch said.

"So was I," Malone said. "I got the cuffs on one and yanked him along, but he disappeared and left me with the cuffs."

"Great," Lynch said. "Hell of a raid."

"Very jolly," Malone agreed. "Fun and games were had by all."

A cop stumbled up, handed Lynch his cap and disappeared without a word. Lynch stared mournfully at it. The emblem was crushed, and the cap looked rather worn and useless. He put it on his head, where it assumed the rakish tilt of a hobo's favorite tam-o'-shanter, and said, "I hope you're not thinking of blaming *me* for this fiasco."

"Not at all," Malone said nobly. He hurt all over, but on reflection he thought that he would probably live. "It was nobody's fault." Except, he thought, his own. If he'd only told Lynch to come in when called for—and under no other circumstances—this wouldn't have happened. He looked around at the remains of New York's Finest, and felt guilty.

The lieutenant from the local precinct limped up, rubbing a well-kicked shin and trying to disentangle pieces of floor lamp from his hair. "Listen, Lynch," he said, "What's with these kids? What's going on here? Look at my men."

"Some days," Lynch said, "it just doesn't pay to get up."

"Sure," the local man said. "But what do I do now?"

"Make your reports."

"But—"

"To the Commissioner," Lynch said, "and to nobody else. If this gets into the papers, heads will roll."

"My head is rolling right now," the local man said. "Know what one of those kids did? Stood in front of a floor lamp. I swung at him and he vanished. Vanished! I hit the lamp, and then the lamp hit me."

"Just see that this doesn't get out," Lynch said.

"It can't," the local man said. "Anybody who mentioned this to a reporter would just be laughed out of town. It's not possible." He paused thoughtfully, and added, "We'd all be laughed out of town."

"And probably replaced with the FBI," Lynch said morosely. He looked at Malone. "Nothing personal, you understand," he said.

"Of course," Malone said. "We can't do any more here, can we?"

"I don't think we can do any more anywhere," Lynch said. "Let's lock the place up and leave and forget all about it."

"Fine," Malone said. "I've got work to do." He looked around, found Dorothea and signaled to her. "Come on, Dorothea. Where's Boyd?"

"Here I am," Boyd said, walking slowly across the big room to Malone. He had one hand held to his chin.

"What's the matter with you?" Malone asked.

Boyd took his hand away. There was a bald spot the size of a quarter on the point of his chin. "One of those kids," he said sadly, "has a hell of a strong grip. Come on, Miss Fueyo. Come on, Malone. Let's get out of here."

CHAPTER THIRTEEN

"Logically," Malone said, "there has to be *some* way to catch them." He looked around the hotel room as though he expected to find an answer painted in big black letters on the wall. "Logically," he said again, and tried to think of what came next. He liked the sound of the word, but that was as far as it went.

"That's fine," Boyd said. He sat on a chair, staring gloomily at the floor and rubbing the bald spot on his chin with a single, sad, inquisitive forefinger. "There has to be an answer. You're probably right. But what the hell is it?"

Malone started to answer, and then wondered what he had been going to say. He sunk himself in thought. There was a knock at the door. "Who's there?" he called, glad of any relief at all.

"It's me," a small voice said. "Dorothea."

"Come in," Malone said.

The door opened. Dorothea came in, shut the door behind her, and looked around the room a little awkwardly.

"Did you get a good night's sleep?" Malone said.

She nodded. "I guess so," she said. "Sure. It was nice of you to get me a room for the night. I mean, I guess I was—well…"

"Forget it," Malone said grandly. "You were upset and tired, that's all. Hell, in the car on the way back here last night, you fainted."

"I did not faint," she said.

"Well," Malone said, "you sure looked like—"

"I was tired," Dorothea said.

Malone shrugged. "Okay. You were tired."

"You're not mad, are you," she said, "because I stole your notebook?"

"Of course not," Malone said. "I said forget it, didn't I? Sit down and help us out."

"Help you?" she said.

"That's right," Boyd said. "Help us figure out how to catch this bunch of maniacs before they steal everything in New York."

Dorothea said, "Maniacs? I—" and Malone interrupted her in a hurry.

"Police Commissioner Fernack has called twice this morning already," he said. "He's screaming about all the burglaries that have been occurring since midnight last night."

"Oh," Dorothea said. "You mean the Spooks? Mike and the others? They've been stealing again?"

"They sure have, Miss Fueyo," Boyd said.

"I guess they're furnishing their new hideout," Malone said. "Wherever it is. Only God knows."

"And even if He told us," Boyd said, "it wouldn't do us any good. Chase 'em out of there, and they'd go somewhere else."

Malone stood up, fished for his cigarettes and lit one. "What we need," he said, blowing out smoke, "is some way to trap 'em and hold 'em. And I don't see how we can do either."

"After last night," Dorothea said, "I really don't see—"

"Wait a minute," Boyd said. "You said *trap*, didn't you?" He looked slowly and speculatively at Dorothea Fueyo.

A second passed.

"Oh, no, you don't!" she said. "Oh, no. Not on your life. I'll help catch him if I can, because I know you don't mean to hurt him or the others. But I wouldn't want Mike to know about it. You're not using me as bait in any trap."

Boyd looked at Malone, shook his head slowly, and said disconsolately, "Well, it was an idea." He returned his gaze to the floor.

The furtive gleam of the half bottle of bourbon on Malone's dresser caught his eye. He'd had it sent up the night before, feeling the need of some medicinal refreshment. Now it winked at him. He ignored it resolutely. "Dorothea," he said.

"Yes?"

"Dorothea, do you have any idea how far one of those kids can go when he teleports?"

"No," Dorothea said. "I really haven't any idea about any of it. Mike tried to teach me once, but I guess I just don't have the talent."

"Oh," Malone said.

"I wish I could help," Dorothea said.

Silence fell, and gloom followed it.

Time ticked by. The bourbon bottle resumed its seductive winking.

"There is one thing," Dorothea said suddenly. "He did say one thing about it."

"What?" Malone said eagerly.

"He said you couldn't teleport to some place you haven't been before. You've got to be able to visualize where you're going."

Malone said, "Hmm." It seemed like the right answer. Dorothea's statement was a fact, certainly, but he didn't see how the fact fit in anywhere.

"He didn't mention anything about distance, and I don't think any of the Spooks ever tested it for that," Dorothea said.

"There probably is a distance limit," Malone said. "At least if Dr. O'Connor's theories are right. I just wish I knew what the limit was."

Silence fell again. Malone sighed. Dorothea sighed. Boyd sighed, looked around at the others and muttered, "Damn thing's catching." He got up and walked over to the dresser and picked up the bottle of bourbon.

"You, too?" Malone murmured, but Boyd didn't hear him.

"I don't care if it is early in the morning," he said, resolutely. "I need a drink. I need something to take the fog out of my head, anyhow." He poured himself a shot, held the bottle aloft, and said, "Dorothea? Malone?"

The girl shook her head.

Malone was tempted but he put Satan behind him with decision. "No," he said firmly. "The way I feel now, one drink would probably immobilize me."

Dorothea chuckled. "You sound just like Mike," she said.

"Mike doesn't drink in the morning either?" Malone said.

"Of course he doesn't," Boyd said. "Mike is a nice kid. A swell kid."

"You keep quiet," Dorothea shot at him. She turned back to Malone. "Mike never drinks at all," she said. "He says it immobilizes him—just what you said."

Somewhere in the black galactic depths of Malone's mind, a very small hot star gulped, took a deep breath and became a supernova.

The light was tremendous! It shed beams over everything, beams of a positively supernal brilliance. And in the all-pervasive brightness of that single inner light, bits of data began to fall into place with all the precision of aerial bombs, each falling neatly and exactly into its own little predetermined bomb crater.

It was beautiful. It was magnificent. Malone felt all choked up.

None of the Silent Spooks drank. He remembered Kettleman telling him that. And the Queen never touched the stuff either.

"What's wrong?" Boyd said.

"Malone, you look green."

"I feel green," Malone said. "I feel like newly sprung grass. I feel as if I had just hatched out of something. I feel wonderful."

"It's the strain," Boyd said. "That's what it is, strain. You've cracked at last."

Malone ignored him. "Tell me," he said to Dorothea with elaborate casualness, "when your brother says that, what does he mean?"

"What?" she said. "Oh, I don't know. I—" She stopped and her eyes widened. "You don't think that—"

217

"I don't know," Malone said. "But we can sure as hell find out."

Dorothea blinked. "What can you do?" she said. "I mean, to find out. You can't force them to drink or anything, can you?"

"No," Malone said. "I can't do that. But it does give me an idea."

Boyd held his untasted drink in his hand, staring at Malone and the girl. "What are you two talking about?" he said. "Or is this the special Captain Midnight code? I left my code ring home this week."

"Boyd," Malone snapped, "get on the phone."

"Are you sure it will hold me?" Boyd said.

"I want you to call Dr. O'Connor at Yucca Flats," Malone said. "Shut up and listen."

There was silence.

Finally Boyd said, "I don't hear anything."

"Never mind," Malone said. "I mean listen to me. I know it's pretty early out where O'Connor is, but that doesn't matter now. Wake him up. Wake everybody up, for all I care."

"Malone," Boyd said carefully, "are you sure you haven't gone nuts?"

Malone grinned cheerfully. "No," he said. "Are you? Now listen: find out what effect drugs have on psionic abilities."

"Drugs?" Boyd said, and then his eyes lit up. "My God!" he said. "We might have something, at that!"

"Get the Queen up too," Malone said. "Ask her the same question. I hope we do have something."

"So do I," Dorothea said.

"And if we get the information we're hoping to get, I want Her Majesty on the first plane to New York," Malone said. "I don't care what strings you have to pull to get that done. Call Burris if you have to. It'll be worth it." Malone paused. "Hell," he said, "call him anyway and tell him what's happened. But get the Queen here!"

"Right!" Boyd said. He dove for the phone and started dialing. Suddenly he looked around. "Hey!" he yelled. "Where are you going?"

Malone, one hand on the door, turned. "Down to see Fernack," he said. "I've got to make some arrangements. I'm betting we're right, Tom!" He charged out the door, slamming it. A second passed and it opened again. Malone's head popped back in. "Dorothea," he said. "When Tom gets off the phone call your mother. Tell her you're going to be away for a day or two—two at the most—and she's not to worry. We'll need you, and her, too, to talk to Mike when the time comes. So stick around."

Then he was gone.

*   *   *

Twelve hours later, Kenneth J. Malone was sitting quietly in a small room at the rear of a sporting-goods store on upper Madison Avenue, trying to remain calm and hoping that the finest, most beautiful hunch he had ever had in his life was going to pay off. With him were Boyd and two agents from the 69th Street office. They were sitting quietly too, but there was a sense of enormous excitement in the air. Malone wanted to get up and walk around, but he didn't dare. He clamped his hands in his lap and sat tight.

They waited in silence, not daring to talk. There was no sound except for the faint whoosh of their breathing through the gas masks they were wearing, and the muffled hiss from a tank nearby.

There was no reason why the plan shouldn't work. Malone told himself.

It looked foolproof. But he didn't believe it would work. This was the time, he assured himself, that his luck ran out. He'd been lucky for too long, and now the wheel was going to turn and he'd be lost. All he could do was wait for it, and hope.

Her Majesty had said definitely that this would be the place the Spooks would hit tonight. She had no doubts about it. And Malone couldn't think of a single reason why she might be wrong. But maybe he'd got the address mixed up. Maybe the Spooks were somewhere else right now, robbing what they pleased, safe from capture....

His hunch about drugs had been correct, or at least everybody had said it was correct. Dr. O'Connor had assured Boyd that the deleterious effects of drugs on psionic abilities had been known ever since the early days of Dr. Rhine's pioneering work, more than twenty years before. And Good Queen Bess had admitted the same thing. She never drank, she said, because on the one occasion when she'd tried it, she'd lost her telepathic ability, and "My goodness, it was just like going blind."

Burris had had to put on the pressure, but it had worked. The Queen had been flown to New York, under psychiatric guard just as soon as possible after Boyd's phone call, and she'd been able to pick up Mike Fueyo without any trouble at all as soon as she was within the same city, and close enough to him.

It doesn't do much good to know where a teleporter *is*, Malone thought. But it's extremely handy to know where he's *going to be*. And if you also know what he plans to do when he gets where he's going, you've got an absolute lead-pipe cinch to work with.

The Queen had provided that lead-pipe cinch. Reading Mike's mind, she'd told Malone that he planned to raid the sporting-goods store with the rest of the Spooks that night. Lucky again, Malone thought; he might have had to wait two or three days before the Spooks set up a robbery.

But, of course, he might just be riding for some kind of horrible, unforeseen fall.

The main part of the sporting-goods store was fairly well lit, even at night, though it was by no means brightly illuminated. There were show-window lights on, and the street lamp from outside cast a nice glow. But the back room was dark, and the four men there were well concealed. A curtain closed the room off, and Malone watched the front of the store through a narrow opening in it. He stared through it until his eyes ached, afraid to blink in case he missed the appearance of the Spooks. Everything had to go off just right, precisely on schedule.

And it was going to happen any minute, he told himself nervously. In just a few minutes, everything would be over.

Malone held his breath.

Then he saw the figure walk slowly by the glass front of the shop, looking in with elaborate casualness. He was casing the joint, making sure there were none left in it.

Mike Fueyo.

Malone tried to breathe, and couldn't.

Seconds ticked by.

And then—almost magically—they appeared. Eight of them, almost simultaneously, in the center of the room.

Mike Fueyo spoke in a low, controlled voice. "Okay, now," he said. "Let's move fast. We—"

And that was all he said.

The odorless anesthetic gas that filled the room had its sudden effect. Fueyo dropped out like a light.

The other seven followed him within seconds. Ramon Otravez, the tallest of them, stayed on his feet a little longer than the rest, obviously trying with all his strength to teleport himself out of danger, but the effects of the fast-working gas had already been felt. He was, literally, too stunned to move.

He too slumped to the floor.

For a second after that, none of the men in the rear room moved.

Then Malone said, "All right, boys. Let's get them out of here. They can't stay too long in this atmosphere." The men started forward into the front room, toward the still bodies. "Boyd," Malone said. "Get out front and wave the ambulance over here. I'll get the air-conditioners working and stop the gas."

He reached down and turned off the valve on the gently hissing tank of anesthetic gas that sat on the floor near him. "You guys get the kids," he said. "And let's make it fast, okay?"

CHAPTER FOURTEEN

"The one thing we had to worry about," Malone said, pouring some more champagne into the two hollow-stemmed glasses, "was whether it was possible to give them just enough synthecaine. Too little, and they'd still be able to teleport. Too much, and they'd be too groggy."

Dorothea relaxed in her chair and looked around at the hotel room walls with contentment. She looked like the proverbial cat who has swallowed the cream. "It looked to me as if it worked," she said. "Mike seemed pretty normal—except that he had that awful *trapped* feeling."

Malone handed her one of the filled glasses with an air. He was beginning slowly to feel less like the nervous, uncertain Kenneth J. Malone, and more and more like Sir Kenneth Malone. "I can see why he felt trapped," he said. "If a guy's been unhampered by four walls all the time, even only for a year or so, he's certainly going to feel penned in when he loses the ability to get through them. It might be just a little claustrophobic." He grinned, proud of himself. "Claustrophobic," he said again. "My tongue and palate are in excellent condition."

"The main thing is," Dorothea said, "that everybody's so happy. Commissioner Fernack, even—with Mr. Burris promising to give him a medal."

"And Lynch," Malone said reflectively. "He'll get a promotion out of this for sure. And good old Kettleman."

"Kettleman?" Dorothea said. "Oh, the funny fat man. He's some kind of social worker or something."

"And now he's getting a scroll from the FBI," Malone said. "A citation for coming up with the essential clue in this case. Even though he didn't know it *was* the essential clue. You know," he added reflectively, "one thing puzzles me about that man."

"Yes?"

"Well," Malone said, "he worked in your neighborhood. You knew him."

"Of course I did," Dorothea said. "We all knew Kettleman."

"He said he had a lot of success as a social worker," Malone said. "Now, I've met him. And talked with him. And I just can't picture—"

"Oh," Dorothea said. "We keep him around—kept him around, I mean—as a sort of joke. A pet, or a mascot. Of course, he never did catch on. I don't suppose he has yet."

Malone laughed. "Nope," he said. "He hasn't."

"And even your friend is happy," Dorothea said.

"Boyd?" Malone said. "Sure. He called his blonde and she was just thrilled at the adventures of an FBI agent, and he's with her now."

"You sound jealous," Dorothea said.

"The hell I am," Malone said, and proceeded to prove his point. Some minutes later they relaxed.

"Mike," Dorothea said. "What?"

"Mike," she said. "He's probably the happiest of all. After Mom and I talked to him for a while, anyhow, and he began to lose that—that *trapped* feeling. Now he's all excited about being an FBI man." She looked worriedly at Malone for a second. "You weren't kidding about that, were you?" she said.

She looked very pretty when she was worried. Malone leaned over and kissed her with great care. After a second, the kiss seemed to gain momentum on its own, and all restraint went by the wayside. A long time passed.

Then, as Malone pulled away and began to recover his breath, he said weakly, "You were saying?"

"Was I?" Dorothea said. "Oh, yes. I was. About Mike being an FBI man."

"Oh," Malone said. "Well, normally you've got to be a lawyer or an accountant, but there are a few special cases. And maybe Mike would fit into the special-case bracket. If he doesn't—well, he'll be doing some sort of official work for the Government. You can be sure of that."

"That woman in the costume—the one you call Your Majesty—certainly threw a scare into the boys," Dorothea said.

"Well," Malone said, "we had to prove one thing to them. We can pick them up at any time. You see, they've got to think about where they're teleporting, and as soon as they do that one of our telepaths—like the Queen—will know where they're going to be. And we can crack down."

"That's what she said," Dorothea said.

"Right," Malone said. "After all, we did them quite a favor—getting them out of all the trouble they'd gotten themselves into. If they try to—"

"That reminds me, Ken," Dorothea said. "All the things that were stolen. The liquor and all of that, Money. What's going to happen to that?"

"Well," Malone said, "everything that can be returned—and that includes most of the liquor, because they hadn't had a chance to get rid of it to the bootleggers around this area—will be returned. What can't be returned—money, stuff that they've used, broken, or sold—well, I don't exactly know about that. It might take a special act of Congress," he said brightly.

"All for the boys?" Dorothea said.

"Well, they'll be at Yucca Flats, and they'll be pretty useful," Malone said. "And, as I was saying, if they try to run away from Yucca Flats, we'll just have to keep them drugged all the time, little as we want to. They can be of some use that way, too. The Government isn't doing all this for nothing."

"But keeping them drugged—"

"I said we didn't want to do it. And I don't think we'll have to. They'll be well taken care of, don't worry. Some of the best psychiatrists and doctors are out there. And Mike and the others—if they can show they're trustworthy—can come home every weekend, or even every night if they can teleport that far." Malone paused. "But it isn't charity," he added. "We need people with specialized psionic abilities—and, for a variety of reasons, they're pretty hard to find."

"You know," Dorothea said, "you're pretty wonderful, Mr. Malone."

Malone didn't answer her. He just kissed her again, not caring particularly whether or not the kiss went wild.

Dorothea pushed him gently away. "I'm envious," she announced. "Everybody gets a reward but me. Do I get left out just because I swiped your notebook?"

Malone kissed her again. "What kind of a reward do you want?" he asked.

She sighed. "Oh, well," she said. "I suppose this is good enough."

"Good enough?" Malone said. "Just good enough?"

His lips met hers for the fifth time. She reached one hand gently out to the light switch and pushed it.

The lights went out.

THE END

Made in the USA
Middletown, DE
22 November 2022

15821881R00135